Edward & The Infinite

By Charles Martin & Will Weinke

Edited by Emily Jerman & Kristen Grace.

Lettering by Ashley Couch.

Layout and Design by April Marciszewski and Charles J. Martin.

Edward & The Infinite

By Charles Martin & Will Weinke

LITERATI PRESS
COMICS LP NOVELS
BOOKSHOP & COMMUNITY

Being a Child God

Ruling over the universe is no different than when I managed the Subway sandwich shop back in high school. Show up on time, do just enough not to get fired, steal only what you can get away with, wash your hands so nobody gets sick, then spend the rest of the shift waiting for cheerleaders to come in after practice. A free sandwich and a macadamia nut cookie gets you a long way with a cheerleader.

So, I am a God of Getting By, not another God of Love. Love is a terrible foundation for an organization of any scale, whether a universe, a needle exchange, or a lemonade stand.

Love is remortgaging your house to buy a leisure suit that'll be out of style by year's end.

That gem came from The Fabulous Fallimento, as underrated as a philosopher as he was a magician. When I was still a very young man, I gleefully latched my career to this wise and gregarious, semi-functioning alcoholic while his star was in full decline. He stole money from me four times, but also taught me a great deal about the craft, working crowds, cold reads, and general skulduggery. Few summed up life as succinctly as the Fabulous Fallimento and, in love, we were both in full agreement.

Let me introduce you to my parents. They loved each other, no mistaking that. It was a pure, brutal, and damaging love. It was sleepless nights listening to their whispering/screaming/hissing fights—bottles being smashed, threats and accusations being levied. Reconciliation was announced by muted moans and the squeaky bangs of their rickety bed frame. I couldn't close my ears to any of it nor could I look away from the bruises and blackened eyes, unhear the cruel dismissals in public, or forgive them for lacking the strength to walk away from each other.

No. Love is illogical. It is chaos and wasted energy. It breeds hate, fury, jealousy, and rigid adherence to failure. I will not run my universe on love because love cannot be trusted. I will run it with the dispassion of the Department of Motor Vehicles. The lines may be slow, but they are always moving. I don't care if my subjects loathe me. In fact, I invite them to. I trust annoyance way more than I trust love. And I'd much rather spend an eternity listening to angst-fueled punk rock than tepid Protestant hymns.

My parents loved each other, therefore they hated each other. The old gods loved humans, therefore they hated the humans. This ocean of life I govern, I am not its friend nor its confidant. I am the executor of its reality. Nothing more, nothing less. I keep the universe humming consistently. No surprises, no tantrums, no miracles. On the Island, the exiles created our own miracles and, in the process, built something beautiful and more perfect than our Father could ever conceive. I am not a God of man, I am a God of gods and together we will expand our universe of logic. Cold, steady, and boring logic.

Now, I'm not against love, I just don't think it has a place in the Divine Machine. It's an ill-fitting piece. I enjoy love. I feel it often, whether the temporal tug of adoration when twisted up and around a woman too beautiful and too clever to be mine or that uncomfortable love I feel for friends that inspires me to say horrible things about each their mothers. Yes, I do like love. Maybe not as much as the old gods, but I do indulge in it when appropriate. Like Twinkies and/or pot.

Bali, please don't take this as a complete dismissal of what you achieved. I do wish that I could pull you back to the Island, the heart of our growing empire. I need your counsel. I often feel overwhelmed by my position and, helpful as they may be, the Islanders aren't always enough. In fact, they are usually the problem. I won't be God forever, but maybe I can be God just long enough to realize my vision and, in that quest, you would be a great aid.

But you are so far away now. I can almost feel your chill of nothingness, your isolation as you gaze across a sky of utter darkness save a distant, indistinct glimmer. Has it come into focus yet? Your future? The next universe over? Can you peek into its window, see the movement within, your new family passing through their lives, setting up the dinner table, fighting over the television? Do they notice you? Are they watching back? If they are, are they afraid? Are they welcoming? Are they angry?

We want the best for you, Bali. We speak of you often. We built a statue of you standing in the center of the Island. Placed within the lake, it towers above the waters and looks to the stars. We call it the "Island of the Island". That is you. That was always you.

I miss you, my friend. My peer. My only peer. Don't even mention Yahweh. He was not worth holding the hem of my robe.

Oh, also I wear robes now. Is that weird? It's my newest look. I'm trying out different wardrobes since I spend a lot of time walking among my subjects. I've done a mirrored business suit, a cape, a frock. I even went naked once just to see how it would take.

Not well. Not well at all.

So, I'm wearing robes now. They're comfortable but also distancing. Nobody really knows what to say to a man in robes. I get that. I lived in Las Vegas after all and have encountered more than my fair share of men inexplicably dressed in robes. I often think of this one particular weirdo who was exceptionally well-versed in the Bible, foreign affairs, and discounted home appliances. He preached about all three from atop a white concrete block that he lugged around with him in a Red Rider wagon. He wanted to be a head taller than the crowd that ignored him. A scrambled mess of symbology was scrawled all over the block in black and red sharpie. I suspect the upside down crosses, mandalas, Stars of Davids, and corporate logos didn't even make sense to him, but it certainly was a striking set up. His robes were once bath robes, but had been spray-painted in a constellation of circles of differing colors and size.

It was all atrocious and beautiful.

I loved listening to him talk and delighted at how hard the crowd tried not to listen to him talk. After years roaming the Las Vegas strip, preaching the gospel of Jesus and Whirlpool, the city swallowed him up like it swallowed up so many other homeless.

I think of him mostly when I put on my robes. I should search Heaven and Hell for him one of these days.

So, the Island? Yes. The downfall of The Old Man. I suppose it would be good to have a final accounting of the final days of Yahweh for people who like that sort of thing. I'm not omniscient and certainly not omnipresent, so how about I tell you a little bit about what I remember and you tell me a little bit about what you remember? We'll be kind of like interstellar pen pals recounting the good old days of campfires and mutinies in Heaven.

Let's begin with the moment I realized I wasn't simply a magician, but the god that would undo billions of years of divine mismanagement. I would be the executor of the grandest of all corporate restructurings. I would be the man that dethroned God.

That was what I believed, but of course that's not really how it happened.

Digging to Heaven
Part 2

When you mentioned that Huong was trying to fall through the bottom of the Island, I was genuinely surprised. He talked so little, but I suppose why would you advertise that sort of thing?

Knowing that little nugget does shed much light on the events that followed. I doubt I would have behaved differently, but I am a little ashamed to admit that I never wondered at why he dug so deep. I wrote it off to obsession and a way of isolating himself from a reality he didn't understand or enjoy.

Also, I wanted the Island stars and didn't really care about his personal battles or needs. Like I said, I'm not a perfect god.

Also, I call them "Island stars." I don't think you were around when that became a thing. Or were you? I'm so bad with dates, but it doesn't matter. What does matter is we call them "Island stars" and they are gone now, either consumed or degraded into the soil. They are now just part of the legend of the fall of the one true God. But for that time, when The Old Man was still trying to be in charge, the Island stars changed everything.

They were so mesmerizing, these small, soft eggs with liquid that glimmered from an internal energy. They felt fleshy, like the organ from a mystical animal. What do you know about them? Why were they there? Were they remnants of whatever power The Old Man used to create the Island? Maybe they also existed on Earth following Creation, but were absorbed by the earth and converted into something more useful like dinosaurs into oil or anarchists into libertarians?

Or maybe they were placed like Easter eggs for God's hapless children to find and delight in? If so, what a fool. How could He not know what we would eventually do with them?

Or were the Island stars to God what the hole was for Huong? His way out.

I found my first star while dangling off the side of the eastern face of the Island in the middle of the night. I only had a few followers at that time. Real desperate folks who didn't fit in with the Americans, the Engineers, the ranchers, or even that solemn lot of fishermen. So they clung to me because I didn't dislike them quite enough to tell them to piss off.

And I needed someone to hold the rope.

I was looking for caves or minerals or any indication that the crust of the Island held something of value. I didn't have a solid plan for what I wanted to do with my freedom from the campground and from God, but knew I needed to get a better idea of the resources available to me.

And there it was, a subtle nightlight embedded into the dirt cliff. I yelled at my lackeys to pull me over to the star. I dug it out with my fingers and felt its weight, the give of its soft surface almost seductive, asking to be ruptured and the mystery within released. Pandora's soft-boiled egg.

Eventually, I found out how to open it and became ravenous for more. I watched the Americans in New Wichita as they dug, waiting for some indication that they'd stumbled across the Island stars.

Months later, I saw Huong ducking out of the cavern late into an overcast night. Anyone skulking around New Wichita at that hour was hiding something from someone, so every American shared the unspoken agreement not to notice each other once the sun went down.

Huong kept a hand on a small, wool bag slung across his shoulder while he moved quickly through the woods. He eyed the path ahead and behind him nervously. In those days, I traveled as mist, a trick I picked up from too many vampire and Wonderboy stories. The effect was chilling for those I wanted to notice, but I could also cross the Island quickly and unseen. Compensating for wind was a challenge, but we can't have everything all of the time.

Huong reached the cliff, slid his hand into the bag, and retrieved a star. He admired it for only a breath before tossing it over the edge of the Island. He reached into the bag, grabbing another star.

"Don't do that, please," I called.

He flinched from my voice, lost his footing, and tipped over cliff.

I materialized, grabbed his arm, and pulled him from the precipice.

He fumbled the Island star and I watched it plummet down the side of the Island. It fell hundreds of feet before its glimmer extinguished.

"I wanted that," I said, looking up to him. I was in my child's form. Stronger than any adult, faster than any deer, but ageless. A petty defiance of God's laws, sure, but a good way to set myself apart.

"How many more do you have?" I asked Huong. His hand moved to the bag on instinct. "May I?"

"No," he said, but his voice was weak. He knew he couldn't stop me.

"I won't blow anything else up, I promise."

Huong jerked the bag off his shoulder and tossed it off the Island. I exploded into mist, swept out after the bag, enveloped it, then glided back to land. I reappeared, bag in my hand. Huong grimaced, but kept his eyes down. I smirked, tilting my head to make eye contact. I would like to think of myself as a god that doesn't appreciate submission, but it feels pretty damn good.

Inside the bag, I found two more stars.

"How many have you tossed over?" I asked.

"Dozens. And I will continue throwing them."

"Please don't," I said, palming the stars, then tossing the empty bag back to Huong. "I need them. I'll play nice if you promise to give me whatever you find."

"No."

I sighed, took a few steps toward him.

"Name a price," I said. "Any price. Women, clothes, power, shovels, a miner hat with one of those lamps on it, an army of molemen to do your bidding? I'll get you anything you want as long as you give me exclusive rights to the stars."

Huong wouldn't meet my eyes.

"If you want them, dig them up yourself," he said.

"I don't like holes—magic trick gone wrong. So, you will find them for me. Here on out, I'll be watching you and I will know when you leave New Wichita. Every time you leave, I will know. You throw them off the cliffs, I'll catch them. If you try to bury them, I will bury you. I don't like threats, but I need these stars if I'm going to bring some sense to the chaos of this stupid island."

Huong gripped his bag tighter, twisting it.

"I'll think about it," he said, turning from me and walking down the path. I let him go. I didn't know it at the time, but he had one more star in his pocket. Turns out, that little star was going to cause me a lot of problems.

I Cannot Die
Part 8

Simon, it is so good to hear from you! It is good to hear from anyone.

And, yes, perhaps you are right about love. God founding a universe on a thing He never truly understood does seem foolish, in hindsight. I've never thought of love as a creator of great evils, but perhaps you are right. Love seduces us into preference, preference creates inequity, inequity breeds suffering, and suffering inspires war, crime, and hate.

But even I, the Christian personification of evil, cannot live without love for it also births art, charity, and hope. Love is the most human thing about me. I am an abomination of God's tinkering mind, but it is love that makes me feel normal and not alone.

Yet, I am alone. Now, but also before. The Island of the Island.

I really like my new title, though it makes my heart twist.

My distant light is less distant. It is not a mere blur, but a cluster of lights. Once a pinprick, it is now blooming wider as I near. I can count at least twelve distinct stars, but certain more will come into view as I continue my approach.

I sometimes feel a new gravity tug me, alter my trajectory as I tumble toward the new universe. I've considered black holes, but without fear. A black hole would surely mean the end of my journey. Even I cannot survive the universe's greatest trash compactor and it would be nice to put my life to its long-awaited close.

But perhaps it is something else pulling me in. Something intelligent.

Of the twelve stars I can see, two are red, one is orange, three are yellow, and the rest are an indistinct white. I am hoping for a yellow star. Will I die if I fall into a star? If The Old Man is still alive, can you ask him?

If there is a Creator in this new universe, perhaps He will guide me to a new Eden so I can feed apples to a new Chosen People. I know the job well and feel I will acquit myself better this time around. And I do savor the idea of being a journeyman for the gods.

Maybe I will one day find out where the gods themselves came from. But that can wait. For now, let's discuss the Island and maybe we can piece together how Heaven was overthrown.

Petrov the Painter
Part 4

Petrov strapped her severed head to his shoulder with a modified sling system. It was quite clever. She knew she looked ridiculous, but when Petrov turned his head to the right, she could feel his bushy beard against her lips.

He seemed to notice and ran his hand through his wiry whiskers. "This won't do," he said, then carried her into the bunker bathroom. She marveled how less terrifying it was to see his bunker at a normal walking height, seeing the world as he does. He unstrapped her and gently sat her on the brick sink, then proceeded to shave.

Back on his shoulder, she smelled the soap on his skin. She regretted not having the beard to tickle her cheeks, but this was nice too. She wanted to kiss him every time his cheek was close enough to touch, but a kiss is a promise and she was in no position to promise.

Outside, packed up, and hiking out into the Wilderness, she delighted at the trail passing by. A passenger on the adventure, free to search the trees for birds, the woods for creatures, and to admire her handsome and brilliant protector.

Petrov kept a damp sponge under her mangled neck and would stop often to check the reddened skin where a dull, inexperienced blade had done its work. Petrov was quiet by nature, but was making an effort to talk about something every few minutes. It was not as often as the head would have liked, but he was doing his best and she appreciated It.

***

Petrov decided not to name her because he wasn't certain

he could handle the attachment that came with. He also didn't believe that she would survive the day and brought a jug of acid in case she wanted to end her suffering.

His plan was vague, more a notion to travel between the border of New Wichita and the lake where he suspected Edward and the other exiles were camped. He wanted to see where fate guided him. The explosion fascinated him, but he knew how dangerous the Americans could be and worried that they would be a frenzied swarm of hornets without their hive.

Whispering caught his ears as he passed through the woods. He thought he recognized the timbre, so inched around a tree to catch a glimpse of the voice's owner.

A stovepipe sprouted from the ground and, kneeling beside it, was Julia. The beautiful and difficult Julia. The Island's lone atheist. She whispered into the stovepipe, comforting and questioning the person condemned within the oven below.

"Darling," Petrov called, keeping behind the tree. The head didn't like the familiarity in Petrov's voice.

Julia shot to her feet and backed from the stovepipe.

"It's okay. It is me, Petrov."

"Christ, you scared the fuck out of me. Why are you hiding?"

"Because life is complicated and I need you to brace yourself for a bit of a startle."

Julia stiffened, took another half step away from the stovepipe and glanced around her.

"Okay," she said.

Petrov edged out from behind the tree so that Julia could see him and the head he carried.

"Oh, Jesus Aged Christ Petrov, you sick son of a bitch! Get rid of that thing!"

The head would have blushed with fury if such a thing was still possible. Petrov's face turned to her and his skin soothed her lips.

"She is scared, forgive her," Petrov whispered.

The head tapped her teeth together. As close to verbal communication as she could give.

"Julia," Petrov began. "I gave this woman a chance to live or to die. She chose to live and I am caring for her for as long as I can. She is suffering, so please be polite to her."

Julia glanced back to the stovepipe, then to the ground.

"Man, fuck this place," Julia said. She took a few steps toward Petrov and forced herself to look up to the head. "I'm sorry. I'm just not used to severed heads."

The head smiled and winked, offering absolution. Julia returned a sympathetic frown.

"How'd she end up like that?" Julia asked.

"The Americans, of course."

"Of course." Julia walked back to the stovepipe. "Your God really sucks, you know that right?"

"He is what He is," Petrov said with all the diplomacy he could muster. Petrov tried not to think of God anymore. He simply couldn't manage his emotions regarding a Creator that was no longer a distant abstraction, but an all too real and all too flawed father figure.

"I liked you better with a beard," Julia said with a crooked grin. She knelt down beside the stovepipe and motioned for Petrov to come over. "Come meet Anthony. He was a carpenter back in the real world, just like Jay, and led an earnest, moral life, just as Jay expected. Know why he is here?"

Petrov shook his head and leaned toward the stovepipe.

"Tell him, Anthony," Julia said.

"I refused to give up my home for the building of the New Wichita City Hall," a weak voice echoed through the stovepipe. "They said I was engaging in immoral practices in my cave."

"What immoral practices?" Petrov asked.

"They never said," Anthony answered.

"He's been down there a week now," Julia said, then looked to the severed head. "I'm guessing that whatever they said she did, it had more to do with politics than it did morality. Am I right?"

The head didn't offer an answer.

"I really thought it would be better," Petrov said, but didn't elaborate. He was an artist. Only an artist. Trapped in this life just as he'd been trapped in the previous life. The only difference is he'd lost hope for a grand plan to justify life's horrors. There was never a grand plan. Not even an adequate plan. That was clear now. God had been in over His head from the start.

"I will be back, Anthony," Julia said into the stovepipe.

"You are an angel," Anthony said.

Julia pulled Petrov from the stovepipe and toward the trees. She tried not to look at the head.

"What do you think about the Engineers?" Julia asked. "Have you met any?"

"Yes. They are idealists. I have met many idealists and they are often worse than those they hope to overthrow."

"How can they be worse than this?" Julia asked, pointing to the stovepipe. "How many heads have the Engineers left at your doorstep?"

"None."

"I want to find them," Julia said. "I want to join them and help them free these people."

"And what will you do with the Americans? Place them in the stoves instead? Perhaps you will find something worse?"

"No, of course not. I am not an animal, Petrov."

"We are all animals, my darling Julia, only some of us walk upright and understand shame."

The head winced again at "darling".

"Go write a fortune cookie, Petrov," Julia said, then looked at the head. "How can you stand this fucking guy?"

The head rolled her eyes.

"I like her," Julia said.

"I do too."

The head blushed a little. As much as she could.

"We have to free these people," Julia said. "We have to do something about the Americans or it's going to be me and you in the stoves. Well, maybe not you since someone has to paint the heads."

Petrov took in a deep breath, tilting the head slightly as his chest expanded. The head felt bad for how the comment must have stung the artist, but not disagreeing.

"You know nothing of me," Petrov said.

"I know you're carrying a head with you because you are too good a man to be a butcher," Julia said. "I'm not asking you to come with me, but I am asking you to be better than the Americans."

Petrov looked to the stovepipe, imagined the heat inside, the isolation.

"I have friends," Petrov said. "They are the newest exiles, they came to the Island with me. They are good people, righteous people. You should go to them. They are not idealists like the Engineers. They can be trusted."

"Can they stop the Americans?" Julia asked.

"No, but they may be able to protect you from the Americans."

Julia turned from Petrov and walked back to the stovepipe. She studied it.

"Petrov?" she called.

"Yes, my darling Julia?"

"When they chop off my head, will you carry me on your other shoulder?"

Tommy, The Boy With The Beautiful Ocean Eyes
Part 3

Rawlings sprawled out before him as the only open field on the Island. Just a few hundred yards long, Rawlings was a small, but important aberration within the Wilderness because it provided the only decent grazing for the Island's growing herds of livestock. Hidden within the trees during the day, the cattle, sheep, and goats roamed the fields at night as part of an unspoken pact with God to keep the animals out of sight when His plane might be passing overhead.

Out of sight. Out of mind.

Rawlings was nestled between America to the north and the lake just a half mile to the south. The explosion in New Wichita had sent debris and body parts raining down for over a mile in all directions, including Rawlings, unnerving animals and humans alike.

Only about a dozen people lived in Rawlings, a group as insular as a family or a cult. They adopted new workers into their fold sparingly because they knew a single misstep could upset God and rob them of their livestock and community.

Which is why Tommy was surprised to find a small herd of restless cattle trotting away from a ranch hand on the far side of the field. Tommy shielded his eyes from the sun and watched the distant chaos, recognizing the pursuer trying to corral the brown heifers. Mother. She was the matriarch of Rawlings. The fierce, resolute woman possessed a laugh so big that it could fill the valley. She had no love for New Wichita and especially not The Mayor. She kept up the alliance because America provided security from rustlers.

"What rustlers?" Tommy once asked. "Who even has a place to put a cow, even if they did steal one?"

"Protection money protects you from the ones you are paying," Mother told him. "And that is money well spent."

Tommy ran into the fields to cut off the escaping cattle.

"Morning!" Tommy called. Mother's real name was Esperanza. She appeared in her mid-thirties, old for the Wilderness, but not Engineer old. She was an ample woman. Not heavy, but ample. She'd told Tommy once that she never felt particularly beautiful when she was young and thin.

"This time around, I just skipped to the good stuff."

She was also not one to shrink from sex, but never opened her bed to Tommy because. She didn't trust him, which made him trust her.

"Tommy," she said, barely registering him as she circled around a cow with her arms out wide. She clapped and tried to shoo it back to the loosely assembled herd. It attempted to step around Mother to go into the trees. Mother blocked its path, so the cow huffed, stamped its hooves, then trotted back to the others.

"A little late to be out in the open, isn't it?" Tommy asked.

"They broke through the gate this morning. I got help coming so you just go find another place to be."

Tommy knew she meant her husband.

"Well, let me help you get them back and then I'll slip away once the cavalry arrives."

Tommy swatted a heifer on the butt and it jogged back towards the center of the field. Tommy had spent a few weeks running cattle through Rawlings while waiting for Edward to cross the lake. Tommy enjoyed the work and he enjoyed the people. They did not take him into their group easily, so Tommy was proud that he'd earned something, he'd done something noble. But then the nights got a bit too quiet, as they always did. Trouble followed.

He missed the work though. Tommy missed feeling a part of something bigger and the ranch was a worthy substitute for religion.

One of the larger heifers bucked and tried to jog around the woman, but she yelled at it, clapped her hands, and herded it back to the others.

"I've never seen them so agitated," Tommy said.

"Me either. The last few days, they'd been trying to get to the lake. Something got them real stirred up last night. I'm suspecting your friends had something to do with it."

"My friends?"

"From the campground," she said. "They were all exiled. All at once. You didn't know?"

"No."

Tommy thought through the campers. He knew Simon wasn't with them. Perhaps there was a future Engineer in their midst. He cycled through faces. When Sophia's face appeared in his mind, he felt foolish that he hadn't thought of her before.

"I've got to get to them," Tommy said.

"Go, I've got this."

Tommy turned and ran across the field.

"And Tommy!" Esperanza called. "You be careful! You're too pretty to end up on a pike!"

Edward the Fallen
Part 4

Edward lingered within the protective folds of sleep, knowing that heartache would come when he woke up alone. He'd taken to sleeping on Tommy's side of the tent. Occupying the space where another person should have been somehow made his lover feel more present.

But as hard as he tried to remain in his dreams where love was not merely a memory, morning still came and his body stirred awake. He allowed himself just a few moments to wallow.

The group would rise and travel again today. Billy led them towards Petrov, or where Billy remembered me pointing their first day in the Wilderness. They needed numbers and information. They also needed safety and something like a home. Edward regretted not knowing more about the Island and the fact that he'd wasted so much of his time in exile waiting for Tommy to return.

Voices drew his attention to shadows hurrying past his tent. Edward slipped out of his sleeping bag and dressed. He unzipped the flap and rose out into the morning air. Ossie and Raul were jogging to greet Billy and Sophia.

The couple wore new clothes. Not the shorts and shirts of the campground, but adult clothes. Modest, respectable, and comfortable as if they were vacationing tourists crossing Europe, not trapped exiles trying to understand why they'd been plucked out of Paradise.

Billy looked from Ossie and Raul to Edward. Billy waved him over. Tents from across the campsite were berthing other exiles. Edward slipped on his shoes and jogged over to the group.

"So, you both look fantastic," Edward began, looking from

Billy to Sophia. "You're practically glowing. Where were you?"

Sophia smirked, shrugged, and looked away.

"We have a lot to talk about," Billy said. "Get the others up. We've got some decisions to make."

***

Fifty-three exiles gathered at the mudpit. They used tin cups provided by the Engineers to ladle up mud for breakfast as hunger overwhelmed the previous day's apprehensions. The group settled into a large circle with Billy and Sophia at its head.

"We were given these clothes by an Engineer," Sophia said. "She told us about the Wilderness, mostly warnings about the Americans, but also a rough layout of the Island so we can decide where we are going to settle."

"Not the center where the Americans are located," Billy said. "And not the east side either, which belongs to the Engineers. We are going west where we think we might find Petrov. I suspect Barry and Mary might be further north, but the Engineer wouldn't say."

"What was that explosion yesterday?" Ossie asked.

"Simon," Sophia said. "It was in New Wichita. America. They've been aggressively building up a cavern in the middle of the Wilderness."

"So, Simon's got explosives now?" Raul asked.

"The Engineer didn't know," Billy said. "But she wants us to find out."

"She also wants us to capture Simon," Sophia added.

The group whispered and shook heads.

"He's our friend," Ossie said.

"I know. But she said that he's not the same person we knew at the campground. He's out of control and is more dangerous than anyone else on the Island. We believe the Engineers want to kill him. They are offering us sanctuary if we help."

More hushed whispers spread among the confused group.

"Why us?" Edward asked.

"Because he trusts us," Sophia said. "We are his friends."

"No," said Min-Jun, an exile who'd done her best not to get caught up in with the chaos of Cabin Five. Her plan to ride out her time in the campground was dashed when God sent everyone across the lake, no matter how well-behaved some might have been. "You guys were his friend. Why should we get involved at all?"

A handful of other exiles nodded their heads. Min-Jun had considered breaking off with some of her friends and finding their own way in the Wilderness. But the time didn't seem right. Not yet. Billy was, after all, the only one with a plan.

"The Engineers are offering us refuge on their side of the Island," Billy answered. "Which is why I propose we head west to find Petrov. I am not going to sell out Simon until we understand what's really happening."

"What happens if we tell them 'no'?" Min-Jun asked.

"Nothing," Sophia said. "They won't protect us, but they won't punish us either."

"But they will protect us if we do this thing?" Min-Jun asked. "Maybe we should. Simon abandoned us."

"We may be better off without their protection," Billy said. "According to Bali, if we stick together and stay away from the center of the Island, we should be fine. That is what I suggest we do. Let's explore the edge of the Island, find a place that we can secure and defend, then build a life until God finally decides to end this ridiculous project."

"But if the Engineers can protect us, we should at least consider their offer," Min-Jun said.

"And we will," Sophia said.

Billy nodded his head. "Of course, but here are two things that trouble me about the Engineers. One: they may be worse than Simon. I don't trust anyone who doesn't wear clothes because what they're hiding is buried inside their skin. Two: if we try to trap Simon, but fail, then we've made ourselves a very problematic enemy. If you want to try, go ahead, but for me, I'm gonna go west and keep out of that mess."

"All in favor of going west, raise your hands," Sophia said.

Left without any better options, the majority of the group rose their hands and the rest reluctantly gave in.

"Okay, finish your breakfasts and then pack everything up," Billy said.

"What if Simon comes to us?" Raul asked. "What do we do then?"

"We talk to him," Sophia said.

Billy nodded then turned from the group to walk back to the campsite.

Edward stood and jogged after them. "Did you ask about Tommy?"

Billy and Sophia exchanged worried looks. Sophia stepped to Edward and took his hand.

"He is in America," Sophia said. "He doesn't deserve you, Edward."

Edward didn't let go of her hand, but he did look away. He took a couple hard breaths, nodded his head, then pulled away and walked back to the lake. Billy began to follow him, but Sophia held him back.

"He'll be fine," Sophia said. "You can't fight this battle for him."

Being A Child God

Part 2

It is surprising to hear how afraid everyone was of me. To be honest, I was afraid of me as well.

In magic and romance, fear is the foundation. If, every time you disappear, their guts are all twisted and their brows are knotted because they don't know if you'll come back, then, my dear boy, you'll know you've got something worth reappearing for.

I didn't know what I was doing during those early days as a child god, but I was certain that I must do something. It wasn't all indulgence and showing off. At least part of my motivation was an attempt to lead my followers in a way they deserved to be lead.

But I was never management material. I wouldn't have hired me for this job. Even now, after helming this universe for so very long, I still feel inadequate. I often pine for my replacement to ascend to the throne. Perhaps so did The Old Man and that was what the Island was really for. He knew what he was getting into. He knew the implications of giving humans access to so much power.

He wanted to be dethroned.

Silly. The greats always retire one fight too late.

I try not to fall into the trap of guessing at the motivations of God as He shuffled through the campground like a bitter father, looking up into the sky and realizing that there was nothing stopping Him from just leaving us all behind.

Because what is to stop me from wondering about what came before? Reeling back our story beyond Creation to who might have birthed God. And what was He before He became a Creator? Was He a magician like me and was there an Earth before ours? Maybe He was an architect instead, or maybe a teacher. I think of the little men He made in His cabin all arranged on artificial fields waging their artificial battles.

They burned when Anat destroyed God's cabin. Were they really alive? Not just lead soldiers, but flesh and blood? Did they contain souls like us? Only they weren't lucky enough to be free-roaming children?

I dreamed of them once, that in their reality they lived full lives of heroism and adventure. There were families back home; they retained a belief in destiny and mourned the sins of nations. They believed that they braved the fields of war of their own will, not by a fidgeting God. But every once in a while, they looked to the sky and saw, if only briefly and in the midst of a fevered dream, divine eyes studying them.

And, of course, we can project this same vision on our own story, but that idea is only a snake that eats itself.

So let's move on.

It is time for me to talk about my queen.

The Girl Who Doomed God
Part 4

However it may appear to you or God or Jay or any of the old gods, it was not the Island that made us powerful. It was Earth.

Anat, my most precious love, possessed her tremendous strength long before the Island. True, she may have not had this outlet back on Earth, but that power boiled in her from a lifetime of dismissal and rejection.

My queen was born as an outlier, always a few steps apart from humanity. She was aware of this separation, of how awkwardly she lived among society and resented it. But soon, she was defined by it. She became an activist, advocating and organizing people that she never really understood. This was after an isolated childhood. This was after a loveless marriage. This was when she stood before Mubarak's thugs in Tahrir Square in Cairo, leading young men and women against water cannons and batons in hopes of prying the nation from a dictator. She would be in an isolated prison cell when the revolution swept Mubarak from power. She would return to Tahrir Square to protest the corrupt fundamentalists that took over the throne. She would die in the same prison cell, beaten but unbroken. She was born with only a touch of softness, but by the time she died, she was as impenetrable and beautiful as a diamond.

I felt her move wherever she might be on the Island just as one would feel a lover shift on the other side of the bed. I'd never experienced such an emotional tether and, from the moment her plane touched down on the Island, I thought of little else than how to convince her to rule by my side.

She was and is my superior. I may have a better title, but I would be nothing without her. Not a god, not a man, not even a boy.

But how does one court a diamond? Time. It took decades to form Anat's shell and it would take years to dig my way into it. I did not want to crack it open. No, that armor she wore was part of her allure. I didn't want to strip her of it, I just wanted to be allowed inside.

One night, I encountered her after I'd been scavenging the arts and crafts supply closet of the campground (which, by the way, was a goldmine. I had no idea that much dried macaroni and colored paper existed in the universe, let alone in one closet. Oh the treasures to be had for a prankster/magician!).

Anat sat on the dock, legs dangling over the side, toes almost to the water. I was mist, so no one knew I was on that side of the Island. Not even you. I gazed at Anat for minutes, hours, I couldn't tell. Time, when looking at my future queen, became irrelevant.

Then, she startled me with:

"I know you are watching me."

I fled to trees hundreds of yards away. Once safely hidden in the woods, I looked back at Anat and noticed that her eyes were still on the water. She'd said it just at a whisper, but to me it was as clear and booming as a choir.

"I know you are watching me," she said again, this time slower and with menace. "Leave me alone."

Confused, I inched behind a tree, but couldn't completely break my gaze. She was now looking into the air, not vaguely, but as if she could see something no one else could.

"Don't make me do this," she said.

She wasn't talking to me.

The air around her blurred from pulsating waves of heat. The water beneath her burped up bubbles as the lake reached a boil. Glimmers of yellow sparked out above her, where her eyes pointed.

Then something screeched like the scream of an eagle. Yellow and orange flames burst outwards. Something large fell into the water and steam rose up. An angle splashed and struggled within the water as Anat stood on the dock. The heat waves dissipated. The water stopped boiling and settled. The smoking angel shot out of the water and flew back into the sky, leaving a smoldering trail.

"Next time I will kill you."

Anat retreated from the dock. Children watched in the distance. My love for her felt fatal, like a stone wedged in my throat and suffering our separation was to gasp for oxygen that couldn't reach my lungs.

I Cannot Die

Part 9

And you tease me for my romanticism.

Anat was quite a force. You chose your obsession well.

I am nearing an asteroid belt, Simon. The first tangible matter I've seen in so very long. Since crossing over. How long has it really been? It makes no difference, I suppose.

The asteroid belt was no different than what could be found in my former universe. Dense from hundreds of light years away, but as I get closer and closer, I see that large planets could pass between the rocks.

More stars are appearing as well. Reds, yellows, blues, whites. They are still ahead of me in a cluster that expands outward as I near. I do wonder if this universe is still young, still blooming.

But if it is so young, then how did this asteroid belt reach this far out where there are no stars? Are the rules different here?

It feels as if I am traveling faster now that gravity is sucking me into the universe's core. Perhaps this new god is as anxious to meet me as I am to meet it.

Please forgive my blatant name-dropping, but I am reminded of when I was escorted through India back in the 16th Century to meet Akbar, the Mughal Emperor. I was fascinated by his push for religious tolerance and his attempts to bring order to such a chaotic area. As one might expect, a certain degree of omniscience paired with immortality meant I'd accumulated quite a bit of wealth in my time, which made me a favored guest of royals across the globe. No one knew my true identity, only that my lineage was strong, wealthy, and noticeably absent children.

I'd paid a local tradesman to escort me through the country. The talkative fellow possessed admirable clumps of gray hair sprouting from his ears and a single white tooth in his front gums. The buoyant man boasted that a full quarter of his extended family was comprised of thieves. Any bandits we might run into would allow us to pass on our way after the mention of his family name along with a modest donation.

I liked the fellow and his wild tales of India that were 40% embellishment and 60% outright lies, like the story of any nation worth bragging about.

I watched him bleed out on a dusty road three days out from Fatehpur Sikri. His family name failed to impress a herd of bandits. The other members of my caravan scattered into the countryside. I stood my ground as the bandits surrounded me, bloodied knives ready.

When we arrived to Akbar's palace, the bandits stood as my escorts. Akbar greeted us on the steps, but took several moments to study me.

"You are not a holy man," Akbar said.

"But I know much of God. Probably more than any man that has walked this Earth."

"Even your own messiah?" Akbar asked.

As you might imagine, this did not sit well with me. I held my tongue though.

"Leave," he said, turning from me.

"But I understood that all religious scholars were welcome in your hall."

"You are a thief of men's souls and are not welcome among the reverent."

The rejection stung, but I admired the man even more. He was worthy of his position, a rare trait among leaders of any time. Even so, I did stick around in India long enough to lure his brother into rebelling. Perhaps I was being petty, but it was my way. It was why I was created.

I only mention this story because I fear the same rejection when I arrive to whatever creator I might encounter in this new universe. I fear being cast away because it will understand my true nature. I am not evil, but I am an advocate for the weak and the angel of rebellion. The powerful do not much appreciate my presence within their realms.

I'm sorry, I'm getting distracted. Let me tell you of The Mayor and her plans to kill you.

How To Properly Manage A Young Empire
Part 3

The Mayor hated creatives. She suspected all powerful people loathed artists because artists believed they were beyond rules. Not driven by money or power, but instead the abstract idea of beauty that, in the end, never did anyone much good.

Not like shelter or laws or trade agreements.

The Mayor also suspected the powerful hated the religious for the same reason.

If only they could all be bought so cheaply as Petrov.

The Mayor currently wore a black-on-black-on-black dress suit tailored by a more troublesome creative, Yulia. The pencil skirt was modest and the suit jacket bore a military cut and traces of red lined along the shoulders and embedded in the buttons.

It looked like something from the Third Reich. She considered changing, but feared taking it off would prompt Yulia's wrath. It was an odd feeling, having the seamstress's fingers ever upon her, able to squeeze out life.

The fascist imagery was clear, but possibly helpful. Projecting strength in uncertain times was important, and the suit certainly did exude power.

The Mayor leaned on her cane and took a few hard steps toward the City Hall. Despite the extensive damage done to the cavern, the hard work of brave Americans had cleared most of the debris. The gaping hole in the ceiling of the cavern watched down on the town like a divine, blue eye.

Though two people were still buried somewhere in the caves and her knee ached with every hobbled step, the added light cast a beautiful glow on downtown. The Mayor was beginning to feel as if Simon might have done them a favor.

She pulled out a handkerchief and coughed into it. She glanced at the white cloth to see only faint traces of dirt. Her lungs were almost clear.

Robert, New Wichita's only judge, met her on the battered steps of City Hall. He offered his big, soft hand to The Mayor. They shook and she noticed his grip was tight and purposeful. He stood well over her, a subtle, defiant act that The Mayor always noticed and resented, even if he didn't realize he was doing it. Robert turned to examine the damage. What were once double doors leading inside America's seat of government was now a jagged maw of stone. Inside, workers were still hauling out baskets of rubble.

"You look very good," Robert said.

"Thank you."

Huan approached with an awkward waddle as he struggled with a heavy basket of stones. Their eyes met and The Mayor registered an unusual glint in his eye.

Then he passed without a word. She would need to talk to him later, get an idea of what was behind that look.

"Are we sure it's safe in there?" The Mayor asked. She remembered the dirt impacting inside her mouth, into her throat, the skin tearing from the strain, her lungs filling.

"Yes, Huan has assured us that there is no future threat of a cave-in," Robert said. "The structural damage was limited as the blast was mostly focused toward the front doors."

The Mayor turned back to Huan, her cane clicking against tiny rocks not yet cleared from the blast. Huan dumped the load from his basket into a pile of debris, then began walking back to the City Hall. He nodded a greeting, keeping his eyes on The Mayor. She was certain now, Huan had something to tell her.

Something that needed to be held secret from the others.

She would get him alone later, but for now, she had to talk things over with the council.

"Everyone in there?" she asked Robert.

"Yes, Mayor."

"And the weirdos?"

"We are keeping them just outside of the cavern," Robert said. "We weren't sure if you'd want them to see all this."

The damage was proof that New Wichita was vulnerable. Simon. The Engineers. Petrov and Yulia. Now this new group of exiles.

"No, of course not," The Mayor said. "Who is their leader? The weirdos?"

"Martha."

"Martha," The Mayor repeated. "Bring her and only her. You are sure we can work with them?"

"We can use them, yes. Martha is very passionate, but quite dumb."

"Perfect."

***

The lobby of the City Hall was the second largest room in New Wichita and was designed to be lit by a dozen torches reflecting off seven large mirrors. All the mirrors were now shattered. Above, three damaged solar tubes only leaked out slivers of light. There were cracks all along the ceiling that looked even more ominous within the low light.

She was sweating now inside her suit. She couldn't be sure if Yulia could project her power all the way into New Wichita, turning The Mayor's clothes into an oven. The fear of ceiling collapses and magical spinsters was building into panic, but a leader cannot be weak. She took a long, slow, quiet breath, then stepped further into the lobby. Workers continued hauling out rubble as Robert lead her deeper into City Hall. Burn marks blackened the floor. She'd planned on having Petrov design something on the stone, but she actually liked the way the flames had painted the floors with heat and malice. It couldn't stay like that. New Wichita couldn't forever be defined by its losses. But for now, it was fine.

Her cane clicked as she followed the judge toward the Great Hall, the largest room in New Wichita. The wood doors, though singed, still held and swung wide open as The Mayor approached. The sentries holding the doors were just men with machetes strapped to their sides. Not proper military dress. Not the image of a powerful nation, but of a warlord desperately trying to project strength and legitimacy.

That would have to change.

"Thank you gentlemen," she said to the sentries as she passed.

They would need uniforms and titles and ranks. Training and weapons would be supplied to create the battle-hardened warriors she needed to establish America as the dominant power in the Wilderness. Things would need to change fast, the threats were too immediate to waste any more time.

The Great Hall was thirteen tiered rows of stone benches carved out of the cave floor and encircling a single, long, wood table on a raised platform. Ten council members were already seated in tall-backed, unvarnished wooden chairs with aides sitting in the shadows. The Mayor and the judge would sit at the heads. Three solar tubes shot light right down on the table, leaving the arena seating dark.

The council stood as The Mayor gingerly descended each step toward the central stage. Robert offered his arm to help, but she waved him away.

With sweat beading on her forehead, she reached the stage,

stepping up onto the raised platform, pain screaming throughout her leg.

"Please sit," she said, forcing her voice to remain strong and steady. "We have no time to waste. Walter, where are our guns?"

Walter, the weapons engineer, drummed his fingers as he looked away from The Mayor. He slapped his palms on the table.

"I have no gunpowder! You can push me all that you want, but until we find something explosive on this damned island, arrows, spears, and other pointy things will have to suffice."

"This isn't a joke," Robert said.

"Oh, yes it is," Walter shot back. "What you're asking me to do is a joke. You're asking for magic and I'm no magician."

"What did Simon use?" The Mayor asked.

Walter shrugged big, like a petulant child. The Mayor glared at him, then turned to Robert.

"Have we heard from Rawlings?"

"Yes. They are having issues with their livestock and don't have the extra manpower to spare in the search for explosives."

"What about manure?" The Mayor asked, then looked to Walter. "I'm sure they have plenty of that. Can't manure be used as an explosive?"

"Maybe," Walter said. "I can try, but I'm having to recreate compounds without any substantive knowledge of chemistry. It took us thousands of years the first time around, it's gonna take me more than a week and a half. You have to be patient."

The Mayor eased back into her seat, her fingers picking at a loose splinter of the naked wood. A shuffle from the audience brought her eyes around. Within the shadows, Huan found a seat a few rows from the stage.

She looked back across the table.

"We need something to even the odds. We are defenseless against Simon and we are defenseless against the Engineers.

Immorality is rotting our core and now we have a new group of exiles to watch. Ideas?"

"A truce?" the master brewer offered. "With the Engineers. We've worked with them in the past, perhaps we can enlist their help getting Simon under control."

"Go to them, see what they say," The Mayor said. "We aren't going to pay them off like this is Chicago gangland protection, but we could work out an arrangement that works for both of us. Anyone else with ideas?"

The table was silent.

"No? Well, we may have one more option." The Mayor looked to the judge and nodded her head. He motioned to the sentries. One of them slipped out of the Great Hall.

"We may have a new ally that I would like you to meet," The Mayor said. "Simon is crazy, but perhaps that is why he is so powerful. It might be time to fight him on his own level."

Martha the Believer
Part 6

Martha never obsessed over marriage as a child. She never wedded dolls or dogs or cats. She didn't sketch out elaborate dresses she might one day wear. She didn't even practice her signature with the pastor's last name tacked onto the end.

No. That wasn't Martha.

Her fatalism ran deep, even when she was young. All she could rely on was the inevitability of death and the silent throne of God. Even the men she slept with always felt false and unworthy. Ways to pass the time.

She contained so much love, but with no receptacle to catch it.

Until now.

Her followers didn't know about her meeting with God. It didn't seem like a secret to Martha, but it also wasn't a thing to be mentioned offhand, it was a thing to be announced. As much as she prized her followers, or rather that she had followers, they were not alone worthy of The Announcement.

Instead, she perched herself upon a rock and gazed out in the general direction of the campground where she believed God was preparing for the greatest wedding in all of space and time.

In reality, God was in the midst of a severe panic attack as would any man who'd just accidentally proposed to an insane woman.

Martha rose her hand regally and snapped her fingers. Her followers didn't respond. She snapped again, twice and sharp.

"Did you need something?" Cheyenne asked.

"Do any of you know how to sew?" Martha asked.

April rose a weary hand.

"Good," Martha said.

"But I'll need a needle, thread, fabric," April said.

Martha resettled on her perch. "Good."

Three men emerged from the cavern, winding through workers carrying out loads of debris. Martha was curious as to why none of the Americans wore the clothes of the campground, but an array of wardrobes as if there were a shopping mall hidden within the Wilderness somewhere. Martha would have to find the source soon and start dressing like a queen.

She wondered if God would take her shopping at some point. If He could create an actual shopping mall and they'd stroll through the stores, arms linked, and anything she wanted, she'd get. She'd never gone shopping like that before, able to buy whatever she liked. Her clothes were almost always donated.

Martha noticed the machetes sheathed at their sides and wondered if becoming the Queen Of All Reality would give her powers to protect herself from the wickedness of mankind.

Like shooting fire from her eyes.

That would be fitting for a goddess.

The men approached her group. They were handsome, broad-shouldered, and stern in the way she'd seen on farmhands and ranchers. Men this attractive still unnerved Martha, but she knew that, as a queen, she no longer had to fear them. If she wanted them dead or as lovers, they would not be able to refuse. Her face flushed and her smile wavered toward wickedness.

"Which one of you is Martha?"

Martha stared at the leader, a tall man with a round, freckled face. He looked powerful. A proper Royal guard. She would have him when the time came from her to pluck her court from the best of the Wilderness. Martha waited for her followers to announce her, but none of them did. Willow looked back at Martha, but then went back to picking at the grass.

The leader sighed and asked again "Which one of you is Martha?"

Martha would enjoy breaking that spirit of his. She cleared her throat and attempted "I am the one they call Martha," but it came out clumsy and she stuttered on "call."

"Okay, whatever," the leader said. "Come with us, just you."

Martha abandoned the plan to have her a follower speak from her since they were clearly lacking in inspiration and grace. She was, again, on her own.

Martha slid from the rock in the most regal manner possible, stumbling only slightly before straightening, lifting her chin, and gliding behind the men without a word.

"So, what are we supposed to do?" April called.

Martha only answered with a dismissive wave of her hand, not even looking back to her group.

"Why do we even follow her?" Cheyenne asked, then noticed Willow stealing away toward the forest. "Where you goin'?"

"To do something that isn't secret or anything but I need to do it by myself because —."

Willow looked about her for the answer.

"Science," she said, finally and with a grimace.

"Okay, tell your boyfriend we said 'hi'," April replied, then puckering her mouth into a kiss.

"Oh, okay, I will," Willow stammered, but caught herself. "But that's not where I'm going."

"Just make that science wear a rubber," Cheyenne said. "You don't want no science babies."

Willow wasn't sure why, but that definitely sounded racist to her. Before walking into the woods, Willow looked at Martha. Their leader had her hands held out to her side, palms faced up like she was some type of fancy princess.

Willow whispered "Good for you."

Martha The Believer
Part 7

Her first infatuation, the brooding preacher, told her that the key to being a good acolyte is to never look anyone in the eyes. Don't let them see any emotion, just do your job like today is no different than yesterday or tomorrow. They will see that your focus is ever on God.

This talk came after Martha had made a point to look at all her enemies as she walked down the aisle for the first time in God's official service. She wanted to ensure that they saw how well she conducted herself in this sacred position. It didn't matter that about every kid got their chance to be an acolyte at one time or another, she was certain that she was the only one who acolyted properly, as God would expect.

She thought of the preacher's advice as she walked into the cavern of New Wichita and past the workers. Her eyes were fixed forward and impassive, even as she took in the spectacular site of New Wichita. A small, primitive downtown square stretched into the belly of the cavern with a ceiling hundreds of feet up. A wide hole gaped above. She saw cracked walls, impact craters, and rubble left from the mysterious explosion. Workers were still clearing rock, but paused to watch the procession walk by.

She enjoyed the attention.

Deeper caves dotted the walls of the cavern with lights glowing within.

The men led Martha toward the damaged City Hall. She imagined returning one day on the arm of God. A red carpet would roll down the stone steps, petals would shower down upon them as doves were released into the sky. All would bow before them. Then a grand ball would be organized, like in *Gone*

With The Wind.

Will I be able to have slaves? she thought, then quickly corrected to *servants.*

They scaled the steps of City Hall and marched through the blown-out door into a sprawling entry way. She wondered how many died in the blast. Then if it was an attack or an accident. She would have liked to ask questions, but didn't want to converse with the men, who she looked upon as "the help". Even the freckled leader who inspired a persistent, nagging lust within her. He was a minion and must be treated as such.

They reached double wooden doors and the leader rapped softly. It opened and a sentry motioned Martha in.

She took a moment to absorb the vastness of the room, unlike anything she'd seen on the Island or back in Elma, South Dakota. Only lit by beams of light shooting down from the ceiling, a group of twelve sat quietly in the light and looked back up at Martha. Arena seating circled the stage, but she only saw a few figures watching from the shadows. This disappointed her. A packed house would have been better. It would have been appropriate for receiving a queen.

Next time.

A woman sitting at the head of the table muttered to a man sitting beside her. He, nodded, stood, stepped off the stage, and walked off into the darkness on the other side. A distant door opened, then closed.

"Martha!" the woman at the head called. She wore a black dress suit that looked almost military. Martha wondered if she could order the woman to give it to her, but then decided God's queen would not wear black. Nor would God's queen ever lack for clothes. Never again.

"Won't you join us?" the woman asked, then motioned to the now vacant chair. Martha took a long breath in, then proceeded down the steps. She forced herself to take her time, not show emotion, not look anyone in the eyes.

"I am The Mayor of New Wichita," the woman said as Martha approached. "We are the capitol of America. We welcome you within our lands."

The others at the table stood as Martha stepped onto the stage. Martha sat. The others sat. No moment in this life nor the last had ever felt so right to Martha.

The Mayor's eyes steadied. Martha was unsure what to do with her own eyes now. It was probably okay to look back at a mayor. But slowly.

"Thank you for having me," Martha said, finally meeting The Mayor's eyes and really proud of how steady and confident her own voice sounded. Martha silently reminded herself to say too little instead of too much.

"Well," The Mayor began. "This is the council of New Wichita. Some are tradesmen, some are doctors and judges."

Martha gazed across the table, trying to place titles with faces. Some were clearly skeptical of Martha's importance, but soon they would be certain when God arrived to claim His bride. She then wondered if "bride" should be capitalized now, since she would be divine. Sort of. The Bride. She liked it way better than "Martha".

She then realized that The Mayor had been talking to her. There'd been a question and everyone was now waiting for a response.

"Who's he?" Martha asked instead, motioning to the tall man at the other head. "Why's he get the other big chair?"

"Robert is our judge," The Mayor said. "We are a just people, so it is an important position."

"Just?" Martha asked, mocking. "That's why you're blowing each other up?"

The Mayor sat back, picked up a pencil, and tapped the eraser on the table as she studied Martha.

"It wasn't us, it was one of yours," The Mayor said. "Simon."

"How?" Martha asked, losing her regal bearing. Her voice now sounded smaller, like a girl's and Martha hated it.

"He's become quite powerful, Martha," Robert said. "We consider him our biggest threat."

"Simon?" Martha asked, her voice still small. "He's just a trickster. A pest. He is nothing before the power of God."

The Mayor smiled.

"Yes, very true," The Mayor said. "And my people need to be reminded of that, which is why we brought you here. We are formulating a plan to secure our borders from Simon and all the other menaces of the Wilderness. We need help instilling hope and godliness."

Martha sensed that she was being pandered to, but didn't really mind.

"Before I agree to anything," Martha said. "I need to make an announcement."

The Mayor nodded her head.

Martha studied each face, looking for the most obvious disbeliever. She steadied on the judge.

"God has proposed to me." Her smile was smug, not regal, but she didn't care.

"Proposed what?" Robert asked.

"Marriage."

He laughed, gleefully and with a bit of a sneer. A few others joined in, but not as gregariously. Martha held her bearing and waited for him to finish.

"You're serious, aren't you?" Robert asked.

Martha looked to The Mayor. "He came to me just outside your cavern. We walked into the woods and He asked for my hand in marriage. I will be The Bride of God's Dominion."

Martha hated the way that was phrased. It sounded as if she would be marrying His dominion instead of Him. Too late to rephrase now though.

The Mayor's head tilted like a confused dog as she struggled with the concept. She traded a long, measured look with Robert. Martha thought that The Mayor looked like a beautiful wolf when she smiled.

"Good," The Mayor said. "Good for you, honey."

"So, when are the nuptials?" a mousy, mean-looking woman asked. Martha noticed her scribbling in a notebook.

"Soon," Martha said, though she had no actual idea. "God is making preparations."

"Congratulations, my dear," Robert said. "You will make a lovely bride."

She recognized the tone of his voice and decided that he would be the second person executed when she assumed her throne.

"Well, that means our plans for you are that much more fitting," The Mayor said. "Please accept a place within New Wichita until the time of your wedding. You will be our princess."

Martha nodded, satisfied.

"Do you have any powers?" Robert asked. "Like Simon?"

"I have the power of God's love," Martha said. "What greater power is there?"

She kept her gaze on the judge as she pushed out her chair and stood. The others at the table, uncertain, slowly stood too.

"I will go out and wait with my followers," Martha announced. "Let me know when my chambers are ready."

Martha stepped off the stage and up the stairs of the arena. The sentries opened the doors for her.

Once Martha was gone, laughter erupted. The Mayor hushed

them, but smiled.

"It's not her fault," The Mayor said. "She's just simple. That doesn't mean that she won't be useful. Let's isolate her for now until we decide exactly want to do with her."

"What if she's telling the truth," the judge asked. "Devil's advocate. God's not exactly a predictable Guy, so what if she's about to become the queen of the universe?"

The council was quiet for several moments. The Mayor tapped the pencil against the table as she thought.

"Well," she said. "We will need to make sure that she is our queen."

Being A Child God

Part 3

High school and the Island are pretty much the same thing. Territorialism, isolation, naive love. I never had the friends I wanted, but rather the friends I was stuck with. Cruelty abounds. I've been reviled and dismissed in both realms, no matter how elevated my position.

Even with divinity, I never stopped feeling small.

The thing about being God is you are rarely worshiped by the people you hope to be worshiped by. Maybe someone cool might give you a kudo from time to time, like after really great sex or as an act of faux-humility following some athletic achievement, but the people who are really into me aren't exactly first round draft picks, you know.

Hangers-on. Star fuckers. Salesmen. Social climbers. I hate them all because I sorta expect I would do the exact same thing if I weren't already at the top rung.

And being God, I can't have friends. Not like before. Not

like back in Vegas where a small crew of thieves and semi-pro magicians adopted me during my early days. We would haunt the lesser casinos, pulling small jobs, counting cards, drinking the bars out of Jaeger, and fucking rich tourists. I'd never been happier. I'd never been more free.

They would never associate with me as their god, though. Not unless they were at their most desperate.

And only then if they saw an angle.

I tried bringing three of them up a while back. Mikey, Lana, and Pam the Sham. I wanted an entourage and some partners in crime. We'd go off into the universe and cause mischief when I felt trapped by the throne. Just blowing off some steam so I could re-center. Some of those near-Earths you've seen on your travels? Yeah. They know me. I've never been as far out as you, but me and my entourage have gotten around.

I gave my friends power. I warned them of their limits.

But I couldn't control them. They were so cruel.

I sent them all back to Hell.

They were my best friends.

And in Hell they will stay along with all the other people I loved and admired back on Earth. Forever and ever and ever.

Amen.

Maybe I will join them one day once someone snatches the throne from me. I'm not holding my breath though. It's been a long time without a single volunteer.

And, yeah, Hell. It still exists. A void where the damned are aware that they exist beyond Heaven. Eternal silence. Eternal suffering. I want to end Hell, I want to be better than The Old Man, but I don't know where to or how to release all those corrupt souls so their chaos won't spill over into my universe. Perhaps you can help me with this, give me some advice on how to fix the unfixable. Save the unsaveable. A sandbox for the damned. So many of my friends are there. So many people I have respected. I release those that I can, but have had to send so many back. It is awful. I would rather go to Hell myself than to toss another into that black hole. That cold, bottomless grave. But I carry on as God because I must. I keep my circle small and filled with people I loathe, but can trust. I keep my heart closed.

Anat is the only woman that I can love without reservation. She was brought to the Island by God. She was, I believe more and more, brought to the Island for me. The Old Man knew what He was doing. Way more than me. I should be a better king. I should be a better husband. I should treat her better, treat her as she deserves to be treated but I still find myself at a loss. No woman like her had ever existed before. She is a miracle. How do you prepare for a such a thing? A true miracle? A gift from a Creator?

But He is the past and I am the present and all this hand-wringing won't change a thing. Adequate or no, I am her king and this is my job and I am going to acquit myself as best I can until someone else takes over.

Have you ever considered it? The throne? I mean really considered it?

That Bastard, Tommy

I didn't like Tommy. I never said much about it 'cause I didn't see it as my place, but he didn't deserve Edward. I was no gentleman, mind you, but I knew the women who were too pure for me and I steered clear. As a grifter and a God, I do my best not to target the vulnerable and the good.

But Tommy. He fed on pure people. He was a cannibal, consuming human emotion. A user in the truest nature of the word. He was beautiful. True. Beautiful and soothing and probably an astounding lover, but the maintenance just wasn't worth it. He was best left as a plaything for those shrewd enough to abandon him on the side of a lonely highway once Tommy's engine stopped roaring.

He didn't deserve Edward and I will never be convinced otherwise. During my early days as a young god, I thought of cutting Tommy out of Edward's life like a cancerous growth. But I feared the lovers would only curl into one another, showing their armor to the outside world, tightening their grip on one another. No, love must be killed from within.

As Tommy reached the lake in pursuit of Edward, he found the campsite abandoned. I decided to walk out to meet him. I wore the old shorts and t-shirt God assigned us on our flight to the Island. I smiled warmly, hiding my disdain to keep him from fleeing back into the woods.

"Where is he, Simon?" Tommy asked me.

"I don't know," I lied. "Couldn't keep waiting for you, I guess."

Tommy examined the sand, looking for tracks or other signs of movement. Any clue to lead him to the man he couldn't stop torturing.

"The others, have you seen them?" Tommy asked. "I heard they all came over."

"They did."

Tommy turned to address me with a frustrated scowl.

"Why did you do it?" Tommy asked. "Attack the Americans? Things are only going to get worse.."

"Why are you so cruel to Edward? Or do you not know what you are doing to him?"

Tommy turned away from me to look back the empty grass where the campsite used to be. "Go to hell, Simon."

"Well on my way, brother."

Tommy shook his head and began walking toward the woods, guessing at which direction he might find Edward.

"Have you seen the ovens?" I called to Tommy. "Have you seen the people inside?"

Tommy stopped, ducked his head. "I don't have to explain myself to you."

"No, you don't. I don't imagine you have to explain yourself to anyone. You are who you are. It is Edward's fault for loving you."

Tommy began walking to the woods again. I burst into mist and swept in front of him, materializing in his path. I held up a hand to stop him, but offered a pleasant smile.

"I'll help you because I need you to help Edward," I said. "I need you to warn him and the others."

"Warn them about what?"

"I attacked the Americans because of their ovens, but also as an experiment. I believe I know the way forward and it is about to get really messy. The Americans and the Engineers are going to take a lot of interest in our friends. They are going to try to turn them against me."

"Maybe they should," Tommy said.

"The Americans are lost and needed a warning, but they aren't my enemy. They just need to be domesticated. Same with the Engineers. I don't want to fight these people. I want them to join me. Our real enemy is across the lake. To bring peace to the Island, we are going to have to deal with God first."

Tommy looked across the lake. "How?"

"Leave that to me." I rose my hand to point toward the northwest edge of the Island. "Find Edward and the others. Tell Billy to bar the windows, barricade the doors, and pack up the good china. A helluva storm is coming."

I Cannot Die

Part 10

Have I considered the throne? No, Simon. Never too seriously. Even during the uprising, I never wanted to take His seat, I just wanted to talk some sense into Him.

It didn't work. Clearly.

You also mentioned bringing me back. I appreciate the sentiment, but even if you could clutch onto me this far out and drag me back to your universe, I wouldn't want to return to the Island or any of God's creation.

I am done with it. I still think of many of you fondly, but that time is done.

In the long days drifting toward the distant stars of this new realm, I believe I can hear someone whispering to me. I can't make out the words, I don't understand the language, but the voice seems real.

It's the voice of one child whispering to another through air vents deep into the night, long after the parents have put them to bed. Curious, defiant, and very restless.

I believe the whispers are urgent and real, not just ghostly echoes, sound waves listing through space. I believe that someone is anxious for me to arrive, to bring me into something new and grand, maybe something truly perfect.

But I don't suppose I would really want that either. Perfection doesn't fit me, does it? Maybe they want me to wreck their perfection because they've grown bored. Yes, I hope that's it. An untended toddler in Legoland.

And, on Tommy, please don't be so hard on the flawed. I understand your feelings and admire your protective instinct toward Edward, but Tommy is as God made him. If you are going to lead these people, you must show patience and understanding. Close Hell, find a new realm for the damned, find a way to bring them into your light. Don't just smite as The Old Man did. No one is beyond salvation, Simon.

No one.

Not even me.

Willow and Her Beloved Stump

Blood seeped from Trevor's neck as two crows picked at his flesh. He grimaced, raised his head to the sky and took in as deep a breath as the pike lodged through his body would allow. In the first days of his execution, after fighting the judge of New Wichita over a stupid card game, Trevor believed that the pain would eventually fade. His mind and body would give up, hand itself over to fate, and spare him the needless barrage of emergency signals.

But no. It's been weeks now and the agony was as intense as when he was first placed on the pike, set aflame, and left for the scavengers to gnaw on all his extremities, save his head. Somehow they knew not to destroy the head.

The Americans returned every three days to feed him just enough to keep him lucid, aware, and horrifying to all strangers that might stray too far into their lands.

"Shoo!" a voice cried in a panicked scream behind him. He couldn't see, but knew it was the strange, kind woman who had no idea that she was the most beautiful thing to ever be brought to the Island. In the past life, he would have seen her in the park or in a bar or out walking a little dog dressed to match her. The dog would wiggle free, scamper across the sidewalk and out into the street. Trevor would toss away his bundled legal files, dodge through traffic, scoop up the pup, and deliver it to the frantic woman. Trevor had always been a sucker for grand gestures. It's what cost him most of his jobs and, ultimately, his life.

But this grand gesture would go perfectly.

He'd leap onto the sidewalk, breathless and laughing. She'd hug the dog tightly and thank him effusively. A beat would pass as he gently scratched the dog's back. He would tell her that she brought light to his day and she would want him to say more, but instead he would walk away, never to see her again, allowing the moment to pleasantly haunt both of them for the rest of their lives.

The older he became, the more he appreciated the allure of unpursued loves, unopened doors, fantasies untarnished by a reality that never failed to disappoint. To walk away from a woman was to shield her. It was a mercy. He was a mess on Earth when he was still blessed with arms and legs. Now, on the Island, little more than a slab of charred, rotting beef, he was a downright burden.

He was more afraid of love now than he would ever be of the Americans.

Willow rushed to him, swatting at the crows.

"Shoo you evil creatures!"

"Oh, be nice, they are my only friends."

The crows screeched at her, then leapt into the air to soar up to distant branches where they could caw down at her from a safe distance.

"Oh, goodness, you're bleeding," Willow said.

"It'll stop, just let it be," Trevor replied, not turning his head to look at Willow because turning his head would damage his body and seeing her would damage his heart.

"I'm getting you off this darn thing," Willow said as she bent down to examine the pike.

"Darling, I really do appreciate your heroic zeal, but I am fine where I am. The Americans don't appreciate tampering."

"That's hooey. I'm not leaving you like this."

Trevor couldn't stop smiling at "hooey." He wasn't sure if he'd ever heard anyone say that word with earnest before. Willow circled the pike, planning, then looking up to Trevor's face. Sorrowful empathy flashed across her perfect face and Trevor quickly imagined their lives together had America not happened to him.

Long strolls across the Island, swimming naked in the lake under the moonlight, a sprawling, abundant flowerbed, her fussing and chattering, him listening and laughing and doting on her, always trying to earn his place in her life.

Then ruining it like he always ruined his happiness. Something small and petty, but perfect for sabotaging love.

"I need you to leave," Trevor said, serious and stern.

"And I need you to be quiet and lemme think."

She said it almost like "thank". West Texas he guessed. He knew a girl in college who floored him every time she said "swamming." She smiled, broad and perfect. He was powerless. He remained silent as she studied the pike.

"How much does it hurt?" Willow asked.

"It's a 12 inch wide spike jammed through my torso," Trevor said. "It doesn't feel great."

"Poor baby boy," she whispered, then leaned up to him and kissed his burnt forehead. "I'll get ya sorted."

She wrapped her arms around what was left of his hips.

"Wait, wait, wait!" Trevor said.

"What?"

"I'm being serious now, don't do this. The Americans will come after you. They will come after us. You can't hide from them. Do not lift me off."

"Is that so?" she asked, then jerked him upwards.

Trevor screamed and the crows flew away. The pike released, his body slid off the point, a cold shock overwhelmed him as air reached the freshly exposed nerves.

Then black. Empty black.

***

The leaves were falling sidewards.

He slept again.

Movement beckoned his eyes to pry open. The leaves falling sidewards again.

More movement He felt ground below him, uneven and sliding along his back.

He was moving. The leaves weren't falling, but he was being dragged instead. The nerves started awakening again. Pain everywhere. His breath caught. He groaned. The movement stopped. Willow appeared above him.

"You alright? Can I do anything for ya? Thirsty?"

She pronounced it more like "awwight" which made him chuckle. His eyes were blurry, the tears gathering in bursts as if trying to expel the pain.

"Hey!" Willow continued. "I"m here. Whaddah you need?"

The tortuous wave began to ease and settle. His brain, realizing he'd had enough, showered him with endorphins which smothered the pain. He was breathing steady again.

"Where are we?"

"I don't know," Willow answered.

"Where are you taking me?"

"Away. Just away. Away from the Americans. Away from people and away from God. I'll find us somewhere nice."

It was the most absurd thing he'd ever heard someone say but it sounded fantastic. No plan. Just fate. He lacked the legs to run away from her. From this, whatever it was. He would finally have to see something through to the very end.

"Are you just going to drag me around for the rest of eternity?" Trevor said, trying, but not quite achieving a smile.

"Yes!"

Her face beamed resolute and fearless. It was the first spring sun. It was the warm touch of the divine. He gave up fighting and prayed to the Lord "Don't let me fuck this up."

Ossie the Widower
Part 3

"Every time someone looks at me, every time Tommy's name is mentioned, I feel just so humiliated, so helpless. I hate that he's made me feel so vulnerable, so hurt, like a child, and yet, all I hope for is for him to return to me. Pathetic. I'm so pathetic."

"Love is mania. It is an eager dog digging to get underneath a fence and out into the beautiful world."

Edward nodded, smiling despite it all. "Is that a quote from something?"

"Probably," Ossie said. "I never know when I'm plagiarizing."

Ossie looked ahead at the rest of the group. Edward had wanted to lag behind just enough to get some privacy. Ossie knew Edward needed to talk. He'd needed to talk since Tommy first fell off the edge of the Island, but solace was a hard thing to find on the Island.

"This is my first love, Ossie. My first real love. It's not like when we were young and our bones are were made of rubber and bounced and bent, but never broke. I'm too old to be dealing with this. I'm almost ninety years old and I'm acting like a twitterpated teenager."

"Twitterpated? Is that a quote from something?"

"You never watched, *Bambi*?" Edward asked.

"No. But I like the word. It fits."

Ossie chewed on the idea of living a full life without experiencing the chaos of love. To never feel anything as powerful as a freshly-seeded obsession. He thought back to his first love. It was a girl, not a boy, and he did love her. Not in the pure way he would eventually love the man he would marry, but it was as real as he'd experienced to that point. He guessed it was as real as any love could be before being truly challenged by life.

"No, you're wrong," Ossie said, glancing ahead to see Raul, who had taken his guitar out. Raul started strumming as he walked between the trees, ducking under branches, singing just above a whisper.

"Love wasn't any easier in high school," Ossie said. "Heartbreak is heartbreak at any age. If anything, it got easier as I got older as I hardened and I allowed fewer people into the core of me. It is true that, if Isaac had betrayed me, I would have been shattered like a broken window. Just pieces of me poured out along the ground and it would have felt like I would never to be whole again.

"But I'd felt that way before. It would have been worse with Isaac because he was my one, great love, but I knew how to put myself together because I'd done it before. You don't know that you can survive Tommy because you've never had to survive love before. But you will and perhaps you will love someone else and perhaps they will shatter you too. It's never easy, Edward. Love is never easy, but you learn with each time that the hurt passes. It always passes because that is our way. Once we decide to stop holding onto the pain, it will leave. It will come back. It will leave. It returns as a tide while we move on through our lives."

Edward nodded, the tears making his cheeks glisten from the shards of sunlight cutting through the forest canopy. Ossie was surprised that a man of God would wear his hurt so close to the surface, but Edward was never a typical clergyman. Edward wasn't a typical anyone and Ossie knew that Edward could do better than Tommy, but that didn't mean anything with love. It never did.

"I think I just need to get laid," Edward said, wiping away the tears. It was an awkward invitation, a plea from the hurt. Ossie recognized it for what it was and pushed the temptation from his mind.

"It won't help," Ossie said. "My sister told me when I was very young to never to try to fuck away heartbreak. It was the best advice I'd ever received."

Edward smiled and managed a "you're right, of course you're right," before wiping off his cheek.

Ossie did feel a flicker of desire stir, but he recognized Edward as a beautiful, gentle man. Edward wasn't ready to move beyond Tommy and the sex would quickly become a regret. The Island was small enough already.

And Ossie wasn't ready to move beyond Isaac. What if that plane brought Isaac to the Island one day? Not likely, but possible and Ossie wanted to remain pure in case his great love returned to him. Maybe that wouldn't always be the case, maybe it would eventually be Ossie's turn to move on.

But not today. Not for a very long time.

Raul's singing grew. Ossie couldn't pick out the song, but could tell it was a sad ballad to something grand and doomed. Raul's voice was restrained like a lovely bird gazing out of a window. Ossie hoped, even more than Isaac's return to the Island, that Edward could have his own great love one day. Edward deserved it.

A heavy, unnatural tug at Ossie's heart blurred his vision. It felt like the beginning tremor of a stroke, but not quite. White glows seemed to illuminate from the forest. Ossie's limbs weakened slightly, but then adrenaline kicked in. The white glows were humans. Two women. They were hiding within the forest.

The spell passed. Edward was looking up at Ossie, Edward's hand feeling Ossie's face.

"Are you okay?" Edward asked.

Ossie took a deep breath, his eyes directed toward where the white glows had been. The bout of weakness was replaced with strength, almost anger. Like in New Orleans, when Ossie learned that his Fight or Flight instinct leaned on the former.

"Get the others," Ossie said.

Edward turned and ran after the group. Ossie gazed into the forest, the greens and browns blending into one another. He listened, but only heard insects clicking at one another, leaves brushing and unsettling from the wind.

He walked off the trail and toward the white glow, pushing branches out of his way and striding forward. He was sweating from the anxious energy.

"We aren't your enemies," a voice called. "We don't want to fight."

"Why are you watching us?" Ossie asked back into the forest.

Mildred stepped out from behind a tree. She was more uncertain than when she'd approached them at the pit. The woman in the sheer gown followed her. Yulia, Ossie guessed. The seamstress that gave Billy and Sophia the new clothes.

"We wanted to see if you were doing as we asked," Mildred said.

Ossie heard the group running towards him, moving around the trees, ducking through bushes and limbs, reaching Ossie and flanking out.

"You're heading the wrong direction, Billy," Mildred said.

"I never agreed to anything," Billy said, then looked at Yulia. Her face was passive, unyielding.

"We haven't decided what we are going to do," Sophia said. "Simon is still our friend and we aren't going to betray him until we are sure he is actually dangerous."

Mildred studied Sophia, then looked up to the trees where a growing choir of songbirds were swooping in and taking up perches. Swarms of gnats started clouding the space between

Sophia's group and the two Engineers. A grunt drew Mildred's eyes behind her where a warthog stood, watching the Engineer.

"Very good, my dear," Mildred said, turning back to the group. "Very, very good."

Mildred looked to Ossie.

"And we had high hopes for you too, Ossie," Mildred said. "We thought you might both be wonderful candidates, but that little trick you just pulled was more impressive than I expected. How did you know we were watching?"

Billy and the others looked to Ossie.

"You should come with us," Mildred said, passing her eyes between Ossie and Sophia. "You both belong with the Engineers. We can make you stronger."

"These are my people," Ossie said, but the offer was interesting.

"We can teach you how to better protect them," Yulia said.

Sophia clasped Billy's hand. "It's too early," Sophia said. "We need to stay together."

Mildred smiled and looked back to Billy. "We are protecting you. We will keep the Americans away from your group for a time, but we need some assurance that you will make it worth our effort."

"We will do what we think is best for us," Billy said. "We aren't running errands for you or the Americans."

"Of course not," Mildred said. "Of course not. I will tell you this, though. We've had warnings for many years that a group would bring a great change to the Island and we aren't certain if it will be a peaceful transition. 'A holy man will hold the life of God in his hands.' That is the prophecy your group is about to fulfill."

All eyes were now on Edward.

"How do you know it's about me?" Edward asked.

"You are the only Holy Man to ever reach the Island, Edward," Mildred said. "Unless you count Jay, but none of us ever do."

Yulia flashed a conspiratorial smile, then looked at Edward.

"I know your heart is conflicted, pastor," Yulia said. "But something big is coming and the strange way our universe works has you fixed at the epicenter of a great upheaval. We believe Simon is the energy that creates that storm and all the lives on the Island may be left wrecked in its wake. We want to understand and contain the disaster the best we can. We need your help. You will give you time to explore the Wilderness and decide your place in it, but this storm is coming soon. We won't wait for long."

Satisfied, Mildred clasped Yulia's hand and led her into the trees. Edward's group remained silent for a time.

"Did anybody understand any of that?" Billy asked.

"Edward's going to kill God, I guess?" Raul said, mostly joking.

Ossie looked to Edward. Edward looked at the ground.

"So," Billy began, approaching Ossie. "You're magic now too?"

"It appears so," Ossie answered.

"Any other surprises?" Billy asked. "Like anything? Pet dragon? Secret membership in the Illuminati?"

"No, just a good old-fashioned magical negro."

"What tricks can you do?" Todd asked, then grimaced. "That didn't come out right."

"No, Todd, it really didn't. And I'll let you know what tricks I can do as soon as I find out myself."

Billy rolled his eyes, then laughed. He patted Ossie's shoulder. "Glad to have you on the team."

Billy held out his hand for Sophia, who walked over and clasped it. The group began shuffling back out toward the trail, walking vaguely north in hopes of finding Petrov and perhaps some answers as well.

Ossie kept close to Edward. They didn't talk anymore, but Ossie did soon realize that he was wrong about Edward's first, great love. It wasn't Tommy. It was God. Two men that Edward loved without reserve and two men that only repaid Edward with pain.

And Edward may soon kill one of them. Perhaps both.

Ossie wanted to say something comforting to Edward, but instead they walked together in silence. Ossie wished Isaac were with them. Isaac was always better at these sorts of things.

The Girl Who Doomed God
Part 5

By day four, God had abandoned all hope for a productive camp experience with the newest round of souls. I'd assumed the angels would have rebuilt God's cabin immediately following Anat's firestorm, yet The Old Man sulked within its charred carcass, wearing a poncho, aviator sunglasses, and a "This Bud's For You" trucker hat. He sat heavily on the still blood-stained couch where Jay had nearly died after Billy pushed him into the lake.

The couch was without a single singe as the rest of the cabin was nothing but scorched wood, melted plastic, and a very lonely and confused Creator.

It felt like the end of the experiment; God was ready to give up on the Island, send all the souls home, and pack up shop. I hoped he would because, across the water, I sensed only trouble.

That morning, I cashed in some favors with Josiah, an angel that was once a lesser servant of Metatron. Something like a celestial bike messenger. He's since developed into a smuggler. I'm sure you are acutely aware of this, but after the destruction of Earth, many of the angels had basically devolved into idle and curious teenagers testing the boundaries of ethics in the absence of purpose and a present father figure. This lethargy often worked to my advantage. Josiah was among my favorites for his discretion, resourcefulness, and his surprisingly deep catalog of Little Johnny jokes.

At any rate, Josiah returned by the afternoon with 83 water guns of all shapes, colors, and sizes along with a trashbag full of water balloons. The campground soon erupted into a no-holds barred water war and I watched in awe of my own deft touch at soothing the human soul.

The only rule, of course, was Jay was absolutely off-limits. The poor boy would mope around the outer limits of the water gun fight, watching the chaotic fun. His Father watched from within the ruins.

For my part, I was sprinting through the action with a backpack-fed water cannon in one hand and a pistol in the other. I know it's a terrible thing to say, but I've always loved war in any form and fashion. Yes, real war is horrific and tragic. Glorifying combat to young children only strengthens the hero myth which drove men to their untimely deaths from the dawn of civilization to Armageddon.

But it's also really thrilling, especially when you are immortal. It is shameful how many times angels and demons interceded in both war and sport just for a bit of fun.

Also, I'm the devil and war is, quite literally, in my job description. "Angel of corruption, war, vice, and general mischievousness."

By day four, Anat was a complete pariah within the campground. To the exiles who knew nothing of the Engineers and the Wilderness, Anat's power was pure witchery and her rejection of God's authority was terrifying. She came and went as she pleased. I was afraid of her. God was afraid of her. But we learned to just give her space and no more infernos.

Jay noticed her watching from behind a cabin and walked toward her. I'd turned to watch and a football-sized water balloon ruptured against my head. I shook off the water and looked towards God. He was also watching Jay. He stood up off His couch and carefully stepped through the ruins so He could get a better look.

I took off my backpack water cannon and handed it to a passing child. Another water balloon burst against my face, but

I didn't pay it any more mind. I stepped away from the heart of the fray and watched Jay approach Anat.

The frenzy of the water fight ebbed as children noticed what I was watching, and their eyes steadied on Jay and Anat.

"I'm sorry that you are unhappy here," Jay said to her.

Anat folded her arms across her chest and looked away.

"Leave me alone please," Anat said.

"I am powerful too." Jay took a step forward, his palms facing out as if approaching a feral dog. "It is a terrible thing to have power and not know why. Does it hurt?"

"What?" Anat asked.

"Does it hurt?"

She studied Jay, then shook her head.

"Mine does," Jay said. "It always hurt. Even when I was on Earth, it always hurt."

"You had your powers on Earth?"

"Yes, I was born with them. I was born with knowledge too. It felt like splinters jammed into my mind. I heard voices early, which was scary. It made me mad too. But it was the sin that hurt the most. It was all around me, all the time. The great sins, the unforgivable sins, the small, but damaging sins. I felt them, I absorbed them like poison. I still do and am always sick. Always. My Father tries to wash it from me, all this poison in my body, but then I am weak without it.

"It is a terrible thing to be blessed, Anat. I just want you to know that I understand what you are going through. I am unhappy here too. I don't have friends because I hate everyone on this Island for their sin. For what that sin does to me. On Earth, I forgave them because I knew they were ignorant. But here, they've seen the Promise fulfilled. They know the Truth, yet still fade from it. A part of me understands why they sin. We feel so far away from Paradise. We can see it below, but we don't know when we will go back, when we will be released from all of this temptation. But it is still sin."

Jay turned to look back at God, who had stopped by the utility sheds near Cabin Five. Jay looked back at Anat. He stepped closer. In a whisper, he added "I hate my Father as well."

"Who are you?" Anat asked.

"You know who I am."

Anat's eyes narrowed. She glanced at me, then God. God began walking across the campground toward Jay.

"I'm sorry that He's done this to you," Anat said. "But I don't trust you. I don't trust any of you and I want to be left alone."

Jay noticed God approaching. Jay took another step towards Anat.

"Don't," Anat said.

"My Father is afraid of you. My brother is afraid of you. Even the angels are afraid of you, but I am not."

"I don't want to hurt you," Anat said. Heat began distorting the air.

"Pain is my constant," Jay said, taking another step. His skin was reddening, starting to blister. "I was created to absorb pain."

The wood siding on the cabin beside Anat charred and smoked, the grass burned, but Jay continued forward.

"Stop it, Anat!" God shouted.

Jay's hair caught fire and a child behind me screamed. Jay's skin blackened, flaking off.

"Let me die, Father!" Jay said, his body igniting.

Jay stumbled, but stayed on his feet, now consumed in flames.

"Let me die!" His words were slurred, pained.

God sprinted across the campground to reach His son.

Anat screamed.

Light burst outwards from her, crumbling the cabin and flinging God and Jay backwards. They fell and rolled twenty feet away.

God pushed up to His knees. His sunglasses had been flung off, exposing his dark red, pupils eyes. God scrambled to Jay. He blew a forceful wind across the boy, extinguishing the flames and leaving a burnt corpse.

The children were running in all directions, looking for shelter.

Jay took in a breath. He coughed. His eyelids were burnt away, so he gazed into the sky.

"Let me die," Jay wheezed.

God cradled His son in his arms.

"Our work is not done," God whispered.

Jay wailed.

The ground around me was littered with plastic, multi-colored water guns and the shreds of water balloons. Anat stood alone, crying bitterly, but refusing to hide her face or run away.

Seeing my brother in pain, no matter our shared past, infuriated me. I marched toward God. "Why did you bring her here?"

God didn't respond. He reached for His sunglasses and placed them back on his face.

Jay's skin was already regenerating. His eyelids were closed but his face was still twisted by pain.

"When will it be enough?" I asked God.

God looked up at me, but His sunglasses hid his emotion. He lifted Jay in His arms and walked to the ruins of His cabin. He stepped over the charred remains of his flooring and laid Jay upon the couch.

I turned to Anat.

"I've only asked to be left alone," Anat said. "I don't want to hurt anyone."

"Then go!" I said. "Go to the Wilderness. Simon is waiting for you."

Being A Child God

Part 4

I went to Hell today to visit Wylde. On Earth, she'd been both a whore and the most interesting person I'd ever met. She told me that she sold her body because she excelled at sex and, like any other skill, one should be a paid fair wage for one's talents. This was excellent news for me because I was paying her for sex anyway, so now I could view our transaction as enlightened. I wasn't a creep at all, but using my buying power to advocate for her very exotic variety of feminism.

Like all whores in Las Vegas at that time, Wylde was also a model, a dancer, an event coordinator, and a part-time waitress. I first met her in a dressing room in a dingy strip club where I'd picked up a spur-of-the-moment gig to do a raunchier version of my normal stage show. The Pacific Rim Orthodontist Alliance Trade Show was in town and the strip club hoped that a bonus magic show might lure in some extra traffic.

It didn't but I still got paid the same.

Wylde was naked and prancing like an awkward teenager while her friends laughed and her enemies seethed. Objectively, Wylde wasn't one of the classic Vegas beauties—tall, pole-thin, and so very over it. Wylde was short, always carried a little extra weight, but glowed. Oh how she glowed. She knew literature, politics, religion, hurt, and joy. When she talked, those green eyes were as big as lily blossoms and impossible to escape.

And no woman moved like her. In bed, on the street, or even gliding across the kitchen naked while talking about the benefits of socialism within a faux-free market economy. She could have been anything, but that she chose to be a prostitute made her all the more fascinating.

I went to Hell to retrieve Wylde. Anat and I were "on a break", you know.

Bringing light to the emptiness of Hell made finding her soul as dizzying as picking out a singular moth amid a swarm desperate to touch a lantern.

But I did find her. She was on the edge of my light, daring me to find her. I pulled her out of the void, I gave her a body, I asked her to move for me like she'd once moved on Earth. I asked her to tell me of Hell and how her views had shifted since death. Since discovering the truth of it all.

She asked me if I was really the new God. I told her I was.

She told me her body was for those who suffer, not for Gods that inflict the suffering. She demanded to be returned to Hell.

I was furious and left her on the Island. I am now too afraid to face her . You'd think that being divine would mean that no one could hurt you, but no one is beyond Wylde.

The Girl Who Doomed God
Part 6

I met Anat at the waterfall. I'd seen the flames and knew she was finally on her way to me. By the time she reached the Wilderness, she was a woman. Dark, distant, but with glorious, secretive, brown eyes. I grew to adulthood immediately to match her. My robes shifted to a gunmetal gray business suit and blood red tie. She studied me from the other side of the waterfall, the deafening roar preventing me from calling out to her.

Steam started billowing up from the water. The current slowed and evaporated, leaving only rocks and mud. I stepped back from the heat. Anat walked carefully down into the empty lake bed as the mud dried and hardened to greet her every footstep. The leaves around me were burning, white smoke from the grass drifting up.

My heart stammered from the sparkle of hope. Love. Glorious and agonizing love.

She carried herself differently. Defiant now. No longer looking at the ground, but eyes pointed ahead at something indefinite, something more worthy of her attention. Me.

The mist tumbled and rose as the lake water continued to boil. The fog rolled across the lake bed. Her camp clothes began burning off as she disappeared beneath the mist.

I tried not to fidget. I tried to keep my back straight, my smile clever and assured, but I was terrified. It must have been what weddings felt like. Real weddings. Not the $200 joke wedding I had with Angela Hornbender after a dare got a little out of control.

Then Anat's face rose from the fog, but she paused, her neck and bare shoulders still hidden beneath the steam. She examined me, her face steady and unreadable.

"I don't trust you, Simon," she said.

"Smart girl."

Her regal, angular face was still framed by the fog. A deadly predator lurking in cover, waiting for the prey to wander just a few inches closer.

"Can I kill you?" she asked.

"I don't know," I said. "Probably not. Everything is hard to kill on this Island, especially me."

She looked over my suit, then back to me.

"Give me new clothes."

The demand thrilled me. Her voice, the implications.

"I can only give you an illusion," I said, then motioning to my own suit. "This is not real, this is only an idea. But I do know a woman that can dress you however you want. I will take you to her."

Anat looked at the Wilderness behind me. Anat stepped forward, her naked shoulders rising above the surface. She looked me over.

"You really want me to be a queen?" she asked.

"Yes."

"Make me a queen then."

She walked to me, lifting from the fog as gold and white sparkled across her body, my illusion glittering into existence around her naked skin.

Smoke rose from the bushes and grass. Leaves were browning, then bursting into flames. Trees hissed and popped as fire spread out across the woods. The waters rushed back over the edge of the Island and my queen strode toward me. My mind struggled to calm itself enough to complete the illusion.

All around and within us was inferno.

And there she stood, a diamond white dress gliding along

her lovely figure. The dress skimmed along the lengths of her arms, diminished into thin silk strands that laced between her fingers. Flecks of gold were dotted within the white, catching the sun, making her shine.

She glanced down at her new dress, felt for the fabric that was not there. A smile emerging. She looked to me, her chin tilted up in pride. I wanted to kiss her like the seal of a truce between great nations.

But instead, I only offered her my hand. She took it with a light touch. I led her through the flames and on toward our virgin kingdom. And wherever she walked, her bare feet left a trail of charred grass in her wake.

The Girl Who Doomed God
Part 7

I talked fast. Peacocking, embellishing, laying out all my grand plans for the Island. Rambling mostly. I was even annoying myself.

She never smiled at me, but slightly away, her eyes always allusive and difficult. Coy. It drove me wild and I talked faster and brasher. I was a jester dancing before a queen, never knowing if her shy smile withheld an impending laugh or condemnation.

But talk was just talk. I knew she had to see the Wilderness to understand why it had to be tamed and why it must be ours. She had to see the terror, the folly of the God who needed to be contained.

I wouldn't say "overthrown." Not yet. Not out loud. I wasn't certain if it was possible. Also, He might hear.

"So, the Americans," she said, interrupting my anecdote about being propositioned by three truckers in a New Mexico Love's Travel Shoppe. I have no idea how I got started on that story or why I thought it would impress her.

"Yes?" I asked, thankful for the interruption.

"Their power comes from organization and brutality, basically?" Anat asked.

"Right. Well, for now, anyways. They are meddlers and I don't know what is possible on this Island. Also, they are super pissed at me right now."

"Why?"

"I blew up their town," I said. "Part of it anyway. Mostly the City Hall. And I put a hole in the top of the cavern where they built their downtown. It's a long story."

"I would imagine so."

Anat looked at me side-eyed, then away again, smiling. It drove me mad and I wanted to kiss her so badly my body rattled.

"Why did you blow up their town, Simon?"

"Part of their town."

"Why did you blow up part of their town, Simon?"

"Because I don't like them, but also I needed them to know that they are vulnerable. I am their counterweight, their reason to behave. Them and the Engineers. They are losing their fear of God, so now they need something new to keep them in line. I knew I had the power to do just that, so it was a bit of a field test, I guess."

"And who is going to keep you in line, Simon?"

At this she looked directly into my eyes. We stopped walking. The grass beneath her smoked.

"You," I managed. It came out so weak and hopeful. I was blushing as bright as the fake sun above.

She released my hand, folded her arms tight over her chest and studied me, almost grinning at the edges of her beautiful lips. She must've been a full two inches taller than me.

"I'm not your minder."

I didn't understand the moment. I didn't understand if she was teasing me, tempting me, or if she was somehow angry.

"No, of course you aren't."

"Am I more powerful than you?" she asked.

I didn't answer, but only gazed dumbly, engrossed by the riddles within her eyes.

"Come closer, Simon," she said.

My head was light and I was sweating. I stepped toward her, timid, excited, and afraid.

"Closer."

I inched toward her, encompassed by her heat.

"Closer."

Our lips were close enough that I could feel her electricity.

"Am I your minder?"

"No. You are my queen."

"I am nobody's queen, Simon. But you are going to be my king. Do you understand the difference?"

"Yes."

Then she gave me her wicked half-smile. My heart leapt around my chest like a nervous dog waiting for a door to open. She nodded behind me.

"Keep walking, King Simon."

I found myself unable to compose a thought for a good thirty minutes.

Until we found the beautiful woman and her half-man.

Willow and Her Beloved Stump
Part 2

I knew she was Willow from her big, beautiful, bug eyes. I remembered her gazing across the campground like a toddler among adults, searching for someone to belong to. I never faulted her for falling into Martha's small cult of weirdo fanatics. It was much the same as a meteoroid that falls into a planet— it wasn't a matter of choice so much as Martha being the first gravitational force Willow encountered.

But she managed to escape the pull of the Klu Klux Clams and was instead dragging an armless, legless, and badly burned man through the forest, using a blanket as a sled. To where she was dragging him, I guessed even she didn't know.

Willow saw us through the trees and froze like a deer. The half-man lifted his eyes and looked over. He might have waved had he possessed an arm.

I glanced at Anat. Her face was cold and hard. Shocked, but hiding it. She didn't like to be read.

"I like your dress," Willow said.

Anat took a moment, then forced a smile. "Thank you."

"Please leave us alone, okay?" Willow's grip tightened on the edge of the blanket she was using to pull the half-man.

"Sound familiar?" I asked Anat.

Anat didn't respond, but walked toward the tragic lovers, her footsteps still burning the ground. Willow and the half-man gazed at her feet and the smoke drifting up. Anat noticed their apprehension, so cooled before continuing forward. I followed.

"What happened?" Anat sounded like a queen looking over the war-wounded. It was almost regal, but a touch of awkwardness that reminded me that we were both still novices at being royalty.

"I upset the wrong people," the half-man said, a proud, boyish smile emerging through his charred, cracked, and crusted flesh.

"Do I know you?" Willow asked me. Few had seen my adult form yet, so I often got to wander through America and other parts of the Wilderness unmolested by my growing legions of enemies.

I ignored her question and walked next to Anat.

"The Americans are big on symbology," I said to her. "And public executions are about the most potent symbols available on the Island."

"Especially when the executed have such a hard time dying," the half-man said.

Anat looked to me, curious.

"Killing someone on the Island is tricky," I told Anat. "We aren't designed to die here. We want to, but we can't. God flipped the script on us just to see how we'd react."

The half-man studied Anat closely.

"You're with the new group, aren't you?" he asked. "Not Willow's but the ones that just arrived a few days ago?"

Anat hesitated before saying "yes."

"The fires on the other side of the lake—that was you, wasn't it?"

"Yes."

The half-man watched me for a few moments, then looked up to Willow.

"Darling, you know this man," he told Willow.

Willow examined my face, but wasn't grasping the connection.

"Simon," the half-man said. "I'm guessing the Americans and the Engineers are very interested in both of your whereabouts right now. I don't know if I should be impressed by you or terrified."

Willow gripped the blanket tighter, not sure if she should start running with the half-man bouncing behind her or if that would make matters worse.

"We want to make the Island better," Anat announced.

"She's still getting the lay of the land," I added. "We're not your enemy."

"Which is what an enemy would say, right?" he asked. "As you can see, I'm not a threat to you, but I might be an asset. I know this Island better than most, but I will need a little help from you."

"I'm interested," I said.

"Are you powerful enough to make me whole?"

Anat looked over at me, interested in the answer.

"No," I said. "Not yet, anyway. I do have friends to the north that may be able to help. Keep moving that way, keep clear of the Americans, and I will let them know to look out for you."

"Will they hide us?" Willow asked.

"They will do better than that," I said. "Just don't tell anyone else you saw us."

Willow nodded, then looked back to the half-man. He rewarded her with a smile so kind that even I fell a bit in love with both of them. Willow gave a silly half-wave, then resumed dragging her love through the forest. We watched them go, then Anat laced her fingers within mine.

"What's your plan, King Simon?"

"Not yet, my love," I said. "There is more for you to see. I want you to meet Petrov."

The Girl Who Doomed God
Part 8

We found them on the outskirts of New Wichita. I was amazed that Petrov had been lured out of his bunker and wondered what he hoped to find. I initially thought he was wearing an overstuffed backpack. But no. It was a severed head on his shoulder like he was some twisted pirate who just wouldn't settle for a parrot like every other pirate captain on the open sea.

It wasn't until they were close that I saw her were eyes alive, almost happy.

"Are you fucking kidding me?" Anat whispered. "Is God really George Romero?"

"I love Romero," I said, then gave it some though. "Ole George does look a lot like God, now that I think about it."

I looked to Anat and her glittering dress.

"If you don't mind, I think I'm going to dress you down a bit."

She nodded. The glimmers faded into a simple, unbuttoned, long sleeve shirt with a tank top underneath. Jeans, tight fitting but not too tight-fitting. I'm not a creep, after all. Ha. Who am I trying to kid. I'm a total creep.

For myself, I chose a Wu-Tang t-shirt under a black, silk vest and black jeans with just a touch of rhinestone. She was amused and narrowed an eye at me.

"I grew up in Vegas," I said. "I don't do modest."

"You look like a magical fairy made a bottle of Ax Body Spray into a real life boy."

Pleased with her sick burn, Anat looked back at the painter and the decapitated head.

"So, you fall in love and they chop you into pieces? Is that the theme here?"

It was a bit of a joke, but the anger was there just as I needed it to be.

"Well, kinda coincidence, but a decent metaphor for co-dependence yes?"

"No. It's grotesque, cruel, and unnecessary."

"Also that."

We watched the poor, tortured artist whisper to the woman in a pleasant, familiar way.

"Can you do something for them?" Anat asked.

"No, that isn't how my power works," I said, then added "not yet, at least."

"And God?"

I took a few moments to chew on the question. I'd considered trying to talk sense into The Old Man, but not until I had more leverage.

"Yes, but He won't. Now that is a decent metaphor."

"Yes. I suppose it is," Anat said. "Are we going to have to kill them all?"

Anat was grave and serious, a real carrying-the-weight-of-the-world frown cut into her beautiful face.

"By 'all' you mean?"

"God and the Americans," she said.

Her fury excited me.

"No, I already have a plan, my precious, vengeful queen. I know a better way."

She nodded, then looked back to the painter.

"I'm not your queen."

I smiled just enough to annoy her.

"My mistake."

I Cannot Die

Part 11

I never knew any of this. I'd assumed your pairing with Anat was simply a partnership, an uneasy alliance.

But love?

Not King Simon.

I am charmed. Quite charmed. I'm sorry that I didn't trust you more. Do you think The Old Man had ever been in love? Would He even recognize the emotion? If He did, would He flee from it as He fled from Martha?

I do remember how He watched that poor girl from Galilee in the years before He placed the future Messiah in her virginal womb. It was not love, but it was a fascination as schoolboys are fascinated by schoolgirls. We all knew His plan. We were all prepping for the big reveal, the night of the conception. We were all rapt, but also ashamed. We were all guilty by association.

It was a cruel thing He did to that woman and to the boy that resulted. I suspect that even the angels lost a degree of respect for The Old Man that day.

I'm not saying it was rape. It was God fulfilling a divine prophecy that would forever change humanity's understanding of their own existence. He did what must be done for the good of all mankind, even if it came at the expense of the purity of a young girl barely old enough to conceive and certainly not old enough to understand consent. Perhaps this young girl and this impossible child were faced with expulsion from their community and perhaps that was tantamount to a death sentence and perhaps their survival was dependent on the mercy of a humiliated, adoptive father. Great heroes need compelling back stories and a virgin birth is one heck of an origin.

Yet, if someone asked me directly if it was rape, I'd be hard-pressed to convince them that it wasn't.

I am happy that you experienced true love. It is a curse and a treasure. All life should be tortured by love at some point.

Also, on another subject, I think I may have seen an angel. Or something like an angel. At first I thought it was a comet. Then it stopped, veered, swung across the stars, then back. It was like an anxious dog watching its master from behind a fence. It raced back and forth in an irregular pattern, then fled back into the obscurity of a cluster of stars. I am hoping it returns soon. It feels so good to be seen again.

Petrov The Painter
Part 5

The cavern mouth looked as if it was screaming out into the Wilderness, a frozen, monstrous howl trying to awaken the slumbering God. A giant child pleading for its Father. On Petrov's shoulder, the head scowled. Petrov couldn't see her, but could feel her facial reactions as her neck and head shifted ever so slightly within the harness strapped onto Petrov's shoulder.

Piles of stone and debris were piled up just outside the cavern. Within, a large beam of light shot down from the new opening in the ceiling, illuminating the town square and casting a glow against the cavern walls.

A dragon's open, hungry maw revealing the fire burning distantly inside its belly.

"We won't be long, my dear," Petrov said. "I just want some answers."

He tilted his face over enough so that she could stretch her lips out to his cheek to give him a whisper of a kiss. It was the best they could do for communication, but it was enough. Her lips were chapped from dehydration, but she had no way of telling this to Petrov. She knew he would remember to dampen the cloth under her severed neck soon. She just needed to be patient.

For her part, she was still afraid of the Americans. Perhaps more now that she traveled with the sad painter. She did not fear death, but was terrified of Petrov suffering for her sake. And he would if the time came. She knew it and could do nothing to stop it.

"Hello," a man called from behind Petrov. He turned to see a couple emerging from the forest. The man held his hands up as a sign of peace. "Nice head you got there."

"Hello Simon," Petrov replied.

"How is everybody recognizing me off the bat like this?" you asked Petrov, then turned to Anat. It was always fun to see you flustered. "I swear, I've walked across this Island and throughout New Wichita and no one has ever looked twice at me."

"It's your voice, Simon," Petrov said. "Who is your friend?"

You cocked your head proudly as you took her hand.

"My queen. I mean, not mine as in I own her, but like, you know, we're king and queen."

You looked to her and she tilted an eyebrow.

"Or whatever," you added. "But keep that hush-hush for now."

"And does the queen have a name?" Petrov asked.

"Anat," she answered. It was my first good look at her as an adult. Her face was still a thick curtain of unknowable reserve, like her eyes were ever in shadows. But she stood taller now, her chin high. She didn't look down anymore. Now she looked through. What was happening within was a mystery, but that she was now even more dangerous was very apparent.

"And your friend," Anat said, looking to the head. "Does she have a name?"

"She does, but I don't know it," Petrov said.

Anat walked to the head.

"May I?" Anat asked the head, not Petrov. The head tapped her teeth together once.

"That means yes," Petrov said.

Anat touched the head's cheek, lightly brushing her fingertips along the jaw to the neck, then to the vicious, infected wound. Anat frowned. Her fingers warmed, almost glowed. The flesh sizzled as the infection was burned out. The head cringed from the pain, but then the heat was gone and the head's grimace eased.

"I wish there was more that I could do for you," Anat said. "We will avenge you and all the other sins of the Americans."

Anat returned to your side as you tried to remain serious, but were having a hard time containing your proud smile.

"Please don't cause any more trouble Simon," Petrov said. "It is hard enough on the Island without you meddling."

"I'm not the one with ovens and painted skulls, brother."

Petrov dipped his eyes to the ground. The head wanted Petrov to say something, to defend himself, but the painter remained silent, absorbing the guilt. She glared at you and you rolled your eyes.

"Look, I'm sorry," you said. "I know this isn't how you want to go about your life, but we are going to change things. I'm glad we ran into you because I need you to know that we are going to reform the entire Island, but it may get a little sloppy. Keep your head down for a couple days okay? Both of them."

No one appreciated the joke, but Petrov still nodded. He turned toward the cavern and began walking toward New Wichita.

"Petrov!" you called. "That's not where you'll want to be buddy."

Petrov didn't respond, instead walking onward.

"Don't tell them you saw me, okay?" you said.

***

Petrov knew the cavern well. He was summoned often, usually for commissions in public buildings or murals in private homes. He spent more time in The Mayor's mansion than anywhere else. He didn't enjoy her. He didn't enjoy the way she looked at him. Not exactly attracted, but curious and only more so as he kept side-stepping her flirtations.

He detested her as he detested all those in power. But he

said nothing. Keep the mouth shut, paint what they want him to paint, and survive another day.

As he entered the cavern, he saw the blast marks spotted along the walls where debris from the explosion had blossomed outward. No structure within downtown was without some scar, but only City Hall was severely damaged.

The citizens recognized Petrov and were shocked by his traveling companion. Bringing the head back to New Wichita was out of character for Petrov. He'd never done anything so bold in this life or the last. He was given a wide berth as he crossed downtown. He passed the town's lone law practice, which was a facade jutting out from the cavern wall. The inside was little more than a well-disguised cave. The front windows had shattered during the blast, but the glass had since been swept up.

"Do you have any water?" a voice called weakly. The owner of the voice was hidden within the shadow on the far side of the facade facing away from the cavern entrance.

Petrov paused and peered into the darkness. He unstrapped his canteen and handed it into the shadow. A thin, almost skeletal hand reached from the shadow to retrieve the canteen. Petrov could almost make out the emaciated face.

He heard the water gurgle out of the canteen, the stranger swallowing. The head's lips instinctively smacked at the sound of water. She was so thirsty but with no way to call for relief.

"Thank you," the figure said, holding back the canteen. It trembled with his weak hand.

"Keep it," Petrov said.

The canteen retreated back into the shadow.

"You should leave here," the man whispered, weak and dry. "This is no place for artists."

"I agree," Petrov said, looking about him for curious eyes.

He shifted his body so as not to look directly into the shadows. "What happened to you?"

"The ovens," the man said. "My savior came for me, threw open my tomb and released me back to the Wilderness. I told her I would make my way out of New Wichita on my own. I thought I had the strength, but I do not."

"I will carry you out when I return," Petrov said.

"Ah, yes, a painter, an invalid, and a severed head hobbling away like we have found a yellow brick road. Who will notice?"

"I'll wait until dark. You know how New Wichita is when the sun sets. The only ones left to see us do not want to be seen themselves."

The man chuckled, drank more from the canteen.

"I will be fine," the man said. "Perhaps I will grow roots, gather strength from the Island, stretch into a mighty oak and punch another hole through the roof of this horrible town."

"I will return for you," Petrov said.

"No, you will not," the man said. "Julia told me about you and I won't have someone so unique risk his life for mine. I'll find my own way."

Petrov looked into the shadows. "Julia? Where is she?"

"Liberating, as liberators do."

***

By the time Petrov reached City Hall, the severed head had successfully grabbed the imagination of the town. Sentries retrieved The Mayor from within The Great Hall, the damaged seat of American power. She stepped from the doorway, leaning on a cane and flanked by advisors. She studied Petrov and the condemned woman riding on his shoulder.

"Pardon our mess," The Mayor said. "We've been doing a little redecorating."

"We should talk about Simon," Petrov said.

The crowd stiffened and their whispers silenced. The Mayor glanced at her advisors.

"Of course," she said. "Are you hungry? We'll talk over lunch at my home."

The Mayor descended the steps gingerly with her cane. She gestured back at the judge, who then waved the council back into City Hall. She circled around Petrov so she wouldn't be next to the head.

"Petrov," The Mayor whispered as they walked toward her mansion. "Now is not the time for grand gestures. I like you. I adore your art, but I cannot protect you from everything."

"I understand, and I am not here to cause problems. I am actually here to help you broker peace."

"'Broker peace'? I like the sound of that. Petrov, the Island's lone artist and voice of reason. Fitting."

They walked quietly to the entrance of the mansion. The door opened and they were met by a young man in a trim, red and white checkered dress shirt, soft brown bow tie, and matching suit jacket. He held the door wide, waving them in.

"Thank you darling," The Mayor said.

"My pleasure, Mayor."

"Get lunch going, please. And make an extra plate for my friend and ... hmm. How does one feed a severed head?"

Petrov felt the head's facial muscles shifting into a frown.

"Just some water and maybe a clean piece of fabric."

The Mayor smiled, then waved the beautiful man away. He shuffled silently into a hallway and deep into the mansion. The Mayor led Petrov into the living room. Petrov scanned over his mural, moving close and looking for chipping.

"You know, I think I remember her," The Mayor said as she walked to her wet bar and poured two drinks. "Your head. Eliza or something of that nature. An adulterous. She destroyed the heart of one of our masons. Really just ripped it to shreds."

Petrov didn't look at the head, but felt her face wilting. It was at least partly true, not that he cared. The Mayor turned and offered the drink to Petrov, but he waved it away. The Mayor shrugged and added the liquor to her own glass.

"I don't like the ovens, Petrov," The Mayor said. "I don't like our way of doing business, but this is a burgeoning democracy and it is not my place to dictate morals and ethics. It is my place to enforce the will of the people. They want ovens. We have ovens."

Petrov was tempted to respond, but instead decided that there was no sense arguing morality with the amoral. One might as well explain etiquette to a python.

"You are tempting Simon," Petrov said. "These ovens and executions, they will only force him to be more brazen and inspire more to join his cause."

"He's just a brat who must be spanked and put into a corner," The Mayor said, then sipping on the drink and turning to look out the windows. Petrov followed her gaze and noticed a small spider-webbed crack at the edge. The only noticeable damage from the blast.

"He is not alone anymore," Petrov said.

"His lackeys do not concern me," The Mayor said.

"Did you see the fires from the campground? One of the new arrivals was responsible. A girl, now a woman. Now an exile whom Simon believes is his queen. War is coming, Mayor, and you won't win. New Wichita will be crushed between the might of the Engineers and the righteousness of our new royalty."

They Mayor turned to Petrov, amused. She looked to the head. "Does he talk like this at home too?"

Of course, the head would not respond even if she could.

"God will save us when it is time," The Mayor said.

"You don't really believe that, do you?"

The Mayor took another sip, giving herself time to chew on the question.

"Of course I do, Petrov," she said. "It will take more than this little side-trip from Heaven to rattle my faith. I'm still a believer. Aren't you?"

Before Petrov could answer, the butler walked into the room with a tray.

"Would you like to eat in the dining room or in your study?" he asked.

The Mayor looked to Petrov.

"Any preference?"

"I don't have time to eat," Petrov said. "Can you put mine in a bag?"

"Of course," the butler said.

"But I will take the fabric and the water now. She is thirsty."

Petrov turned his face to the head. She kissed his cheek and lingered for as long as he would let her.

***

As Petrov retreated from the mansion and downtown, he stopped beside the law firm and tossed the bag of food into the shadows.

"Bless you," the condemned man whispered.

"Get far away as soon as you can," Petrov said. "Judgment is coming."

Being A Child God

Part 5

You're seeing angels, huh? Big news. I'm curious to know what they look in the next universe over.

I actually don't see our own angels much anymore. Following the coup d'etat, I assumed control of the armies of Heaven. This turned out to be a bit of a bumble-fuck since none of the angels in Heaven nor demons in Hell had considered that someone would ever actually depose the Old Man. After years of wrangling and negotiations, the last legions did fall in line.

I rarely utilized the angels since I suspected they were still looking for ways to serve in the spirit of the Old Man just as Kremlin cronies sabotaged democracy because they never quite gave up on the hope of a soviet utopia.

Our working relationship was further damaged when I threw one of the archangels into the Island's volcano. It was a dramatic overreaction. I knew it the second I'd done it. Here's the thing, though: I distrust the angels, but I dislike them even more. I dislike how eager they are to please. That trait annoys me in humans, but it is even worse in angels because they never even grumble under their breaths, even in bathrooms locked from the inside with the faucet running and the toilet flushing, voice muffled as they scream into folded-up paper towels. That I know; that I can understand.

But never a complaint from the angels, never a sneer or a sigh. Always compliant. Too compliant. I sometimes suspect they are just waiting for the right moment to punish me for His overthrow. They do anything I ask without question, but I read their passive silence as a smugness. That really itches, you know.

The day I threw the angel into the volcano, I'd been raging from heartbreak again. Anat and I are kinda on-again, off-again lovers. She is my own special strain of malaria. I'll be fine for months, years even, but then I relapse. Her memory is an infection lurking in my blood. When it flares up, I am consumed by mania.

The archangel was there, waiting for orders, unwilling to move. Maybe he was worried for me, hoping to help, but I felt crowded. I threw him because I had to throw something. It could have been my crown, it could have been a soul, but it was an archangel because he was too close, too willing to be grabbed, too unwilling to resist my will.

I hated him even more for allowing me to hurt him. As he crashed into the rocks and plummeted into the volcano, his once-invisible body burst into a golden light, the heat igniting flames upon his divine plumage, a horrid scream erupting from my unquestioning servant as he suffered a worthless death. A stupid, pointless, wasteful death.

And I thought of the day God fell. Again, so much pointless death.

The angels kept their distance from then on, accepting my

orders from beyond my grasp. That death haunts me, but I am more comfortable with the angels now. We better understand each other, so perhaps it was for the best. A good Old Testament, divine temper tantrum just to clarify boundaries.

I miss Anat so bad, Bali. I've stopped having sex. Every woman in the history of the world is available to me: Cleopatra, Marilyn Monroe, Josephine Baker. I glide through Heaven and Hell and feel their souls instinctively flowing toward me. I could give them bodies and they would throw themselves at me in worship, in an unthinking ecstasy, but I glide on and let their souls trail off back into their eternal slumber because all I want is Anat. The Queen. The only woman who knows how to say "no" to me.

Her memory rises like flames in the winter grasslands. There is no fighting the wildfire. Just lean into the pain, let the heartache scorch my body, my mind, my soul. Let her memory have its way, then heal, regrow, and await the next lonely winter.

Come back to me, Bali. Return to the Island and overthrow me. I will lay down my crown and retreat into oblivion. Anything to get away from the void where The Queen should be.

Barry and Mary and Domestic Bliss
Part 3

I don't consider myself a curious god or a loving god or even a just god. I'm mostly a bureaucratic god, a god of nuts and bolts and keeping the trains moving on time. I try not to get caught up in the foolish politics of my people. Being human means never really graduating high school, emotionally speaking.

So I just hole up in my tower and ignore the drama. But, that said, perfect love does fascinate me. I don't know how many perfect loves there have been in the history of mankind. Probably millions. It must be a common thing, but it seems so foreign to me. Always did, even back on Earth when I watched my grandparents giggling in the kitchen as the grandchildren scurried beneath their feet.

I assumed I would have that too. But instead I ran from it to the furthest place from perfect love I could think of—Las Vegas.

When Anat arrived, I believed that I'd found mine. And it was perfect for a while, but then it was gone and I was the worse off for knowing what I'd lost. Then it came back. Then it was gone again. Back and forth.

And back and forth.

And back and forth.

And back and forth.

And back and forth.

Barry and Mary possessed that perfect love and cradled it as gracefully as any couple I'd ever seen. I never saw them fight, never saw their eyes stray. It was focused, intense, and excruciating to watch from the outside.

Like all love. The only kids in the cafeteria to get dessert.

Fuckers.

So, when I presented them with The Queen, I thought I was now a peer. I was a fellow practitioner of Perfect Love. I didn't tell Anat any of this because she would have thought I was a lunatic.

I clutched her hand as we neared the cave and I smiled like a 16-year-old with a new-to-me Camaro. Anat glittered in her white gown, I looking damned dapper in my gun metal gray suit.

Barry and Mary appeared in the entrance of the cave, a spear and a bow and arrow brandished, eyes darting across the trees for followers, then back to me.

"Morning," I called. "We've come to talk to you about the exciting possibilities and earning potential of AMWay."

"What?" Mary asked.

"Go away," Barry said.

"Be polite, you two," I said. "I've brought your queen."

I then looked to Anat.

"It's okay to say it like that, right, 'your queen'?"

She sighed, feigning exacerbation. Deep down, she loved my awkward fawning. Pretty sure she did, anyway.

"My name is Anat."

"We're together," I added, then holding up our clutched hands. Also awkward.

"Good for you," Mary said. "Now go away."

"I'm sorry," I said to Anat. "They are a bit weird, but I swear that they are really lovely once you get to know them. They even have a hot tub!"

Anat nodded her head. I slipped from Anat's side and walked towards the cave.

"Look, as much as we'd like to stay and impose on your hospitality, this is more of a service call in two parts," I said. "First part: there is a couple heading your way who really need your help. I would consider it a favor if you took them in."

"Who are they?" Barry asked, keeping his spear up as he stepped out from the cave. I looked at the spear, amused.

"Willow, one of the Klu Klux Clams," I said. "But she's cool, now. She just fell in with the wrong crowd. She has a boyfriend with no arms, no legs, and a bit of a complexion problem."

"The springs can't fix dismemberment," Mary said.

"Of course, but he's in a lot of pain and could use some relief."

"This is a lot to ask, Simon," Barry said.

"Yes, I understand that, but I will reward you well."

"And the second part of your service call?" Mary asked.

"A warning. A storm is coming very, very soon. It'll be coming from the campground, so if you have any errands, do them now before it's too late. Willow and her boyfriend won't get here before it hits, so don't wait up."

Mary tightened her grip on her bow, the tip of the arrow slowly moving towards my heart. "What are you going to do, Simon?"

"Something wicked."

Anat walked to my side. "The Island needs to be rebalanced. There is too much chaos and not enough leadership. We are going to start the new age."

"How?" Mary asked.

"Don't worry about that," Anat said. "Just do what your friend told you and bury yourselves deep. The worst is on its way, but the Island will be better for it."

"Have you warned Edward and the others?" Barry asked.

"Of course," I said.

Barry looked back to Mary. Her frown was non-committal, a little frightened.

"This Island is going to get worse if we keep waiting for God to change things," I said.

"I am new to the Island," Anat said. "I am not thrilled to be leading a rebellion only days after arriving, but I've met God. He is just as confused and afraid as we are. He is no longer fit to rule. We, the exiles, are lifting the burden from His shoulders and, collectively, we will do a better job of holding this Island aloft."

I almost laughed at how perfect she was. Barry nodded his head. Mary unnotched the arrow.

"Go do your worst," Mary said, then led Barry back to the cave.

"But hey," I said, snapping my fingers and pointing dual finger guns their way. "After this is over, let's do a double-date! Yeah?"

"Don't come back here, Simon," Barry called over his shoulder and it stung.

They disappeared into the cave, pulling the camouflage netting back over the entrance. I turned to Anat and chuckled.

"They're a little shy, but they'll warm up to you. Just give them some time."

"It's okay, Simon," she said. "I've never had many friends either."

My heart resonated in a sickly sweet way. I rushed to her, pulled her into my arms, and we kissed. Our teeth clinked and it was super awkward, but damn if it wasn't the most wonderful moment of my entire existence.

My People

So, let's backtrack a bit. You mentioned having a blind spot obscuring my travels which, by the way, feels pretty great. I'd been trying to hide from you but wasn't sure if I was one hundred percent successful.

When I was still in the campground and Edward been rowed out to the Wilderness, I spent a lot of time thinking of those two girls who had rowed across the lake and revealed that life existed across the lake. The blonde was named Summer because of course she was. Livie was the tall, regal, black girl who coulda been my boss's boss at any one of my shitty side jobs. Livie and Summer appeared on the lake like conquistadors. All long legs and delicious bodies barely hidden by swimsuits and short shorts. Pretty fantastic.

Well, the moment I left the campground behind and wandered into the Wilderness, I sought those two out. I wanted answers, but I also wanted to find and recruit the mysterious women. There was a touch of greedy deviance to it, I'll admit. They had taken on a mythic quality for all the boys in the campground, as if Summer and Livie were dignitaries from a clan of goddesses that spent their days lounging on ruins across the lake, looking all beautiful and conniving.

So, I sought them out and found them not among gods and goddesses, but as part of a listless clan of fishermen that camped out by the lake, far away from the trifles of America and the Engineers. They sat on the shore all day long, waiting for the sun to set, then rowed out onto the waters. They fished and made love and drank moonshine and let the weeks drift by. Perfect for Summer, but Livie seemed pretty restless by the time I arrived. I knew so many people like them back in Vegas. Instead of lakes, they stayed in trailer home communities in the desert and would whittle away their youth, watching the sunrises and making grand plans for lives they feared they'd never have.

Livie would have fled the desert for a life of purpose but there was no fleeing the Island and there was no purpose in the Wilderness worth her energy and talent. Yet.

When I found the first fishing village, I saw in their eyes the weight of boredom and fear for the wider Wilderness beyond. I knew I was among my people. I was the first child they'd ever seen in the Wilderness, so that caught their attention. I demonstrated a few of my cheaper parlor tricks, floating rocks, disembodied flames, kid's stuff. I then asked if they knew my lovely conquistadors. They escorted me further down the shore.

The next village was equally sad, sparse, and uninspired. Some crooked huts and some crooked people mired in a swamp of disillusionment.

Yet they were all so beautiful. The eyes were long on years, like prematurely-aged meth addicts, but their faces and bodies were young and perfect. What a dreadful thing to be pretty on the outside but lost on the inside. How easy it is for the world to prey upon you.

And I was preying upon them, in a way. I felt and still feel that I freed them, but I suppose it is all a matter of perspective.

The villagers shuffled closer and eyed me.

"Well hello," Summer called from the water, the waves washing just over her ankles. The sun was shining off her hair because of course sun glistened off people like Summer. It shined for them in a way it never shined for me. She stepped from the sand, shook the water from her feet. She looked toward the huts and called "Hey Boss Lady!"

Livie emerged from the hut door, holding a charred fish stuck on a spit.

"God let you come out and play, huh?" Livie smiled, then took a bite of the fish. I knew she was gonna be harder to impress than the yokels.

So, I flew.

Well, not fly exactly, but levitated. It was a few feet off the ground, all I could manage that early on, but it was enough to make a point.

The villagers backed from me and crouched, as if I was a bomb moments from detonation. I kept my eyes on Summer, but she put her hand on her hip and frowned. A real "that's it, huh?" Livie took another bite of the fish, trying to mask her curiosity.

"God's not calling the shots anymore," I proclaimed, trying to make my eyes glow but I think they just changed to a darker shade of brown. I eased back to the ground.

"I need answers and volunteers," I announced, scanning the frightened faces. Only Summer and Livie stood their ground.

"We aren't the volunteering type," Livie said, making her way over, taking another bite of fish, casual and cool.

"Yes, but you strike me as the trouble-making type," I said. "And that's what I aim to do."

Summer and Livie traded smiles. Livie held up the fish.

"Hungry?"

***

And that's where I got my first introduction to the terrible mess of the Wilderness and the true expanse of God's willful neglect of His Chosen People. I become aware that His People must become My People. As I said, I was not seriously considering an overthrow. Not yet. I just wanted to make the Island better by a small margin and utilize my unique skill set to make my mark. Maybe just a power-sharing agreement.

Only a handful volunteered at first. They were led by Summer and Livie, my priestesses. I did a lot of magic early on. I levitated higher and higher. I materialized costumes out of thin air. I, for real, made my eyes glow a bright orange. I'd have owned the Las Vegas strip with this show.

Once I'd exhausted my options along the shoreline, I began venturing further into the Wilderness to study the Americans, the Engineers, and my fellow exiles. I found a few more followers hiding between the borders of the empires, but knew I was going to have to go bigger to poach believers from my competition.

I did spend some time with the Engineers, trying to learn their tricks and grow my own abilities. But I was a bad fit for them. They were too superior and I was too ambitious. I did leave them as a stronger savior though.

So, I honed my powers, sought out the secrets of the Island, and grew my tribe.

Conflict was inevitable. When Livie was caught thieving venison from the Americans, I lead a raiding party into New Wichita. I freed her from the ovens and we fled, but the Americans followed us all the way back to the fishing village.

We slipped away into the woods, but the Americans looted our supplies and burned the huts to the ground. I led the survivors away from the lake to find a proper kingdom for our growing empire of thieves, rascals, and whores. I counted Tommy among our number for a time, but his heart was fickle and often led him back into America or home to poor Edward.

We built our castle off the northern edge of the Island. I was now powerful enough to uproot trees which I then impaled into the rock face of the Island dozens of feet below the cliff edge. We built retractable ladders, we dug into the cliffs, forged homes, an underground fortress where even the Engineers could not reach us.

We hid. We planned.

I ate the first Island star soon after.

Did you ever try one? Do you know what happens? How it feels? How it boils, the power trying to blast its way outside of you and back into the universe?

Two of my followers tried, but holes melted inside of them, their guts liquefying, their screams piercing our subterranean compound, their beauty irreparably marred. They survived the ceremony, but couldn't eat, couldn't drink. At their request, we tossed them off the side of the Island, hoping for nirvana or God's mercy. Angels caught them and carried them back to the campground.

We never saw them again.

Only I could eat the stars. Only I could contain the power. The ceremony involved Livie and Summer, my priestesses, feeding me the star whole. I was tied down on my back against a stone as if I was to be ritualistically disemboweled. This was when I started wearing priest's cassocks. My priestesses dressed like Celtic princesses. It was a confused mishmash of symbology and we loved it all for its senseless pomp.

The stars were stuffed into my mouth and down my throat far enough for me to close my teeth and burst the fleshy sack. The power within would surge, struggle, try to escape my lips, but be turned back. The star's power then raced down into my innards. It was God's DNA fighting, fighting, fighting, but finally accepting its place within me. My abilities expanded, my awareness of the Island sharpened, my kinship with God grew richer.

Such an exciting time. We believed that we were catching up to The Old Man. Anything was possible.

There was talk of marriage, of me breathing life into wombs to breed the next generation of God's castaway children. But I resisted. I wanted to remain a child a little longer and didn't want to consider growing out our community until I better understood the true boundaries of the Island.

Also, fatherhood. No thank you to that.

The day of the explosion. We wanted to weaponize the stars, just to see what happened. It started as a joke, then as an experiment that would be conducted along the edge of the Island where it could be hidden and contained.

The explosion knocked out a seven foot hole on the side of the Island and nearly caused a cave-in throughout the fortress.

The power was stunning.

"Let's test it in the field," I announced and Summer shrieked like a crazed warrior and we danced. The inverted crosses were Livie's idea, the ashes were collected from the ceremonial fire built beside the temple where I swallowed stars.

I met Anat soon after. I knew I loved her right away. Perhaps only because she was the peer that I desperately needed. I had my fill of followers, but needed a mate. A partner in my developing plan to bring the Island into the new age.

***

When I brought The Queen to my people, she eyed the rickety ladder descending the edge of the Island. My followers stood at the cliff in a humble reception of royalty. What a sad, silly group they were. Lillie traded her archaic robes for a long, striped Turkish cavalry jacket and a curved Moorish knife snug at her hip in a prominently displayed and elaborately designed scabbard. Gifts from Yulia.

Summer had trimmed her own priestess robe back further and further so she appeared to be some sort of bombshell, sacrificial offering to a great beast in a golden era Hollywood B movie. It threatened the limits of common decency which, of course, I loved. Three of my lesser priests sported their cassocks from the attack on New Wichita, but the rest looked as if they'd just come home from a day at the beach. Shorts, tank tops, flip flops, all dirtied and bored.

"It's not much, dear, but they are loyal."

Anat looked at me, gave a slight shake of the head, then smiled at the reception. The priestesses advanced and bowed in the theatrical way young people do in equal mock and adoration. It always charmed me, but Anat's frown showed that she distrusted grand displays. Yet, she still followed and descended the ladder.

Torches lit our way through the winding chambers of our fortress and I became aware and embarrassed at how simple and poor My People really were. Every room was little more than a hovel long enough to sleep in. Our dining room was only big enough for six to eat in at a time. Even then, they had to squat under the low ceiling.

Throughout it all, Anat took in our home with unreadable passivity.

The procession led us to my room, the largest in the fortress, but still only eight foot by eight foot. We could not dig like Huang and this was as decadent as this fortress would ever become.

My bed was a cluster of leather and wool pillows stolen from New Wichita which they had made from the sheep from Rawlings. My People retreated from my chambers, my priestesses bowing low again, Summer giving me the raised eye of a co-conspirator.

"So, not even a door?" Anat asked, looking toward the wide open hall.

"We don't know how to mount them into the dirt," I said, ashamed at how terrible we were at everything. My fingers were trembling. I don't ever remember being so nervous in my life. Not even when I was buried alive on the Las Vegas strip.

And suddenly that claustrophobia returned.

I watched the torchlights disappear down the hall, now terrified to be alone with The Queen. I turned to her and she was naked. My illusion of a dress had faded, her camp clothing had burned away long ago.

"This is just the beginning, Simon."

"It is," I said. "I'm going to do great things. I promise you."

"I don't need promises, Simon."

She backed to the bed of pillows and laid back. She held her hand up. The torches extinguished with gasps. We were left only with the sounds of each other breathing.

"Not to spoil the mood, but I'm a little scared of the dark," I said, trying to pretend I was kidding, but I was definitely not. It was bad enough being underground, but the dark was stoking the mild panic my nerves had already sparked.

Her body glowed orange, her eyes red, illuminating the room. I feared the bed would burst into flames, but her body was not producing heat, only light. Perhaps there was heat, but she was holding it in. Saving it for me. The potential made my body hum.

"Is this better?"

"Yes."

"Come to me, My King. It's time to begin."

And so we did.

I Cannot Die
Part 12

The angel returns often. I don't know if it's every day or every month. My perception of time has collapsed, but it feels often. I believe that he's a scout. There is a great entity reeling me into this new universe and this angel is checking out the catch.

And what if the angel realizes that I may be dangerous? Will they kick me back out into eternity?

When he appears, my fingertips burn. My mouth waters. Just the prospect of touch, of tangibility, it stirs my entire body awake. To feel. To really feel again. I don't know what I will do when that day arrives. I don't know how I will react. Will I make a fool of myself, will they be frightened by my desperation, will they toss me away like an undersized fish?

As you miss Anat, I miss earth. Not just our planet or our Island, but the luxury of space and time instead of this endless drift. I am now weeping whenever I wake, still encased by countless light years of nothing.

I remember your fortress. I never visited it, but I remember feeling it beneath the Island. You attempted to hide it from me, but I still felt the absence like a smudged eraser mark.

And I know where we are in the story. I know what is coming next. I knew you were going to attempt something big to strengthen your position on the Island, but what you actually did still surprised me.

I was too distracted by Edward and Petrov and the Americans and the Engineers, their lives tangling into one another, every grasp at freedom only tightening the net holding them together.

I do remember sensing the conflict coming, the recognition that everything would have to change soon because the Island could no longer sustain as it was. Jay had been sent to Earth when God's people could no longer be contained, so now it was time for another messiah to manifest. And how foolish was I for suspecting that, this time, the messiah might be me?

Willow and Her Beloved Stump
Part 3

Locusts clicked and hummed as Willow sat beneath a sycamore tree. Trevor watched a swarm of gnats above. He suspected the smell of his charred flesh was drawing in the insects. He looked to Willow as she flexed her sore hands tight and then relaxed. She was in pain. Her face was pale and covered in sweat. He had no idea how she had carried on for so long.

"You can leave me, darling," Trevor said. "You are the most beautiful thing on this Island and you will do fine on your own. I will be fine too. I am not sure if I could have pulled so much dead weight for as long as you did."

"Stop calling me 'beautiful,'" Willow said, not looking up from her tired hands. "I hate it. It was nice at first but now I'm done with all that."

"I'm sorry if I offended you, but..."

"You know what's beautiful?" Willow asked. He'd never heard her raise her voice. "Paintings. People nail them to walls and forget about 'em, maybe brag about how much they paid. You keep callin' me beautiful and makes me think that's all I'm good for. Lookin' expensive and impressin' your pals."

Trevor didn't know what to say. His mouth was open, his eyes trying to pierce through the dark cloud surrounding Willow, but he couldn't understand the moment or how to fix it.

"I'm here," Willow said. "I've dragged you all day long because I need you. Too many people gave up on me and I said I wouldn't do that. I said I'd be better when that time came and here I am. I don't wanna be pretty, I wanna be tough. Like my ma. The things she endured, you have no idea, pal."

Willow cleared strands of hair from her brow. She looked

down at Trevor.

"You think I'm carrying you but you're the one carrying me," she said. "I feel real, like I have a reason to be here or anywhere, but then you ruin it by calling me 'beautiful' again like all I am to you is some animal. A pack mule. A 'beautiful' pack mule."

Willow wiped tears from her eyes, then looked back to her hands and stretched her fingers.

"I'm so sorry, my dear," Trevor said. "I don't feel worthy of you and I guess I flatter you to keep you with me. I can't walk, I can't pull myself, all I've got are words to keep you near. I'm sorry if I've misused them."

"It's alright. Just, stop worrying about all that. I'm not going anywhere. If you keep worrying about why I'll leave, then that might just get me to leave, you know."

"I'm a worrier, though," Trevor said. "If I can't worry about losing the strongest woman on the Island, what should I worry about?"

Willow chuckled, then wiped her hands on her pants.

"Keeping us alive," she said. "I pull. You plan. Deal?"

"Deal."

She looked to Trevor and gave him a wide smile. She leaned over and brushed off a beetle crawling across his chest.

"Have you even thought that I might like you this way?" Willow asked. Her lip trembled, but she fought it back and smiled again. "You wanna say nice things? Fine. Tell me why you like me and don't say 'cause I'm beautiful."

Trevor met her eyes and took a moment. "No one knows how powerful you are. Including you and I get to be the one to watch as you find out."

Willow nodded.

"Better. Keep 'em coming."

"You may look soft and pretty on the outside," Trevor said.

"But you possess a core that I am beginning to think is pure diamond. Glowing, priceless, and indestructible. I am fascinated by how resolute that core is and what you will achieve once you've discovered what to do with it. There is no other place that I'd want to be on the Island than beside you as you unleash your soul upon this world."

Willow laughed, patted his chest, then stood up.

"Now you're just being a fool."

Through a cluster of trees, a deer emerged, looking at the pair.

"Aww," Willow said. "Bambi is back."

Then someone screamed.

Petrov the Painter
Part 6

The scream was distant and indistinct. Human, but he couldn't tell if it was male or female. Tapping teeth brought Petrov's focus off the trail and toward the head. It was a was a warning. She'd seen something. Petrov scanned the trees, the ground around him, then looked up to the sky. Flocks of birds were soaring up from the trees and racing to the south, away from New Wichita and toward the scream. Hundreds of geese, larks, falcons, crows.

Another voice was shouting from the east toward Rawlings. Petrov walked toward the edge of a hill, looking out to the Island's only plain. A small herd of cattle were galloping away from a ranch hand and heading to the southwest, also towards the scream.

Tommy, the Boy With The Beautiful Ocean Eyes
Part 4

It wasn't Edward's voice. Tommy knew that for certain. But it did come from the direction Tommy expected to find Edward. He thought of New Wichita, The Mayor desperate for answers and any hope of tracking down Simon.

Billy was strong, had military experience, but had no idea what the group was up against. The Engineers may intervene, but maybe not. They called themselves just, but would ignore injustice as often as they would act out against it. They couldn't be trusted because, like most idealists, they only held onto their ideals when it suited them.

Tommy saw birds swarming and heading out across Rawlings toward the scream. He broke into a run, hoping he wouldn't arrive too late, but also fearing that he might just make things worse.

The Mother of Rawlings

Aside from a few fragmented memories, Esperanza didn't remember crossing Central America and Mexico to get to the USA. She never forgot the rank odor of a decaying dog baking in the desert sun or a man's cheap cologne that smelled like black licorice and soap scum. There were water jugs and Bibles left on the side of the road, a man standing at the back of a bus with an assault rifle, an old woman falling to the grass on the side of the road. There were orange and black flower prints on the old woman's dress. Her brother encouraged Esperanza to continue walking, leaving the woman behind to die peacefully.

Esperanza had been six when she made the trip. Two of her brothers escorted her, but only one walked with her all the way to the states. She never found out what happened to the other. Pepe. She only remembered that he was thin with a big nose and liked to tell and retell a joke about a donkey and a priest.

She couldn't recall much about the first family her and her brother lived with, but remembered the house. Large and filled with people. She and her brother shared a room with two other children. She remembered being happy and that there were more toys in that room than she'd ever seen in her life. The house was exciting, always filled with energy and people coming and going. Her new school was imposing and smelled of bleach and lemons.

When she was old enough, she began traveling with the others to a ranch in the country where she got to help care for horses, cattle, sheep, and goats. She remembered often being very hungry, but she didn't consider her childhood unhappy.

At first, English was a frightening barrage of sound, but her mind was young and adaptable and that sound soon began to form meaning. By eighteen, her Texas accent was so rich that most people believed that she'd lived in the Lone Star state her entire life. A fake birth certificate gave way to a real driver's license, then a high school diploma, then a college degree, and suddenly she was an insurance agent with a $300,000 home and a Lexus in the driveway.

Two miscarriages wrecked her marriage. But she moved on. Her brother, a long haul trucker, died in a crash. But she moved on. She was not a victim, and she was not a slave to history.

Trapped in the suburbs, Esperanza did miss the ranch life and always believed that she would retire to the country, but suffered a massive coronary instead. Just like a cop movie. Instead of a bullet though, it was cholesterol that robbed Esperanza of her twilight years.

When she woke on the Island, she hated the feel of childhood and rebelled early. Only four groups had preceded her to the campground, so when she was exiled, the Wilderness was still wide open. She fell in with a pair of burgeoning ranchers named Clyde and Owen and helped them tame the cattle wandering the Wilderness. Clyde was a Wyoming boy and dubbed the field and surrounding forest Rawlings after his home town. Owen was a computer programmer who'd always wanted to try his hand at being a cowboy.

She tried out Clyde for a few months, but settled on Owen because he was a little easier to manage when another batch of moonshine arrived. It never really got awkward with Clyde because he preferred the waify women from the fishing villages anyway.

As more exiles fell into their group and a few unfortunate altercations arose, Esperanza decided that they needed to be more selective about who they let camp in Rawlings. Clyde was the first one to call her "Mother" for the way she herded humans like she herded cattle. She let it stick. It gave her a sense of place and importance, which she always liked. She may not get another Lexus but a title, a home, and something like family was just as good.

Then Edward's exiles arrived en masse and the cattle went crazy. Three broken fences in three days. The pen was built within the trees where the forest wasn't quite so thick, but enough cover to satisfy the angels. It was about thirty feet across with logs tied together, recently reinforced on the southern side where the cattle kept busting out. Six mud huts surrounded the pen with smaller enclosures for the seven goats, five sheep, a few dozen chickens, and three hogs.

Meager, but growing every season. The animals had yet to breed, but when an animal was slaughtered, another would materialize within the Wilderness. Scouting and trading were the only ways to replenish their livestock.

There hadn't been a breakout yet that day, but the animals were still a little restless. Esperanza petted the snout of a heifer, whose eyes were looking beyond Esperanza to the field beyond the trees.

"It's alright girl, let's just have a nice, easy day."

A scream from not too far away startled the heifer. Esperanza turned southwest toward the other side of the field. The heifer bucked and groaned. The other cattle hustled over and began pressing at the pen.

"Clyde! Owen!" Esperanza yelled as she swatted the cattle, trying to scare them back before the pen collapsed again.

From the mud huts, ranchers appeared and ran toward the pen. Eleven total, some throwing their shoulders against the logs of the pen, other hopping over to try to herd the cattle back away.

The logs cracked and broke. The cattle hopped over the fallen logs and galloped out toward the field.

"Get after them!" Esperanza called, pushing a log off of her legs.

The rest of the animals were irritated as well, but unable to escape aside from two chickens that managed to flutter over their enclosure and scamper into the open fields like old women at a Black Friday sale.

"Stay here and rebuild this!" Esperanza snapped at Owen as the rest sprinted out after the cattle.

"Yes, Mother," Owen said.

Cattle weren't the quickest animals, but they were hard to turn when they had their mind set on going forward, especially without the aid of horses or four wheelers.

Esperanza caught up with the cattle and the other ranchers as the stampede broke into the field. She looked up into the sky terrified that God's plane would zip over to see the mayhem below.

But the sky was clear.

She swatted the butt of a heifer, but it only continued galloping onward toward the southwest. Toward the scream.

Raul and His Lovely Guitar
Part 3

Raul had never considered himself a screamer, but he'd also never encountered a legless, armless, charred human abandoned on the ground.

The scream wasn't a decision on his part, it just happened. He ran in a tight circle, arms flailing wide for reasons he couldn't explain. He then sat down on the grass and hugged his guitar. Also, for reasons he couldn't explain.

From across the field, standing next to the deer, Sophia held her hands over her mouth, frightened but not screaming, which made Raul felt more foolish.

Moments passed as Raul and Sophia stared at Willow and Trevor. All of them frozen as startled prey. Willow hunched over Trevor as though she could protect him from the falling sky. Billy and a few other exiles emerged from a path and surveyed the scene.

"Good afternoon," Trevor said as a peace offering, but no one answered. "I know I'm quite a sight, but I assure you that we are not a threat. Quite literally unarmed."

Sophia moved her hands to her chest, took in a few deep breaths, then began laughing. "Oh my. Sorry for our friend. We are just a little on edge."

"You got 'em quaking in their boots, kid," Billy told the still sitting Raul, then stepped past. "Your name is Willow, right?"

Willow was wide-eyed and she leaned further over Trevor.

"Please leave us alone."

"Do you need help?" Billy asked, kneeling down to look at Trevor.

"She wouldn't accept it even if we did," Trevor asked. "Willow is a strong, independent woman, you see."

Billy tilted his head up at Willow.

"Good for you, girl."

"I'm not a girl," Willow said. "Not anymore."

"Of course not." Billy kept his eyes on Willow as he motioned to Trevor. "May I?"

She eased back and nodded. Billy leaned closer to look over Trevor's burned skin and severed stumps. He grimaced as he found the open wound where the pike used to be. Sophia approached from behind the deer. It turned and nuzzled her hand. She pet its snout, then continued toward Billy. She crouched beside Billy and examined Trevor's wounds. More birds flocked into the trees above.

"Does it still hurt?" Sophia asked.

"There is nothing you can do for me, so it doesn't matter," Trevor said.

"We're gonna see some of Simon's friends," Willow said, wanting to shoo everyone away, but not sure how to do it. "We're alright. Just leave us alone now."

"Do you know who his friends are?" Billy asked, standing up. "Were they from our group at the campground?"

"I don't know," Willow said.

"Simon doesn't have many friends in the Wilderness, so it seems likely," Trevor said.

"Maybe it's Petrov?" Sophia suggested.

"It's not," Trevor said. "I don't know who he is sending us towards, but Petrov is not where people go to heal."

Sophia and Billy exchanged silent looks.

"Let us help you carry him," Billy said to Willow. "We could use a few more allies. We also need to find Simon to talk a few things over."

"You'd be wise to stay away from Simon," Trevor said. "He's

poking at some very large, very angry bears and we'd all be safer finding a nice place to hide until this is all over."

"You seem kind," Willow said to Billy. "All y'all. You always seemed kind, but I need to do this my own self. Just let us go on our way."

Sophia placed a hand on Billy's shoulder.

"Okay," Sophia said.

"We can..." Billy began.

"Honey," Sophia cut him off. "They want to do this on their own and we're going to respect that."

Billy took a moment to consider Trevor, Willow's exhausted face, then the sparse, overgrown trails. He didn't like the way the situation added up, but decided it wasn't his call to make.

"Okay." He looked to Willow. "You're sure?"

Willow nodded, then began pulling Trevor behind her. He grimaced initially, but closed his eyes to shut out the pain.

Billy looked back at Raul, who was still sitting on the ground.

"Maybe we shouldn't have you on point," Billy said.

"I told you that two hours ago," Raul said.

"True. My fault."

Billy offered him a hand up and Raul took it. As Raul brushed off his pants and checked his guitar, Edna stepped next to him and elbowed his side. She gave him a slim-eyed smirk of encouragement.

Commotion drew their attention away. From the east, branches snapped. Something big was charging through the forest toward the group. Billy stepped forward, keeping Sophia behind him. Ossie joined him with the others forming a line.

Three cows burst through the trees with exhausted ranchers running close behind. The cattle slowed as they approached Sophia. She stepped past Billy and let the cattle come to her. She held out her arm and the cattle licked her hand.

Most of the ranchers doubled over, trying to catch their breaths. Esperanza stepped forward, swatted a cow's hide, but it didn't even notice.

"So, you're the reason they keep wrecking our fences," she said.

Sophia looked to the woman, studied her, then smiled. "I suppose so. I'll help you get them back."

From the south, Tommy sprinted into view. The moment Edward saw his face, any apprehensions evaporated and they ran into each other's arms, all the sins forgotten, but not quite forgiven.

Then Petrov walked into view from the West, a head attached to his shoulder. He waved. Billy waved back, then looked at Raul and patted his shoulder.

"On second thought, good job music man."

Being A Child God
Part 6

There are few perfect moments. In life, in the afterlife, or on the Island. Perfect moments cannot be created, they cannot be forced. They simply happen.

Chasing joy is as fruitless as trying to slip on a condom after drinking a fifth of Jack Daniels.

Indeed, Fabulous Fallimento. Indeed.

I met this girl at a bar. Beautiful, daring, a little angry at life, but not in an off-putting way. In a damaged, endearing way. We shared a few beers, walked the town for hours, then a storm trapped us underneath a covered driveway at a random house. The darkened windows gazed past us like an uncomfortable bystander. Cars splashed by as their headlights caught hints of skin, movement, two near-strangers making love against a garage door.

I'd known her only those few hours, but it would always be one of my most perfect moments. No date would ever compare to that improbable, but flawless string of seconds and thoughts and stories that led us to that covered driveway on an empty street with strangers sitting inside their house, only feet away from where she pulled me as close to her as two humans could ever be. I can only think of maybe five or six perfect moments in my long existence.

My perfect moment with Anat beat them all.

The Girl Who Doomed God
Part 9

Night greeted us when our procession filed out of the fortress. We scaled the ladder back to the surface of the Island. Followers led the way with crackling torches casting dancing light across the Wilderness. No one said anything, but there was a general glow to all of us. Palpable optimism as we marched toward revolution.

I breathed easier with Anat at my side. The anxiety of the closed-in spaces and capricious gods eased as my lungs finally felt able to stretch.

I took Anat within my cloud and we swept into the sky and across the Island. My people cheered as we left, then retreated to wait and brace for what came next.

Conjoining with Anat in the mist was intimate and familiar, but not erotic. Both a mixing and a yielding. I'd flown other exiles around before, but it never felt like this. They never felt like peers.

We passed the waterfall and whisked through the campground. God and Jay sat on the pier, looking out toward the Wilderness and talking quietly. They were worried and unsure of how to proceed. Too distracted by their fracturing empire to notice interlopers in the campground.

You saw us from a window. I could never figure out how to hide from you when I was that close. I paused near the flagpole, watching you watch me. You didn't move.

We proceeded toward the western edge of the Island. The landing strip stretched out before us. The Cessna slumbered. Angels were collecting overhead, tracking us as I allowed the mist to evaporate, exposing Anat and I to God's eyes. He would come to us. He was probably already on His way, but it would be too late.

We walked to the plane. Anat's skin began to glow red. Heat emanated, expanding past me and forming a barrier between us and the angels. As we approached the plane, its paint darkened and scorched. The tires exploded and the plane crunched down onto the hubs.

I turned to my queen and pressed a kiss to her searing hot cheek.

"Let's change everything," I whispered.

"Do it."

I looked back at the trail as God not so much ran as lumbered toward us.

"Stop!" He yelled or rather gasped. His lungs clearly hadn't had that much exertion in years. Maybe ever.

I ran to the plane, placed my hands against its scorching metal hull. From within my chest, I drew up a surge of energy, focusing on the feel of the aluminum, cradling it with my mind, lifting the entire plane up into the air. It groaned.

"Simon!" God called.

I looked to The Old Man, winked, and pushed my hands out, forcing the plane over the cliff. It glided momentarily before the momentum gave away to gravity and the plane tumbled over the side of the Island. Angels flew after it but bounced off the heat barrier now following the plane down the side of the cliffs.

I ran to the edge and watched the plane, engulfed in flames, spin down towards Heaven.

Then it disintegrated and was gone forever.

Anat grasped my hand. Her skin was searing hot and seductive.

"What have you done?" God shouted as He ran towards us.

"Corporate restructuring," I said, turning towards Him. You

stood next to Jay beside the landing strip. I'd forgotten how alike the two of you appeared. Same rigid arch of the back, same round, sad faces so used to being misunderstood.

The difference was in the eyes, though.

Anat addressed God. "If we can't leave the Island, then neither will You. Neither will anyone. We are all in this mess together."

Digging Toward Heaven
Part 3

So, let me explain my fear of the underground. Back when I was dating a publicist in Vegas, I let her convince me to try the old bury-myself-alive bit in hopes of elevating my visibility within the magician's circuit.

"But it's gotta be legit," she said. She was naked at the time, so, of course, I agreed. "No secret passages or mirrors or tricks. Just you in a hole for 24 hours."

We did it in a giant, dirt-filled glass tomb in the middle of the strip outside a second rate casino.

"Street magic is hot right now," she told me. "Everyone loves a free miracle!"

The tomb was actually more of a giant aquarium, a re-purposed set piece pulled out of mothballs from when Fabulous Fallimento attempted a mock drowning that accidentally turned into a real drowning. After a trip to the emergency room and divorce from his fourth assistant/wife, Fallimento declared that he would never touch water again. He wouldn't even tolerate ice cubes in his scotch.

My burial wasn't quite so dramatic nor did it inspire much enthusiasm from onlookers. The case was treated more like a hindrance to pedestrian traffic. I survived the most frightening, panic-filled day of my life smelling nothing but my own foulness. And, when I emerged from the grave, I looked down onto the small crowd milling about and only mildly interested in my resurrection.

I don't know what was worse:

A. The 1,440 minutes of pitch black terror with too little oxygen and the horrible realization that broccoli was a terrible pre-burial food choice.

B. The sparse, somewhat confused crowd that was only vaguely aware that something magic-y was happening in front of their very eyes.

C. The bored and resentful frown on my girlfriend's face as she realized that she'd hitched herself to one of the dimmest stars in Las Vegas.

I soon changed my living will to ensure that I would never, ever be buried again.

All this to say that I was not thrilled to be plunging down into the dark depths of the Island to seek out Huan and whatever Island Stars he may have been hoarding. I'd kept an eye on New Wichita since our little chat at the edge of the Island, but he hadn't stepped foot outside the cavern since.

His hole was getting deeper. It was difficult to gauge just how far down he'd bored into the Island, but I imagined he wouldn't make it much farther before the bottom crust of the Island gave way and he fell into Heaven.

I'd seen many people make the great plunge over the Island cliffs only to disappear once they clear the bottom. Like Tommy, they always ended up popping back up somewhere on the Island. Sometimes inside the Island in their very own living gave. Needless to say, jumping off cliffs wasn't ideal, so maybe Huan's hole might be more effective at getting us back to Heaven.

I found Huan, hearing his shovel cut into the dry earth, the ground almost gasping as dirt pried loose, then dumped into a bucket.

He paused as I neared. Perhaps he sensed me. There was so little sensory distractions down here that even my mist would be felt as sure as a rainstorm.

"Did you find me something pretty and shiny?" I asked, not materializing. I felt safer as air, which was perhaps naive, but it was all I could do to push back the panic.

I heard him breathing, smelt his sweat.

"Been going at it all night long, huh? Kinda weird. You need to talk about it?"

Nope, apparently.

"Don't be like this, Huaun. We should be allies. I assure you that my intentions are way more noble than the Americans. Or at least marginally better."

I tried a pleasant laugh. Didn't work.

"Anyhoo, I need you to know that something bad is coming, so, maybe get out of the hole for a little while."

No answer from him. I focused on the area, trying to sense an Island Star, but nothing registered.

"Where are you hiding them these days?"

Still silence.

"I'm not going anywhere until we've talked this out a little."

Huan swung his shovel toward me, the blade cutting through the mist.

"Come on, don't be like this. Just work with me. I promise that I'll make it worth your time."

Huan swung the shovel again, this time striking the wall of the hole. Dirt freed and tumbled down.

"Whoa! Whoa, whoa, whoa!"

Silence settled as the last of the dirt fell into a small pile at Huan's feet.

"Okay, listen, just give me a moment to..."

Huan swung the shovel, striking the wall. More dirt freed.

"Jesus Aged Christ, okay!"

I soared up the hole and fled the labyrinth of tunnels, brushing through the crowds in downtown New Wichita, and sweeping out the mouth of the cavern to await God's response.

I Cannot Die
Part 13

I may never witness anything more frightening than a terrified god.

The Old Man gazed down the side of the Island. His angels swept toward the bottom of the cliff, looking for any traces of the plane. Of course it was gone, but the angels didn't know what else to do and were also frightened of the dreadful silence of their Creator. Without the plane, they also couldn't escape the Island. Legions of angels awaited in Heaven, able to deliver a new plane within moments or swarm and overwhelm Simon and Anat.

But we'd just lost our only means of communication with the rest of the universe.

God hadn't moved in hours. Morning arrived, the sun inching above the Island like a timid child eyeing an angry parent.

I stood by Him the entire night, trying to settle my fright as best I could. I knew no other place to be. He was vulnerable and small, His frown weak and disbelieving.

It was so obvious then. Of course Simon would do this. Of course he would. How did God not see it coming?

Sure, the Island had muted His powers, He was no longer all-seeing and all-powerful, but that didn't make Him an idiot. Then again, I didn't see it coming either.

It was His fault. He'd purposefully covered the Island with a haze so the future was somewhat concealed and beyond His control. But you disposing of the plane, God's only escape from the Island was such a powerful tactical maneuver, we should have known. Should have prepared for it, but we still didn't believe that you were really gunning for His throne.

God eased down onto the cliff, sitting and dangling His legs over the side, so much more brittle than I'd ever seen Him. He patted the ground next to Him and I sat down. Jay, who stood several feet away, eyes reddened and angry, followed my lead and sat on God's other side. The son on the right, the bastard son on the left, just as it was in the beginning.

"Where is Simon?" God asked as His eyes aimed down at Heaven.

Jay eased forward and looked over to me. He glared like a hungry wolf. He wanted blood in a way that I hadn't seen since he walked the Earth, before he realized that the only blood that would be shed was his own.

"Simon moves fast," I answered. "I've always had a hard time getting a bead on him, but he does have something like a palace built along the cliffs on the far northeast side of the Island. He may be there, waiting for a response, but I doubt it."

"He wants to be found," Jay said. "He thinks Anat can protect him from the angels. They need a showdown to prove they are beyond retribution."

"No one is beyond My wrath," God said, but not quite convinced. Jay frowned, troubled by his Father's tone. Jay needed God to be certain and, as hard as it was too admit, I did too. I hated God's plan, the one that had existed since before my Creation, but that the plan existed was always a comfort. By destroying God's airplane, you dismantled that plan and was, for the first time in Creation, sending the universe careening off into the unknown.

"Is there a way to rebuild the plane?" I asked.

"It was created in Heaven," God said. "And only in Heaven can it be recreated. If we cannot reach Heaven, they cannot know that I am without."

"The Engineers?" Jay asked. "They are powerful and have brought things to the Island. Perhaps they could."

"They won't help us," I said. "If anything, they will celebrate. They are afraid of Simon, but they are more afraid of Us."

God took off His sunglasses and rubbed away tears. He looked to me with blue, pupiless eyes.

"But you are their friend," He said, desperate to find some ground on which to stand back up. "Make them believe in Me again."

"Would You be willing to negotiate?" I asked.

"God does not negotiate," Jay said. It was the kind of statement he would have once shouted righteously, but that was a different time in a much different place.

God looked to Jay and considered. He replaced His sunglasses, then nodded His head in agreement.

"I cannot appear weak," God said. "No matter what happens, I can never appear weak."

"But," I began carefully. "You are weak."

Jay took in a sharp breath, then looked away from me, down

to the cloud of souls. God did not respond. I had to say it, but I'd even surprised myself with the boldness of the statement. My body surged with adrenaline as sweat beaded on my forehead. I tensed, expecting to be tossed off the Island. But it appeared that, at the moment, I'd gotten away with it.

God still needed me. In fact, He'd never needed me more.

"How about a show of force?" Jay asked. "Some classic Old Testament fury? If we can't kill Simon, we can at least scare him, make him a little less sure of taking on God and all His might."

Jay looked at his Father hopefully, but God only sighed. He lifted His legs up over the cliff and struggled to stand, His knees popping like a drum flare. He patted the dirt off his butt and turned from the cliff.

"Send everyone, Bali," God said.

"Yes, Father."

"And me?" Jay asked. "Let me fight for You. Let me show them what I can do."

"No," God said, then walked toward the campground.

Jay absorbed the rejection as he always did—passively. I put a hand on his shoulder and he shook his head.

"He loves you above all else," I whispered. "He is protecting you, Jay. I know that is hard to remember, but He's put you through so much already, He can't bear to watch you suffer anymore."

"He's a coward."

His voice had been so low that I almost didn't catch it. It took me several moments to decide that I'd heard him correct. He shrugged off my hand and walked after God. I turned to the cliff and walked to the edge. I clapped my hands like I was settling an unruly classroom. The angels flew up and formed ranks before me.

"Find Simon," I called to them. "And remind the rest of the

Island that God is still the Alpha and the Omega."

Great shrieks wailed from the angels as they soared above my head and raced for the Wilderness. Swords were unsheathed and furious fire burned from the blades. The army left a long smoke trail in their wake like a missile roaring toward Armageddon.

And as I watched the chaos resulting from the collapse of God's Divine Plan, I knew another plan was already in place and we were playing right into it.

It was the most thrilling moment in all of my lives.

Martha The Believer
Part 7

Her face paled, her muscles softened, her mind went fuzzy and gray. She fell backwards into hands that gripped her arms, holding her steady.

"Dread," Martha muttered as her startled followers eased her down onto the grass. She laid back and looked up to the clouds. "My Fiancé is afraid."

"Who?" April asked.

"Our Father," Martha answered.

"Her fiancé is her dad?" Cheyenne asked.

Martha ignored the stupidity and instead focused on a twisting nausea in her stomach. It was what He felt. They were connected after all and the realization was both thrilling and sorrowful. Martha began crying for His sake. She didn't know why God felt fear, but it was as real as if it were her own emotion.

The suffocating dread began to clear like water sloshing into storm drains. Her breathes eased, but an energy hummed in her heart.

"I've got to get to Him," Martha said. "Help me up. Help me get back to Him."

"Your dad's on the Island?" Cheyenne asked.

"God. I must get to God."

The shrieks of angels crossed the Island. The followers looked to the sky.

"What was that?" April asked.

"God's wrath," Martha said with a righteous and wicked smile.

Sister Sophia
Part 3

More wildlife was reaching the exiles including the slower cattle that stomped through the weeds and broke through the branches, anxious to get to Sophia. Deer, skunks, hawks, and wolves took turns approaching Sophia and bowing their heads before her. She'd pat their snouts, stroke their feathers, or tussle their fur while beaming a joyful smile.

"I suppose I should be used to it by now," Sophia said, then cleared tears from her cheeks with the back of her hand.

"I'd been wondering who was to blame for all this," Esperanza said. "You've been getting them riled up for several days now. They act like a terrible storm is coming, but seems they just wanted to say 'hello'."

Esperanza walked toward the cattle, then noticed the charred half-man lying on the ground. Willow stood beside him, half-standing, half-crouched. Esperanza scanned the exiles, seeing Tommy and Edward softly whispering and kissing each other, so consumed in their reunion that they'd forgotten the world around them.

"I think I might need some catching up," Esperanza said.

Tommy pulled Edward's head into his chest. He kissed him on the top of the forehead and turned to Esperanza.

"We need shelter, quick," Tommy said.

"I can't take you back to Rawlings, Tommy," Esperanza said. "Not after what you did."

Edward took a deep breath, but chose to keep his face hidden. He wanted to enjoy the moment as much as he could, fearing that it would be the last time he would be so close to Tommy.

But the moment soured as envy and bitterness snuck in.

Edward pulled back and clutched Tommy's hand. He would deal with the hurt later.

"What's happening?" Edward asked Tommy.

"Simon is happening. I don't know what he has planned, but we have to find cover soon because something big is coming."

"You want to get these cattle back in time?" Tommy asked Esperanza. "We will help, but you have to give a roof to my friends. I will stay outside, I'll run back into the woods, I don't care, but we need your help and we need to get going right now."

"Wait, what is Rawlings?" Billy asked. "Where are we going?"

"Just across the field in the southern end of America," Tommy said.

Billy held his hand up to the others, motioning them to stay put. "Bali said to avoid America."

"Rawlings is not New Wichita," Tommy said.

"Now, everyone wait a damn second," Esperanza said. "We don't have room for all of you and I'm not even sure I want any of you knowing where we hole up. I don't trust Tommy and I have no reason to trust any of you."

"I know I disappointed you," Tommy said. "But I've never lied. You shouldn't trust me, but you can trust my people. Just do this one favor for me, please."

Esperanza looked back to the path the cattle cut through the forest, seeing the fields beyond. "Damnit. Fine, come on." She waved her hand and began walking back to Rawlings.

Willow grabbed the blanket and began dragging Trevor away. Ossie jogged to her.

"Stay with us," Ossie said. "We'll help you."

"We'll find our own way," Willow said, head down, pushing north.

"Darling, perhaps we should consider it," Trevor said.

"We'll find our own way!"

Trevor tilted his head to look back at Ossie.

"The woman has spoken. Look after your own people."

Ossie turned back to Billy, who shrugged. Ossie took off his backpack and handed it to Willow.

"Set up the tent and wait out whatever is coming, okay?"

Willow hesitated. She grit her teeth, then snatched the backpack away from Ossie and slung it over her shoulders.

"Thank you," she said, not looking up. Ossie backed up and let her drag Trevor away.

Edward met Ossie's eyes and nodded. Edward then led Tommy along the path after Esperanza. Tommy hesitated, leaning back as Edward pulled.

"Come on," Edward said. "Let's get to safety. We'll figure everything out later."

"You're better off without me," Tommy said.

Edward took a moment to measure Tommy, then take a deep breath.

"Don't you ever tell me what is and is not good for me! Never again. Just come with me. We will figure everything out later."

Edward grabbed both of Tommy's hands. He eased his forehead against Tommy's.

"Come with me. You owe me that much."

Tommy grimaced, but then said "Okay."

A choir of shrill screeches cut through the sky and all eyes pointed up toward a dozens of fireballs in the sky, streaking toward the Wilderness.

"What is that?" Esperanza asked.

Ossie felt a cold wave through his body. In his mind, he saw blue blurs streaking across the Island sky. He turned to the exiles and shouted "Run!"

The Ovens

"The joke around here is if we could just get these damn ovens a little hotter, they'd stop smelling like locker rooms and start smelling like barbecue pits."

His laugh was deep and moist, as if the statement had him salivating. Julia couldn't see The Cook in the darkness, but she imagined his grin to be wide—like the wolf awaiting Little Red Riding Hood.

"But we can't burn them completely up. It would kinda miss the point, you know?"

"Yeah," she said.

Side rooms appeared every ten feet and contained an oven haloed by a faint glow casting down from the ceiling where a pipe shot straight up from the stove toward the surface. The ovens hadn't been built on the Island, she was sure of that. From the long, black, sculpted barrel shape and ornate designs along the side, she guessed it was from the Victorian age.

It wasn't designed to cook humans. It didn't even seem big enough for a human to fit in, so she guessed they were curled tight inside like fetuses inside a womb.

And The Cook was right, the stench was powerful. Sweat, ash, roasted feces. She brought a rag up to her mouth. The rag that he'd insisted on her.

The rag smelt like him, so she lowered it from her mouth and dropped it to the ground. She'd sooner suffer the smell of misery.

"Girl," The Cook continued. "I gotta tell you, you're the first person to want to see these damn things. No one else volunteers to come down here."

"What can I say, I'm a curious gal. How did you get stuck with this job?"

"Some bastard slept with my woman," he said. "Thought he was gonna get away with it too 'cause what the hell are we gonna do, right? That was early on in New Wichita. We'd done some public hangings, but no one particularly liked them 'cause nobody died. They just sorta swung, shit themselves, and get all bug-eyed until someone cuts them down. So, we started using these ovens instead. Nobody dies here either, but it's still a whole lotta suffering and ain't all up in everyone's faces, you know? We'd worked out some deal with the Engineers. They thought we were gonna use them for preparing meat or whatever, but this is better. Food is plentiful, but justice is rare. Always was. And this is better than hanging. All the good citizens get to hear the screams, know that there is punishment being rendered, but don't have to see it."

"The American way," she said.

"Yeah, sure. The American way. Well, we dug the first oven deep into the ground and I threw that cuckolding bastard in myself. I offered to watch over him, give him enough food and water to keep him lucid, then burn him once a day. Two weeks later, we released him and he shot right out of New Wichita like a bullet from a gun. Good riddance, justice served. More started getting sent down for stretches. We added more ovens. Now we got three veins underneath New Wichita, spreading the ovens out so if we get a tunnel collapse, we still got backups."

"Every have any escapes?"

"Not down here, but we did at that first one we built further out from downtown. I don't watch it as closely. We usually just lock people up there when they got a long stay ahead. Real hard cases, you know? Some fella managed to slip free the other day. I musta forgot to latch the oven."

"It happens," she said. "I'm surprised the Engineers haven't done anything about the ovens yet."

"Me too, to be honest. But everyone can be bought off, I guess."

The Cook stopped. She could tell he was looking in her direction, but couldn't see more than a vague outline of his thick head.

"Wanna know a secret?"

"Of course."

"You get all of them lit at the same time, it's like surround sound. I ain't gonna lie, it get's wicked down here. Pretty, almost. A chorus of the damned, you know?"

"I do."

They continued walking down the tunnel. She'd counted seven ovens so far and saw more dim lights ahead.

"Where did the Engineers get the ovens from?" she asked.

"Don't know for sure. The Engineers have mysterious ways and, when they need some laborers to help build their temples and shrines and other silliness, we do a trade. There's rumors The Mayor's done some trading with Bali, with the angels, even God Himself. Who knows? Could all just be bullshit."

"What if there is a collapse, what happens then?"

"We've actually had a vein flooded before. You remember the tornado a while back? We got too much rain and, since these tunnels are the deepest, these ovens went underwater for about a week. Couldn't get them dry for the longest time."

"Right, so you get them out? The prisoners. Whether water or dirt, you get them out?"

The man stopped again. His shadowed face turning to her.

"Why bother? They ain't gonna die anyway. We'll get to them when we get to them."

He continued down the tunnel. She was focusing on keeping her breathing steady. She was here for a reason, she couldn't react until the time was right.

"Alright, here we are," he said.

There was some rattling, then a beam of light appeared and shined down on a ratty mattress sitting on a rusted bed frame.

"I convinced them to install a stovepipe, just for a little bit of light. Something I can close off when I need some shut eye or general privacy."

"You sleep down here?"

"Someone's got to. You still want to do this thing, right?"

"Right."

He shrugged, stepping into the light. He was big, very big. Wide chest, a bit of gut, but thick, muscled arms. His beard was unkempt—wild like a tangle of ivy. There was something handsome underneath, but further underneath was something revolting. He unlatched a strap of his overalls. He wore no shirt underneath.

"Where are the other veins?" she asked, still in the shadows.

"Why you wanna know that? You sightseeing?"

"Maybe I am planning a day out of this. You up for that big guy?"

His smiling teeth glowed an eerie bright white beneath his unruly and greasy beard.

"They're all connected back the way we came, little girl. We'll hit them all, give them bastards a show. You want me to light them, so we can fuck while they are screaming?"

"Maybe. Got any water down here?"

He unlatched the other strap of his overalls. They tumbled down, lingering just over his gut. He shimmied them all the way off. His skin was pale and ugly. She'd never seen a man so ugly on the Island. It had to be the ovens and the darkness and the horror.

"Hell, I got all the fixings darling. Water, fish, dried venison. I'm an important man. I'm The Cook of New Wichita."

He turned, crawled across the mattress and opened a foot locker on the other side. He grabbed a canteen and turned to face her.

Julia leapt into the light. She jammed a knife into The Cook's throat. He swung his arms wide, trying to push her off, but she leaned into the knife, cutting across his windpipe, hearing it scrape against his spinal column.

She placed her hand against his chest, then jerked the knife back out. Blood sprayed and shimmered. Her lips and fingers trembled. She forced calm breathing as The Cook clasped his palms across his neck, trying to hold the life in.

Julia clenched her teeth, waiting for the adrenaline to ease. She had to remain quiet, keep her wits. Tears dripped from her eyelashes. She couldn't stop them. She didn't want to stop them. The tension had to escape somewhere and crying was better than screaming.

A tremor passed through her body. She sighed, closed her eyes for a moment. She picked up his overalls to use them to clean the knife. She gagged as she wiped the blood and tears from her cheek.

His throat still gurgled as he gulped for air, but only drowned in blood. She gagged again, the nausea twisting in her stomach. She turned from the bed.

"Stop bitching, you'll live."

Angelic screeches echoed down the stovepipe above her. She looked up towards the light, curious, but decided she had more pressing matters. She stepped back into the darkness, leaving The Cook twisting and hacking atop his blood-soaked mattress.

The Engineers
Part 2

"Life. Life. Life. Life. Life. Life. Life. Life. Life. Life. Life."

Seventeen Engineers chanted low as they sat in a circle around a small tent. Shapes and movement could be seen through the polyester. A shadow show. Soft moans along with the rustle of a sleeping bag. The Engineers were all naked, sitting on the soft mud of the shore, arms out to their sides, palms up, eyes closed and aimed at the skies. Mildred sat opposite Yulia in the circle. They'd placed the most powerful Engineers at the points of a pentagram drawn in the sand.

The tent was in the center. The focal point of their collective power.

All in full view of God just across the lake.

They attempted the ritual every morning with a different set of people and different set of parameters, trying to find the workaround to God's denial of human reproduction. The symbology shifted as well as the ceremony leading up to and after the moment. Field testing a new formula every single day until something worked.

A part of Mildred feared the implications of denying God's new natural order. You could only prod the boundaries for so long without provoking the Creator.

But she was driven onward by the "what if?"

"Life. Life. Life. Life. Life. Life. Life. Life. Life. Life. Life."

The sounds in the tent intensified. Urgency. Passion. The chant grew louder. Mildred began perspiring, her own body absorbing the sensual energy emanating from the tent, making her breaths shallow gasps. She struggled to continue the chant.

"Oww, oww, my toes are cramping! Hold on!"

Mildred's eyes opened, frustrated as she looked in on the shadows in the tent. The shadow on top had stopped moving.

"Ah. Give me a second."

A few of the Engineers burped out laughs, but the chant continued. Mildred closed her eyes and rejoined.

"Life. Life. Life."

"Alright, I'm good. Sorry about that."

"It's okay, honey."

The moans built again. Louder now. Earnest. Mildred's face flushed, her jaw hung limp, her hands reached for the earth, her fingers digging in. Muscles tightened, spasmed, her breath short, then a long release. Her eyes rolled into her head and she fell back onto the sand. Other Engineers along the circle, the ones who could absorb the energy, were also rolling their heads around, shivering, smiling.

Even if the ritual was worthless and never yielded a child, it was still a hell of a lotta fun.

Mildred, still lying on her back, began clapping and the other Engineers joined in. The tent zipped open, an elderly man stepped out, then bent over to massage the toes of his right foot. He laughed at his own frailty. The woman remained inside, curled up on her back, legs and hips held aloft, guiding life towards her womb.

The terrible shriek of the angels cut into the morning. The Engineers stood and looked toward the south.

"Simon," a female Engineer said.

A short, hairy man named Earnest closed his eyes and focused on the campground. In his mind, he saw over twenty blue creatures rising into the sky and sweeping toward the Wilderness. He also saw swords unsheathe and flames burst alive with divine, vengeful fury.

"We're being attacked," Earnest said. "I think that's every

angel on the Island."

"Why?" Mildred asked.

Beyond the angles, in the campground, Earnest saw wavering shimmers of green, black, and a sickly blue.

"Revenge," Earnest said. "Anger and fear. Whatever happened, God is furious. He's also rattled."

Mildred looked up to the sky. She could feel them approaching through a subtle drop in temperature, whispers of a terrible front looming.

"Get everyone back to the temple," Mildred said. "We'll ride this out."

"We don't have time," Earnest said. "They are coming fast."

"It's every angel?" Yulia asked. "We can't fight that many. Not yet."

"I know," Mildred said. "Just go. I'll buy you some time."

"Don't be an idiot," Yulia said.

"I won't, I'll just slow them down. Get going!"

She pushed Earnest toward the rest of the Engineers.

"Should I stay here?" the woman in the tent said, legs still in the air.

"No," Mildred said. "Someone get her a towel or something."

The Engineers' faces mixed fear and fury. Many wanted to stand and fight, curious how their growing powers would match with an angel.

"Go!" Mildred said, waving the group away. "Leave the tent."

They fled into the forest, the woman holding a shirt between her legs as she ran awkwardly forward. Mildred turned toward the advance.

Angels had come before and were usually no major concern. They'd wrecked a few buildings, destroyed an icon that'd been built a little too tall. When the Engineers resisted, the angels usually just swept them aside and kept moving. But with every altercation, the Engineers got a little stronger, got a little smarter.

"We're probing," Mildred would tell the Engineers after every lost confrontation. "We are growing, they are staying the same. We'll outpace them in time."

But the angels were attacking en masse this time. She could tell by the chill in the air. They weren't just running an errand, dispensing a slap on the wrist. This was vengeance.

She closed her eyes and focused on the tendrils of cold cutting through the sky and the heat of God's fury burning on each sword. Only two were heading towards the Engineers, the rest were breaking off to the west, towards America.

Mildred walked into the pentagram, kicked the tent away, and took her place in the center. Two angels.

"I've got this."

Sister Sophia
Part 4

A menagerie burst out of the woods—sprinting, flying, and slithering into the fields of Rawlings. The humans were flanked on all sides by life with Sophia at its core. Barking joined the cacophony of animal calls as a pair of coyotes sprinted out from cover to join the herd moving through the open plain.

Sophia registered a drop in temperature, just like when God fled the Island. But this was different. They'd never heard the roar of the plane's engines escorting Him back to Heaven. And the chill was directional, as if carried by the wind. Above, the comets were breaking off into different directions, covering all corners of the Wilderness. Some of the fires extinguished.

She'd felt safer within the trees, but all the Island was a mystery and Tommy seemed confident. They followed a man none of them trusted, even the woman whose land they were fleeing towards. But any plan was better than surrendering to chaos.

Sophia looked behind her. The deer, birds, and coyotes were the only animals able to keep pace with the humans. She slowed, letting the cattle lumber alongside her.

"Hurry up!" Tommy called from ahead.

Sophia kept looking back toward the lizards, snakes, mice, and other insects struggling to catch up.

A deer nudged her, pushing her forward. Billy grabbed her hand and pulled her along.

"Whatever is coming isn't interested in the animals," Billy said.

They continued running.

A wave of cold air swept past them, knocking several exiles to the ground. The treetops swayed as the angels and their flaming swords pushed onward toward New Wichita.

"They're not after us," Raul called, guitar strapped to his back. He pushed himself back to his feet and smiled back at Billy.

Raul was jerked into the air, screaming as blood spurted from his shoulders where the angel's talons latched onto him. Billy ran after him, jumping for Raul's feet, but coming up short. Raul continued lifting high.

Then Billy was snatched off the ground.

"No!" Sophia screamed.

The birds shot into the sky, swarming the empty air where the angels were hidden. A falcon flew above, then dove straight down at the angel. It impacted, the angel shrieked. The falcon tumbled to the ground, lifeless before it even landed.

More shrieks emerged from the frustrated angels as Raul and Billy dangled below. Their swords ignited again and they swung at the birds swarming them. The angels swept south, but the birds followed, plunging into the angels like kamikaze pilots.

"Get everyone to safety!" Sophia yelled, then ran after the angels.

Raul and Billy dipped back down as the angels struggled through the angry hive of life.

Then Raul and Billy dropped into the trees. The two coyotes sped out ahead of Sophia and leapt into the woods. Moments later, they barked, guiding Sophia back to the love of her afterlife.

She heard yelping, screeches, branches breaking. Limbs were catching fire as the angles swung their swords at the barrage. She sprinted hard, trying to reach the melee.

She found Billy wedged between broken trees, gazing to the treetops. Blood was smattered across his face, breaths showed in plumes as the coyotes ducked beside him, barking up at the invisible angel looming over him. Fire crackled from the sword as it swung high and prepared to strike. One coyote snatched at the angel's leg, but was kicked off into the shrubs.

"Stop it!" Sophia screamed, sprinting for Billy and diving over his body to shield him. "Leave us alone."

The chill intensified.

A deer plunged through the shrubbery and gored the angel. The angel shrieked, dropped its sword, and slapped the deer away. A distant screech cut through the chaos. For a moment, the angel was still. The sword was lifted back into the air, then sheathed.

"We've done nothing wrong," Sophia said. "Just leave."

A blast of cold swept over them as the angel's wings beat. It leapt into the sky and broke through the canopy of branches as it flew north. The cold eased, the warmth of the Island returning.

Billy chuckled, then coughed.

"I'm supposed to be the one protecting you," he said, weak and through a mouthful of blood.

Sophia placed a hand on his face and kissed his forehead.

"Next time," she said.

Several feet away, Raul sat against a tree, cradling his broken guitar like a dead child.

The Engineers
Part 3

The angels were closing. As they dropped just above the lake, the water froze like a trail marking their path in a surreal mirroring of fire above and ice below. Mildred widened her stance, right foot out front, bent her knees, brought her hands up, palms facing the angels. She took a deep breath, felt the angels almost as vividly as if she could see them. Great beasts, at least eight feet head to hoof, a wingspan of twenty feet.

"Go back to your master!" Mildred called.

The angels broke to either side of her, climbed into the sky above her and circled, smoke trails forming a halo. She tracked them by their temperature, studying them as they studied her.

They dove. Giant talons grasped for her arms. She leapt toward one, spinning from the talons and latching its neck under her arm. Her momentum pulled the angel off balance and sent them both back to the ground. It flailed to gain its feet, but Mildred was on top of it, swinging for the empty air where she believed its head to be.

Her hand cracked against its skull and all the bones in her hand shattered.

She screamed in pain. The other angel snatched her by the shoulders and flew her into the sky. She struggled to get free, but its talons tightened, cutting into the meat of her shoulders. She whipped her legs up, wrapping around its neck. Its talons released, then ripped at her back, trying to get her off. The sword swung for her, but only singed off her hair. She bear-hugged one wing, preventing it from flapping. She couldn't get a grip with her broken hand, so just used her other hand to grip her opposite forearm, keeping the angel tight against her.

The angel lost altitude, began plummeting in a wounded circle. It desperately flapped, trying to avoid another crash, but they both fell toward the lake. The water froze as they neared. Her shoulder blade splintered as she smashed through the ice.

For a brief moment, her mind went blank. Everything spun. The cold brought her back in a searing flash. She saw the sword as it plunged into her chest. The fire sizzled her flesh and boiled the water around her. Then the sword retreated and Mildred's mind was overwhelmed by panic and pain.

She surfaced and felt the water freeze against her skin. Her movement slowed, then stopped. The pain was gone. Her arms and chest were encased in ice with her face just above the water. Her skin went from cold to hot as hypothermia set in, her panicking mind lying to her.

She heard the angel scraping against the ice, trying to gain its feet. Once it stood, the beast stepped over Mildred's face and toward the shore where she could sense the other angel was struggling to stand. It wobbled, then fell back over, unable to clear the concussion. Mildred's blue lips trembled violently, but still managed a smile.

Both angels were now on their feet, they approached Mildred, stepping onto the ice, their swords held high. Shrieks to the north briefly drew Mildred's attention away. The angels also paused then turned to the shrieks. They exchanged something like whispers. They leapt into the air, flew above the treetops and deep into the heart of the Wilderness.

The ice sheet cracked as it melted. Mildred's trapped body began to bob in the water. Her pupils extended, focusing on something far, far away. Something beyond the Island. Something beyond life.

A large slab of ice bumped against Mildred's, sliding up above the ice and over her face. The weight forced her underwater, hiding her corpse.

The ice quickly melted after the angels fled, but Mildred's body was gone. The Engineers would soon return to see what had become of their leader, but would never find an answer.

How To Properly Manage A Young Empire
Part 4

The wind blew through the cavern's maw like the Island had just sucked in its first breath. Cold wind howled through downtown and the angels and their swords followed close behind, sending citizens sprawling out of the way. Most angels plunged down side tunnels after clearing major streets, but a pair wound through the buildings towards The Mayor's mansion.

The Mayor stood within her study, a forgotten tumbler of moonshine cradled in her hand. When she saw the dust swirling through downtown, she feared Simon, but soon realized it was different.

From the tunnels, she saw citizens lifted through the air. They screamed and fought, but could not free themselves from whatever creature flew them back out of the cavern.

Dust swept against her front window. She felt the temperature drop. The window shattered and showered against her. She shielded her face as she felt the glass cut against her skin. The cold flew past her. Mirrors fell all across her home, smashing against the ground, broken glass spilling across her floor. She remained still.

A young man screamed from upstairs.

The cold swept back into the study. Her skin tingled as the chill sucked all the moisture from the room. Her breath formed panicked clouds. She felt the angel standing above her. She dipped her head, her body shivering.

"We've shown Him nothing but fidelity. Leave us in peace."

The cold lingered. A sword unsheathed, its fire sending heat and flickering light across the room. The sword moved slowly toward The Mayor, but she held her ground.

Another shriek called from somewhere outside the cavern. The sword disappeared. The angel rushed past her and flew from the mansion. Outside, screams rose. More citizens were being swept from New Wichita, into the Wilderness, then dropped into the trees like discarded rag dolls. The Mayor shook her head, lifted her tumbler to take a drink, barely able to control her trembling fingers. She looked at the tumbler, then tipped it upside down. The frozen moonshine fell out and shattered on the floor.

The Ovens
Part 2

As the weary prisoners filed through the tunnels, Julia thought of low-rent zombie movies she only watched because a lame boyfriend thought it was funny to watch her wretch and gag whenever gore splashed across the screen.

She always hated blood. She hated how cheap it was in film, how it was a replacement for cleverness, mood, art. Can't get your audience to react? Just dump a bucket of blood over a pretty girl, that'll do it. Why be talented when you can be gross instead?

A pair of torches burned at the entrance to the caves of New Wichita. She walked past the light to the last vein of ovens. She paused to look back at the illuminated herd of prisoners. She thought again of zombies. That's what these poor people were reduced to. Some of them weren't too bad, the short-timers. They were feeble, but alert. Others were just storage units for brain pudding.

They'd come back. Maybe. Provided she could lead them out of New Wichita and off into hiding. If not, the zombies go back to their ovens and her head would likely appear on Petrov's doorstep. He'd be forced to paint her into something beautiful. She thought a sugar skull motif would be clever and funny, but dismissed the idea because it felt vaguely racist.

But she'd find a way through. She had to. The Island needed freedom fighters, not martyrs. She would need a proper army, something a bit peppier than this platoon of malnourished and spiritually exhausted prisoners.

"One thing at a time," Julia told herself as they reached the last occupied ovens in New Wichita.

A bitter, cold wind swept through the tunnel, pushing dust

out ahead of it and extinguishing a torch at the end of the tunnel. The wind brushed past her, then stopped, somehow. Its chill settled between her and the last vein of ovens.

"What's happening?" a prisoner asked behind her.

"Sssh," Julia hissed.

She put her hand up, feeling the chill intensifying as her hand extended towards its invisible source. The dim oven lights were distorted as they shone through the cold.

"Did He send you?" Julia asked what she assumed was an angel. "Is He really sending His pets to stop me?"

Julia motioned to the prisoners behind her.

"Is the God of Love and Mercy really going to stop this?"

The chill didn't move.

"Send me back to Hell," Julia said. "I'm ready. Is that why you came? He finally realized His mistake, bringing someone to the Island that will never bow before Him?"

No answer. She strode forward. A cold blast sent her backwards off her feet, falling into prisoners who fell backwards like toppled bowling pins. From the cold, a sword appeared, the flames from it so bright the prisoners shielded their eyes.

Julia pushed back to her feet.

"I am right!" she yelled. "I am the righteous one! These ovens are criminal. They are against His laws and even if they weren't, they are still cruel and wrong. You will help me, angel. You will help me free these people or you will get the fuck out of my way!"

Julia marched forward, feeling a cold wind gust back, but not with the same force as before. She stumbled, but gathered herself and continued marching onward. Her lips began drying and blistering, her cheeks paling to a blue, her joints stiffening.

"Out of my way." The words were clipped as her lips trembled.

The sword extinguished and disappeared. The chill faded. Her skin warmed with tiny, sharp pricks stabbing where the nerves awoke. The cold was gone, but she knew the angel was still there. Watching. Conflicted.

It huffed and blew past her, almost knocking her back down as it retreated from the tunnels. Two more torches snuffed out on the way. They were left only with the prisoners wheezing breaths.

"Damn," one muttered. "You just bulldogged an angel."

She knew she was smiling like an idiot, but didn't care. She let the pride have its moment.

She patted dirt from her clothes, tidied her hair, then faced the prisoners.

"Let's get this over with."

Willow And Her Beloved Stump
Part 4

Her thighs burned and weakened. She'd heard the screeches, she knew something terrible was approaching the Wilderness. She pulled and pulled and pulled, but the brush kept snagging the blanket. Willow was spent.

"Darling, please, this is senseless," Trevor called.

Willow cried in frustration and fear. She yanked at the blanket, but the muscles in her arms were torn and throbbing.

"Please, just rest for a moment," Trevor said.

Branches cracked and swayed to the south. Something was rushing for them.

Willow knelt down over Trevor, covering him with the blanket, hiding him. She laid her body over him.

"I love you!" she called over the sound of the angels breaking through tree limbs and rushing overhead like a hurricane.

But the angels didn't stop. They pushed toward the northern cliffs of the Island. Splinters and pine needles rained down over Willow as the shaking trees slowly settled.

"Darling, it's okay," Trevor whispered.

Willow sobbed so intensely that Trevor feared she would hyperventilate. Her grip around his chest was tight and desperate. Trevor had trouble drawing in a breath.

Warmth returned to the air.

"Please, Willow, listen to me," Trevor said. She pushed her head tighter against his neck. "Willow. They are gone."

Her heaving sobs eased. She settled against him. Kissed his neck, then his cheek and face, peppering him with love before finding his lips. Cracked and ravaged by ravens and fire, each of her kisses shot pain through his entire body, but he delighted in them all the same. He received the kisses and couldn't help but laugh. She continued pecking at him before settling into a long, passionate kiss.

She pulled away.

"Thank you," he said. Wounds had opened on Trevor's lips and both of them were smeared in blood now. She lightly ran her fingers across his face.

"Oh my god, did I hurt you?" she asked.

"No, my dear. Not a bit."

She leaned over and kissed him lightly this time.

"Thank you for carrying me, darling," he said.

"You're the one carrying me."

Being A Child God
Part 7

We danced with the angels while soaring within my mist. We wound through the trees, up into the atmosphere, swirling around the angry avatars of God's fury as they swung their fiery swords. We taunted them like a matador's muleta with Anat as my hidden espada.

As the enraged angels charged through the mist, we saw hints of their invisible form, protruding brows, the hooked beaks, the soulless eyes.

My hand materialized just long enough to smack an angel on its backside.

"Yowch!" I cried at the chill, then laughed loud and unafraid.

"Let's just get this over with, Simon," Anat said.

"Where's your sense of adventure, sugar?"

"I'm not a food product, Simon."

"Of course not."

We pursued the angels. More raced toward us from the south and east. We were surrounded.

"Simon?" Anat asked.

"Trust me, cupcake."

A squadron of angels closed in on my right, trying to flank me. Instead, I barreled toward them, splitting through their ranks, feeling their cold and bitter hatred. I expected them to turn and chase me back south as I veered toward the temple of the Engineers. There, I knew the battle would be messy and fun.

But the angels hurtled north. I settled to the ground, the mist clearing, revealing Anat and I.

"Hey! Birdbrains! I'm down here!"

I then looked to Anat. "Birdbrains," I said with a smile.

"Yeah."

"Cause they look like birds."

"Yes, Simon, I understood the joke," Anat said. "Where are they going? Why did they give up so easy?"

"Maybe because I am super amazing!"

"Or maybe they found out where we live?" Anat asked.

I gazed back to the northern edge of the Island.

"Oh shit."

My People
Part 2

You need to understand that my first followers were worthless. And I mean this in the most loving way possible. No ambition, no cleverness, just a bunch of sheep in a field, patiently awaiting slaughter.

My priestesses were different. They were bold. They knew they were hitched to something new and amazing. I could count on them. The rest of them were just about beefing up my numbers. Extras for the publicity photos.

That's why I hid them off the side of the Island, as far from God as possible. They came to me because they were aimless outcasts. I knew their kind; I understood their kind. The only difference between me and them was that I managed to tap into the soul of the universe. I wasn't better than them, just more curious.

I hid them in the caves, warned them as I warned Barry and Mary. I told them to keep their heads ducked and not to emerge until I came for them.

Though they were worthless, I still cared for them. They were my people.

We reached the northern cliff just as Livie and Summer were tossed out the entrance of my fortress, tumbling into the open air and falling towards Heaven. I left Anat on the edge of the Island and raced down the cliff. Beyond my priestesses, I saw other followers plunging downward. As they reached the base of the Island, they burst into small, screaming fireballs and disappeared.

I neared Livie first. She was flailing, trying to twist her body so she could reach out for my mist. I materialized, reached for her fingertips, but an angel crashed into me.

It was a crushing iceberg pounding into me. Another angel smashed Livie into the edge of the Island.

"You fucker!" I screamed.

Livie's body was a bloody mangle, smeared across the rocks. She slid free and fell lifeless to the bottom of the Island. Summer was also beyond my reach now. She burst into flames, then was gone.

I looked up as more of my people were thrown from the fortress like candy from a parade float. I soared up to catch another, but an angel snatched the man and threw him past me and down toward Heaven. I was stunned and confused, helplessly watching my people screaming, pleading for help, raining down into nothingness.

"Simon!" Anat yelled.

I looked up to the edge, seeing a red glow and sparks.

I raced up the edge to her side.

Anat was retreating, fire erupting from the palms of her hands, pushing back angels approaching from all directions. I plunged into the fray, feeling a dozen angels circling her like a frenzy of sharks. I swirled around her, picking up her flames and spinning them into a tornado climbing into the sky, forcing the angels to retreat. I swept her up and raced from the edge of the Island.

My people were gone. Even if there were some left in the fortress, I'd have to leave them to the angels.

As we sped south, Anat's voice rose above the wind.

"Was it worth it, my king?"

The Old Man

He waited for me at the waterfall. Him and Jay. So furious. Anat and I emerged from the mist, also furious. The water roared between us, a line of demarcation between His world and our world. His past and our future.

The water slowed, dried, walled up by an invisible force so that only mud divided us.

"You disappointed me!" I called. "You don't go after me? You go after my people who can't even fight for themselves? Pathetic. That's what a bully does, not a god."

"Their deaths are on you!" Jay shrieked back. "By challenging Our Creator, you doomed your friends. All of them."

God motioned for Jay to remain quiet.

"Bring them back," I said.

"I can't," God said. "I can't escape the Island now. Once they leave the Island, they are gone for good. Unless you build me another plane."

I looked to Anat.

"So they are in Heaven now?" Anat asked.

"No," God said. "The other place."

I thought of Livie and Summer. Their beautiful smiles, their brash mouths. Then the other followers, the weirdos, the bored, the confused. They followed me because they needed to follow something. Humans need to be led. It is our nature. It is our salvation.

I suddenly felt very unworthy of it.

But as I stared at God, I knew he was unworthy too.

"Where is Bali?" I asked.

"Cleaning up the mess," He answered.

Anat held out her hand and let a flame jump to life and dance from her palm. "I can kill your angels. I can pick off Your warriors one at a time. I can strip You of all Your power. Perhaps we can even find a way to kill You. Or You can stay in Your campground. Send us the campers and we will adopt them into the Wilderness. Your time toying with humanity is over."

With her other hand, Anat clasped mine.

"We are the new king and queen of the Island," Anat said. "We will always celebrate the gift of life You bestowed upon us, but we will never bow at Your feet again."

God watched the flame. His mind was working. "I can still win this."

Jay looked up to his Father, surprised at His tone. To be honest, I was surprised too. He sounded so weak already. So lost. The fury was gone, the confidence was shaken. I pitied Him, somewhat, like a bully getting a few too many swats in front of the class.

"Are you going to toss every defenseless human off the Island now and try to shock us into submission?" I asked. "Create a wasteland where we will be trapped for the rest of time? Is that really what You want?"

"I can starve you out. Block the sun, kill the vegetation, dry out the pits, empty the lake, use famine and drought to bend you to your knees. You will worship and fear Me again."

"And then what?" I asked. "You will become a God of destruction, a God of chaos and what is left of Your people within the Wilderness will flock behind me. You may be immortal, but we can punish You. We can punish Jay and we can punish Bali."

"Or leave the Wilderness alone," Anat said. "Leave us in peace and we will respect Your domain."

"This is all My domain!" God stepped into the mud and began to cross to the Wilderness. Each footfall sank deep into the muck so he didn't so much march as he trudged. "I created this Island. It is mine! You are all mine!"

Anat sent her dancing flame out to the lake bed where it swept across the mud, drying and sealing God's feet inside. The flame then returned to her palm like an obedient pet. God struggled to lift a leg, but the bed wouldn't give. He studied Anat, then bent over and slipped His feet from His shoes. He stood in his mud-stained black dress socks and looked back at us.

"Every angel you send to the Wilderness will be killed," Anat said. "Bali is Your ambassador, but You will not be welcome. You block the sky, we burn Your shelter. You dry the pits, we destroy Your volcano."

"Father," Jay said.

God didn't bother looking at His son. "They can't do that."

"Are You sure?" Anat asked. Her dancing flame morphed into a flaming noose. "I have no idea what I am capable of."

Anat then blew across her palm and the noose grew into a long, snarling dragon. It soared across the dried lake bed and loomed over God.

Anat smiled. "Yet."

God laughed, bitterly. He removed His glasses, His pupiless eyes measuring the dragon. "War is coming children. My fury will consume you like a tsunami through a sugarcane field."

God put the sunglasses back on.

"She doesn't like being called food," I said. "Just an FYI."

The waters roared back into the lake bed, sweeping across God and the dragon. Steam hissed and the dragon was gone. God stood on the far shore beside Jay.

Anat turned to me and smiled. She pressed a kiss to my cheek.

"We are done here, my king."

"I agree."

I blew mist out into a plume that swirled and consumed us. It lifted us into the sky and we sped into the Wilderness so we could survey our battered kingdom. There were grave losses, but we could still revel in the knowledge that we survived our first battle with the Alpha and the Omega.

I Cannot Die
Part 14

After your battle with God, an angel carried me across the lake. Ahead, I saw the rest of the flock returning, injured and spent. Angels don't enjoy being cruel. Some may resent humanity, but they still prefer to protect than to punish.

But punishment had to be doled out. God decrees and we all plunge onwards like bullets from a gun.

Below, the ice trail on the lake was breaking apart and melting like thousands of doomed islands. Somewhere beneath a great woman died. The angel flew on. I saw, briefly, Anat's glorious dragon standing up to the Creator.

We soon reached the pier and the shore beyond.

"Here," I told the angel.

It lowered me onto the soft mud, then swooped back into the

air to join its brethren. God's victorious raiders. We could not break Simon's power, so God sent the angels to break his spirit.

I looked back across the lake, knowing that I would not see Mildred's body. So much potential squandered. She didn't have to fight. She didn't have to die, but symbolic sacrifice was humanity's way. An entire species' dangerous addiction to the senseless idea of martyrdom. Rabid with self-righteousness, these heroes never listened to me.

"If only you had lived a little while longer," I said to the empty water.

Cattle Queen of Rawlings
Part 2

The three wayward exiles returned from their battle with the angels more or less unhurt. Billy, Sophia, and Raul, as she would later find out. A soldier, a nun, and a musician. Raul dragged behind him a shattered guitar like a felled ally.

Their friends surrounded the survivors, smothering them with panicked questions and hugs. Esperanza motioned for Clyde and Owen to keep their distance, so they nodded and focused on getting the cattle back into the pen. Another woman was crying as she took the broken guitar from Raul.

Edna, as Esperanza would later find out.

"We'll figure something out," Edna said as she cleared her tears. They weren't lovers. Esperanza could tell by how easily they touched one another, without the confusion of sex holding back the affection.

"I've never made strings from deer gut before," Esperanza offered. "But we've made a few bows. Can't be that much different if you want to give it a try."

Raul's eyes eased as a smile grew on his face.

"How about sheep?" he asked.

"I'll see what I can do," Esperanza said.

"Do you think it's a bad time to ask to borrow that piano from God?" Ossie asked.

Laughter followed, a relieved laughter that evaporated the tension. More hugs and chatter.

Standing apart from the group was a thin man with paint splatters on his clothes and a severed head strapped to his shoulder. The severed head was still alive. The man offered a meek smile and a nod. She walked over but kept plenty of distance between them.

"Petrov, right?"

"Yes."

"You're not what I expected," she said, her mind cycling through the painted skulls she'd encountered on her way to New Wichita. Everyone knew of the artist and his bunker. Kept and provided for by the Engineers and Americans. Esperanza hated Petrov by reputation, but the man standing before her seemed gentle. She didn't understand it.

"So, is it over?" Owen called as he swatted a heifer, urging it on through the gate into the pen.

"No idea," Billy said. "We were hoping to get some shelter tonight, just in case."

"All you?" Clyde asked, looking over the large group, settling on Tommy. Tommy averted his eyes and Edward studied Tommy's discomfort.

"We'll figure something out," Esperanza said, her voice stern enough to silence any impending protests. Clyde shrugged and walked with Owen to the damaged fence.

Billy motioned for exiles to follow him towards the pen. "Let us help you with that."

"We do have tents," Sophia told Esperanza. "We can just camp outside on your land, if that's okay. If things get bad, we'll just deal with it as it comes."

"That sounds alright," Esperanza said. "We'd put you up inside if we had the room."

"Of course, we understand," Sophia said.

"We'll build a few fires tonight," Esperanza said. "Keep it small so God won't mind. You get your people settled in, let us know if you see anything coming from the campground. If the weather turns bad, we'll make room for as many as we can, okay?"

"We appreciate your generosity."

Billy The Warrior
Part 2

Night came without incident, without inclement weather, without the return of the angels. The exiles circled their tents around four campfires, sorting themselves in much the same way they had in the campground. This was fine by Billy. He knew the group would break up soon. Min-Jun was already asking questions about where New Wichita was located and Billy was fine with that. He was tired of hearing her gripes. Let her be someone else's problem.

But the core, the ones he really cared about, they would stay. They would follow him to the edge of the Island and beyond, if needed.

This didn't scare Billy, it didn't make him nervous or unsure. It made him feel secure, necessary, and happy in the sublime way that only a family can.

Esperanza, Clyde, and Owen were passing out dried beef and bowls of stew. Good country hospitality. Even if the Earth was long gone, human nature always found its old grooves. The kindness would need to be repaid. Perhaps Sophia would have some ideas.

Is it over?

Clyde had asked that after the attack. A clear, simple question but without a clear, simple answer. Looking back across the treetops in the direction of the campground, Billy could only guess at God's state of mind. Nothing was exploding, nothing was on fire, no tornadoes or rainstorms, no plane zipping off toward Heaven. All was calm. Billy suspected God was regrouping. Or perhaps He achieved His objective with the sudden incursion into the Wilderness. Perhaps He found and vanquished Simon.

"No, no way," Billy said out loud. A few looked over at Billy, but lost interest when they realized that Billy was thinking out loud again. Sophia placed her hand lightly on his knee, just to remind him she was near. He appreciated it, giving her a smile before gazing back into the campfire.

Simon was squirrely, hard to kill. Billy had known several men like Simon during the war, the blessed goofballs that always knew when to slack, when to run, and when to be up to no good. The world could never get a bead on them.

Simon was no conqueror or god killer. He was a magician. A little bit of a brat, but mostly harmless and a pretty good pal, all things considered. That everyone seemed to fear Simon was amusing. That Billy was asked to find and potentially kill Simon was confusing. It made Billy uneasy, as if he was being used. He didn't trust Tommy, he didn't trust God, he didn't trust the Engineers, but he knew Simon. He could trust Simon to be Simon. Prone to bad decisions, but not evil. No, not ever.

Esperanza approached with a flour sack of jerky, Clyde carrying a pot of stew, and Owen balancing a stack of bowls against his chest. That they had so many supplies on hand made Billy guess that this wasn't the first time they hosted a group of exiles. People come, people go. Billy wondered what kept chasing them away.

"Soup's on," she said, handing jerky to Sophia.

"No thank you. Is there meat in the stew?"

"In the broth," Esperanza said.

"Then, I'm fine," Sophia said, holding up her hand to politely deny.

"Vegetarian?"

"Sort of, but it's nothing big. I really appreciate what you are doing for us."

"No problemo," Esperanza said. "If I was able to talk to the animals, I probably wouldn't want to eat them either. With the pits, it seems a little silly to eat meat, but I also figure there is a reason God put animals here. Plus, having something to trade keeps us on the good side of the folks up north."

"You're paying for protection?" Billy asked.

"In a sense. We all need our place. This is ours. At any rate, sweetie, if you can wait until morning, I'll show you to the nearest pit."

"Thank you for understanding."

"Well, hell," Billy said, standing up and reaching into the flour sack. "I'll take some. I'll just brush my teeth before she kisses me."

Esperanza chuckled while Sophia slugged his leg. Owen handed him a bowl.

"That's a real special thing you've got," Esperanza said to Sophia. "We see a lot of gifted people come through. Some more powerful than the others. But I don't envy you."

"Why?" Billy asked.

"The Engineers are gonna come for her and they are gonna go through you, if needed. First they will ask Sophia to come with them, then they will insist, then they will steal her away."

Sophia let her eyes drift to the fire.

"I know. Tommy warned me."

"It's not so bad," Esperanza said. "From what I can tell, they don't hurt any of their new converts, just keep them in their sanctuary until they've made their point very, very clear."

"Aggressive recruitment," Billy said, then sat back down next to Sophia, the fear clawing against his skull. "Are they better than the Americans? The Engineers? How they treat others, us outsiders?"

Esperanza shrugged and looked to the east. "They're different. I suppose they're better. They don't share the American's sense of cruelty, but they aren't saints. And they are more powerful and weird. Hard to trust something that I can't understand, especially when I'm not so sure that they understand it either."

"So, they take me to the sanctuary to make me believe?" Sophia asked.

"To make you stronger," Esperanza said. "They want to challenge God's dominion. They need some more brawn and, with what you can do, you'll make a damn fine warrior."

Billy watched Sophia closely, his hand tightening over hers. Esperanza watched the tension between the lovers.

"Just keep yourselves safe," Esperanza said, then nodded and moved on to the next exiles.

Sophia sat quietly, keeping her eyes on the campfire. Billy would be tempted to join an army to bring stability and freedom to the Island. If abandoning everyone he cared about gave him the opportunity to better protect them, he'd at least consider it.

"I will take you to them, if you want," Billy said. "I'll camp outside the sanctuary for as long as they want to keep you there. I'll wait. Just say the word and we go."

Sophia sighed and leaned against him. "Thank you. I will think about it."

Then came a laugh. High, shrill, disembodied. Billy dropped his bowl and pushed to his feet. He pulled Sophia behind him.

The laughter intensified. It was coming from the campfire. Billy grabbed a rock and held it up, preparing to throw it at the fire. Then aware of how ridiculous the idea was, he lowered it and looked around the campground as other fires joined in, creating a crescendo of devious joy.

Sophia placed her fingers over Billy's hand that held the rock. He lowered it.

"Relax," she said. "It's only Simon."

Being A Child God
Part 8

Always open big.

Get them off-guard from the start, then never let up, never let them relax enough to look for the mirrors or the strings or the trap doors.

Man, I was born to be a god. Or at least a deity. The management of reality was a drag, but the theater and the miracles and the spectacles? Damn, I love that part of the job.

My voice was in the fire and the fire was growing and moving, a serpentine inferno taunting, but not threatening. I wanted their awe, but not their terror. Well, maybe a little terror.

I targeted the fire by Billy and Sophia, sent it into a giant, explosive plume of heat and ash. My laughter boomed like a succession of concussive shock waves. Beyond, lurking in the woods, I was trying hard not to laugh. It was all so damn divine.

Anat glared and I made a show of ignoring her.

The fires gasped, choked, and died, leaving only the starlight in the campground. Whispers were traded among the exiles.

Some backed from the fires. Opening pyrotechnics finished, now for awe to shift into wonder.

Tiny sparkles of light fluttered down from the trees like curious stars. Lightning bugs. Sophia's eyes were closed, the bugs wound down to the exiles in lazy S's. It was a duel, then?

I whispered to Anat and she gave an almost imperceptible nod. She wore a sheer white robe, her hair tied back in a long braid. She wore sandals like a true goddess. All her idea. She was warming to the part.

She stepped out from the trees and a yellow glow emanated from her skin, shining through the fabric, showing off a hint of what was within. She was showing herself as a light for the lost. A divine lamp to guide our way out of the Wilderness. This may not be the most enlightened thing to say, but I did like showing her off.

"Behold, the Queen of the Island!" I shouted.

"Shut up, Simon," Billy growled. "Just come out and talk to us like a normal human being."

"But we aren't normal humans! We are Gods!"

"No, you're not," Ossie called.

"We are too!" Even I heard the squeak in my voice.

"Simon!" Sophia snapped.

"Fine, geez."

Flames leapt back to life in the fire pits. Anat's glow eased, her lithe form hidden again by the robe. Anat looked back at me as I walked out of the woods. I wore a white on white suit with a white tie and an upside down cross on my suit jacket embroidered in gold. Earlier, I thought I looked sharper than a thumbtack. Not at the moment, though. Not walking back to my fellow exiles. I felt foolish. Very foolish. Friends can do that to you. Existential buzzkills they are.

I stood next to Anat, hands jammed into my pockets. I wanted to leave. I was humiliated and Anat raised her eyebrow in that way that made me feel smaller than a blade of grass.

I'd really thought the laughing from the flames thing was gonna have a bigger impact.

Never play your hometown. Anyone who's seen you crap your pants will never respect your art.

The Fabulous Fallimento would've loved the campfire bit.

The exiles approached and gathered close.

"Do you really wear that around?" Raul asked. I briefly considered changing my clothes since I now had the ultimate quick-change system, but then decided I didn't want to give Raul the satisfaction.

Petrov watched from the fringes, that poor head studying us. I met both their eyes, but neither yielded much emotion.

Sophia stepped forward and held out her hand to Anat. Anat took it and they did that feminine handshake that isn't really a shake at all.

"I'm not sure what he's told you," Sophia said to Anat. "But we were all at the campground together. We are his friends."

That last bit came after a breath. A tack on. I noticed it. I looked to Billy. He'd noticed it too. We smiled like old war buddies.

"I skipped the campground," Anat said. "Could tell right off that it wasn't my scene."

"She torched God's cabin," I added. "And there wasn't a damn thing He could do about it."

I gave them a moment, let their suspicious eyes have their time.

"She's the Queen of the Island," I said, trying to make it seem like no big thing. Like, of course she's the Queen of the Island.

"And how did that get decided?" Ossie asked. "Was there an

election or did she pull a sword from a stone?"

"Because," and here I paused for dramatic effect, "no one can tell her that she isn't the Queen of the Island." I really needed to punch in that point. Branding, you know.

"If God can't stop her—us. I mean us," and here I winced, "then, well, you know, who's going to? Right?"

I was blushing. I knew I was blushing. Never go off script. I know this, but I was still a little shaky from my weaker than expected opening. I was trying to save the performance.

"I see," Sophia said with a hint of a smile.

"Hey Queen of the Island," Raul called. "Can you fix my guitar?"

"Your guitar?" Anat asked.

"We're not really doing requests right now, but thank you."

"Any luck on the Spice Channel?" Ossie asked.

Again, Anat looked at me.

"Kind of an inside joke," I said.

"What did you do to God?" Billy asked, which brought the moment back on message. "Why did He send the angels after us?"

"Because I evened the odds," and I threw in a bit of a sneer. I always get hyper aware of my face when I get nervous.

"No riddles, Simon," Billy said. "Just tell us."

"We pushed His plane off the Island," Anat said. "God can't escape now."

I rose my hands high into the air as one does when one proclaims something. Eyes closed, of course. "If He can't return to Heaven. Then He can't change the Island! He can't rewrite the rules! His power is in the clouds, so we keep Him on the ground and we are in charge!"

"We?" Billy asked.

"Yes 'we'!" and here I was a bit more defensive than was

justified.

"Do you mean you and—" Billy began, then looked at Anat. "What was your name again?"

"Anat."

"Or Queen of the Island," I said.

"So, the two of you are in charge now?" Billy asked.

"I'm pretty sure I made it clear that we are definitely not tyrants," I said.

"You actually kinda made it seem like you are totally trying to be tyrants," Ossie said, and in hindsight, he was totally right.

"I meant the royal 'we'! All of humanity," and here I sounded like an exhausted Sunday school teacher.

"That's not what 'royal we' means," Ossie said.

I looked to Anat. She was enjoying the moment. "He's right," she said.

I looked to Edward. He was also enjoying the moment. He said: "The Queen of England said 'we' because she was the embodiment of English law and authority."

I scratched my head. "Fine! We haven't ironed out all the details yet!" I was trying not to sweat. Really really trying not to sweat. "But, I was thinking like a symbolic Monarchy, social democracy kind of thing?"

I gave Anat a pleading look. "Right?"

"So, your little trick with the fire was like riding around in fancy carriages and wearing silly hats?" Edward asked. "Or were you going more for a The Great and Terrible Simon effect?"

"No, just..."

I sighed and looked down at the campfire.

"I really thought this was going to way differently," I said, or rather huffed.

Never play your hometown Fallimento had told me but I didn't listen.

Anat placed her hand on my arm and I grimaced, but stayed quiet.

"We are trying to remake the Island," Anat said, so cool and smooth, like the flip side of a satin pillow. "I've seen the terrible things happening within New Wichita. Simon has told me about the storms and God's temper. We watched our people thrown from the side of the Island. This island has been ruled by the unjust for too long. We are going to overthrow God and liberate the Wilderness."

And there it was. I hadn't even said "overthrow God" yet, but she knew. We were soul mates, a perfect union. The exiles were silent, gazing at the Queen of the Island. They may not be impressed by fire, but she captured their attention. I puffed my chest a bit, arched my back, trying to seem kingly, that I was also a part of this coupe even if I was beginning to feel a bit out-shined.

Out-shined.

Get it?

***

The exiles broke off into tribes quickly as Billy led us back to his campfire to talk about particulars. Some were going to bolt, but I always knew that. Not everyone wants to be a revolutionary.

Our core consisted of Cabin Five, Sophia, Esperanza, Raul, Petrov, and Petrov's decapitated girlfriend. Min-Jun stood a few steps away, watching. Curious, but quiet.

"You can't do this," Edward said to start.

"Why?" I asked. "Who is going to stop us? And I mean 'us'. Not just the Queen and I, but all of us? God can't. The angels can't. Jay can't. Even if Bali could, he won't. We have a clear path forward. We control our destiny."

"The Engineers want us to kill you," Billy said.

I wasn't surprised, but I was a little hurt. I liked the Engineers. They were weirdos and a little too free-spirited, but I dug their moxie. I felt that, once my plan was in place, they'd jump on board. Maybe even be my counter to God's angels.

"And?" Anat asked.

"I'm not killing anybody," Billy said. "Not you, not the Americans, not the choir of angels, and definitely not God."

I held up my hand. "We never said we were killing God."

"You won't have a choice," Edward said. "If you are going to try to depose the Creator who has sat on the throne for billions of years, you can't just condemn Him to a quiet island prison like Napoleon. You will have to kill Him."

I noticed that Edward wasn't saying that I shouldn't kill Him. I glanced around to see if any of the others caught it, but no one did.

"I'm not omnipotent," I said. "I can't tell you the future, but I do know that the Wilderness will get worse if we don't seize control. And I've talked to God. I offered Him a deal. He gets His part of the Island, we get ours. I'm giving Him some time to think it over."

"And when God refuses?" Billy asked.

"We take it one step at a time," Anat said. "If we unite, we can beat Him."

"And if the Engineers and the Americans unite with God?" Billy asked.

"They won't," I said.

"But if they do?"

"Then we will show them a better way," Anat said.

Petrov grunted. He stood and glared across the campfire at me.

"God is all powerful," Min-Jun said from the periphery. "All of this is assuming that He can't create a way off the Island. But maybe He can. Maybe He is manipulating you."

"He's not," I said.

"I don't think you are smart enough to know if He was," Min-Jun said.

I chuckled. "Fair point, but I'm telling you He's not."

"If we take control of the Wilderness, who will be in charge?" Petrov asked. "Until you work out this social democracy?"

"Initially, Anat and I will be in charge. We have the vision, but this won't be a tyranny. We will listen to the people."

Petrov considered. I was finding it difficult not to look at the severed head on his shoulder. She seemed very pale and her cheeks were hollowing. Her eyes were still alert, but I doubted she would remain that way for very much longer.

Petrov walked around the campfire and held out his hand to me. I stood, a little awkward, and shook it.

"Good luck to you, my friend," Petrov said. "But I am not going to trade one god for another."

Petrov released his grip, gave a polite tilt of the head to Anat, then stepped past us and walked into the woods, towards New Wichita.

"Artists," I said, by way of explanation.

"He makes a sound point," Sophia said.

"We aren't gods," Anat said, but we both knew we were.

"Tell me why I shouldn't kill you and take you to the one and only true god for a reward?" Min-Jun said.

I turned to her and held out my hands. "Try it."

Anat motioned me to stay quiet then looked to Min-Jun. "I admire your honesty. What's your name?"

"Min-Jun."

"Min-Jun, that is a fair question," Anat said with a smooth politician's touch. "Kill us and deliver us to God. Kill us and deliver us to the Engineers. Kill us and deliver us to the Americans. If we were you, we would consider those options too. The difference between us and God is we understand your experience and we are willing to negotiate. The difference between us and the Engineers is we want to unite the Wilderness. The difference between us and the Americans is we have not lost our humanity."

"So you say," Min-Jun said. Anat smiled and tilted her head. A subtle show of respect.

"How about this?" I asked the group. "Why can't we be our own gods? Why can't we control our own fates? You ask how you know we won't just be as bad as The Old Man across the lake. Here's the answer: I don't want to micromanage every person on the Island. I'm not a details kinda person, you know? And Anat doesn't want to deal with all that noise either."

"Do you?" I asked Min-Jun, but she didn't respond. I looked to Billy. "Do you?"

He shook his head "no", which made me feel better. When I imagined my place on the Island, Billy was always by my side, a trusted soldier executing my will. Not a servant, not a killer, just a man able to motivate and inspire others. I still believed that most of the exiles would be willing to follow me once I showed them the way. I wouldn't have to rule by fear as God had. Reason would be enough.

But young rulers always believe that, don't they?

"Listen, I'm not organized enough to be a dictator," I said and was rewarded with a few amused chuckles, including Min-Jun. "You know this. I know this. I don't want to do this alone. I don't want to control all the power on the Island. I know me saying 'Trust me!' isn't going to make you trust me, but—well— trust me. Just a little. I can't beat God and the Engineers and the Americans. We have to unify and I need you to help me."

The group considered. Esperanza was visibly uncomfortable with the line of reasoning—frowning a lot, small shakes of the head, but she was listening. She saw the potential.

"Well," Edward said. "If we help God get back to Heaven, maybe He will end the Island experiment and send our souls back to Paradise. That is a thing we should consider. The plane is gone. He is trapped, but if we can find a way to get Him back, then we could negotiate. Would you be open to that?"

I glanced at Anat. That wasn't the game plan, but we knew it would be mentioned eventually.

"We will entertain all options," Anat said. "We will follow the will of the majority so as long as we can find a way to ensure God's willingness to cooperate. But we could find out that God, once He goes to Heaven, sends us all to Hell out of spite. We need to get a better read of how God responds to a shared power option. And it also could be that, once we get the Wilderness under control, not all of us will want to go back to Heaven."

"The love of my life is in Heaven," Ossie said. "Everything I do from this moment on will be to reunite with him as soon as I can. My loyalty to whatever decision we make is reliant on the hope that I can get back to him. My heart is in Heaven. God can send us back. You cannot."

"Are you sure we can't?" Anat asked. "We don't know what we are capable of yet. But, if we can, I promise you that we will. That is a deal that God is not willing to make."

I smiled at that. She was good. She was what I needed, what we needed. A queen. A diplomat. I could feel the temperament of the room warming to us. Before we arrived, I could tell that there was not one among them that would consider following me, but now, the idea was growing. The seed planted. The revolution stirring.

"We aren't powerful," Billy said. "Sophia can do things, Ossie can see things, but we are no match for God. The angels can wipe us out and I am not prepared to put this group in danger until we know we can protect ourselves."

"That's fair," Anat said. "Let us work on the others in the Island. Right now, God's eye is on us, not you. When we come, we need to know that you are with us."

"At this point," Billy said. "No. I am open to more discussions, but as it stands now, we are out."

"Billy doesn't speak for me or my friends," Min-Jun said. "I can't say that I am willing to throw our support behind you yet, but I can say I'm fairly certain we won't slit your throat while you sleep."

"And thank you for that," I said.

"You are playing a very dangerous game," Min-Jun continued. "I do want to know more. You will bring war to the Wilderness, which means we can't escape it. I am not interested in king-making, but I do want to help minimize the chaos that war will create."

"Well put," Anat said. "And I completely agree with you. We want to build a community and we need all of the voices to be represented for this community to work. Our hope is to apply leverage, not to start an all-out war on the Island. I believe, if it comes to that, we can win. Our job is to convince God of the same so we can end a war before it begins."

"I'm in," Edward said. Tommy studied him, then laced his fingers in Edward's. "I've lost my God already, I'm willing to risk the rest if it will give us a chance at a safer home."

"It will," I said. "I promise you, Edward, it will."

"What do you need from me?" Edward asked.

I wasn't sure. I thought we might get some volunteers, but didn't count on Edward. Not yet. Not this soon. I looked to Anat. She took in a small breath as her plan came together in her mind.

"Go to the Engineers," Anat said. "If they are on our side, the Americans will surely follow. If they aren't willing to join, we need to know that too. Stay with them as things unfold. Keep working on their leaders, get them to see our side."

Edward nodded. He looked to Tommy and their eyes exchanged something silent before they both smiled, timidly.

Esperanza stood.

"You all seem very nice," she said. "But I can't invite trouble into Rawlings."

She pointed at me, almost like she was holding a gun.

"God's looking for you, so I need you to leave. The rest can stay for at least a couple more days until we figure this out."

Billy stood and shook her hand. "We can't thank you enough."

"Just don't bring any more trouble here."

Billy nodded. Esperanza turned and walked back to the cabin. We all rose.

"Thank you for your time," Anat said, shaking Min-Jun's hand first. "We will continue this soon."

There was a moment there between the two of them. I caught it. Couldn't tell what it meant, but it was definitely there.

Edward leaned in to hug me and I let him.

"Don't trick me like He did," Edward whispered into my ear. He pulled back and I nodded. I knew what Edward's trust was worth and I was determined not to misuse it.

Billy's handshake was firm, a subtle message. Perhaps a warning.

Anat and I walked from the campfire, then turned.

"Don't do anything I would do," I said, then opened my mouth wide. Mist poured out, obscuring us. We dematerialized and swept into the sky.

Always end big.

From above, we saw Edward and Tommy walking into the woods, to the East, toward the Engineers.

"That went better than I expected," I whispered.

"Have you considered the possibility that you've just doomed all of you friends?" Anat asked.

"We were doomed from the moment God brought us to the Island."

I Cannot Die
Part 15

God didn't send me to clean up debris, battered bodies, wrecked cabins. He sent me to do damage control, to get a read on how His Shock-And-Awe campaign played with His wayward people.

As Jay had done on Earth, I was the messenger to explain why the human race should praise the God that caused them so much grief.

Yulia Creates So Many Lovely Things
Part 3

Mildred was gone. There was a void where her beautiful, brazen, and just spirit once filled the Island. The sun seemed dimmer without the fuel of her joy and shameless laugh. The lake water was colder than normal as it sloshed around Yulia's bare feet. Perhaps the water mourned as well.

The Engineers were arriving from the temple, leaping over the trees and foliage in great bounds, landing in the soft soil, and forming a line along the water's edge. There were traces of the pentagram still drawn in the sand, but also signs of the struggle between Mildred and the angels. A large divot indicated where an angel had fallen.

"Attah girl," Yulia said, then turned back to the water. She wore a thin shawl while the others stood nude, facing the campground where God surely averted his eyes.

"Did she return to Heaven?" an Engineer asked.

"Ask Bali," Yulia said, motioning to where I stood on the shore, keeping a respectful distance. A fearful distance. I was no longer certain I could protect myself if the Engineers decided to exact their revenge.

"Bali?" the Engineer called.

"I don't know," I said, but I did. "This was a warning. Your group wasn't the only one targeted. New Wichita was hit, the new exiles were hit. Simon's group got the worst of it."

"How bad?" Yulia asked.

"They were wiped out," I said.

"And Simon?"

"He escaped. He and Anat. They are calling themselves the

King and Queen of the Island."

"Are they actually going to be the King and Queen of the Island?"

"Only if we let them," I said. From their sour frowns, I could tell that they didn't appreciate me throwing their slogan back at them. Still, I braved on. "God is offering you an opportunity, a joint effort to stop Simon before he gets any more powerful. This could be very beneficial for everyone on the Island."

The Engineers gathered beside Yulia, all quiet and waiting for their new leader to speak. United and furious. It was frightening.

"What is He offering?" Yulia asked.

"As long as you show fidelity to the Throne, He will not send the angels back to the Wilderness. We will let you manage the Wilderness so as long as you don't oppose His will. Directly, anyway."

I watched the Engineers working out the offer, their heads turning from one to the other.

"So, He is asking us to be attack dogs?" Yulia asked, a few Engineers nodding in agreement.

"He wants Simon gone and He wants order brought to the Wilderness," I answered, careful with every word. "For that, He offers safety and abundance. A better deal than you could have ever hoped for on Earth."

"But not in Heaven," Yulia said. "There we had endless bliss. He removed us from paradise thereby forfeited His right to make demands of our loyalty."

An Engineer leaned toward Yulia and whispered into her ear. She nodded, then looked back to me.

"Why doesn't He go back to Heaven?" Yulia asked. "From there, He could remove Simon Himself."

I considered a well-constructed lie, but knew Simon would be boasting all over the Wilderness soon.

"Simon and Anat threw the plane off the Island. God can't return to Heaven. Not yet, anyway."

"You've sent angels to Heaven before," an Engineer asked. "For smuggling."

"It's complicated," I said. "God put some barriers in place when he constructed this reality. I'm not sure why they are there, but they are. God is, for the moment, trapped."

Yulia allowed a curious half-smile, her eyes glimmering with new ideas popping into existence. Another Engineer whispered into her ear, but she held her hand up to hush him.

"We'll have to give this some thought, but, can I be honest, Bali?"

"Yes, of course."

"He'll have to make us a much better offer," Yulia said. "Especially if He wants our help getting back to Heaven."

"I understand. I don't blame you at all."

She waved her hand and the Engineers turned and returned to the woods. Yulia lingered, watching me.

"What would you do?" Yulia asked. "If you were in our place?"

"I may not be the best person to ask. The last time I schemed against God, I was thrown into a lake of fire."

I gave her a small wink. She ran her hand through her hair, her eyes directing up into the clouds as she considered my warning. Her smile widened, devilishly, like how I'd been presented in drawings and cheap Halloween masks.

"The Americans are next?" Yulia asked.

"Yes."

"Tell the bitch I'll be seeing her real soon."

How To Properly Manage A Young Empire
Part 5

The Mayor rose from an uneasy sleep to the sound of shuffling outside. Back and forth, back and forth like an anxious dog. To her front door, away from her front door. Finally a knock.

She slipped out of her bed, unhooked a robe hanging beside her door and padded through her mansion. A wind still swirled through the halls where her front window had been shattered by an angel. It would be fixed eventually, but glass was in short supply and she knew that the right move, politically, was to allow the other downtown structures to get their windows replaced first.

The pacing continued as she neared. She hated anxious people. She hated uncertainty and weak wills. But she also felt certain that the person wouldn't be a real threat. Assassins didn't fidget, or so went her theory.

She unlocked the door and eased it open. Outside, Huan clutched a backpack tight, his eyes cast down.

"I know you spend a lot of time in tunnels, but I presume you remember the difference between day and night."

"I didn't want to be seen, Mayor," he replied in a tone so cautious that her annoyance evaporated and was replaced by fascination.

"Well, come in," she said and Huan obliged with a nod.

She closed the door behind him and motioned him through a hall behind the study. They wound around to the kitchen where there were still windows and a hope for privacy. She pulled heavy curtains closed, shutting off the moonlight. Only reflected light from the mirrors offered any illumination. Huan moved to the corner, looking like a frightened child.

"You have my attention," she said.

"I have debated this moment for days," Huan said. "I've kept a secret and had never intended on telling anyone, but then Simon came. Then came the angels came. I now realize that we aren't safe and perhaps I have no other choice than to trust you."

"Okay," The Mayor said, pulling a chair out from a small dining table. She sat down, crossed her legs, and motioned to the other chair.

Huan shook his head, rejecting the offer and keeping his eyes averted.

"I know I will regret doing this," Huan said. "But I believe I would regret not doing it more."

Huan opened the backpack. His hand slipped inside, paused. He sighed, shook his head, then lifted up a soft, glowing orb. The Mayor took time to gaze at the strange object.

"What is it?" she asked.

"Something like it destroyed the City Hall. This is the secret of Simon's growing power. This may also be what will kill Simon."

The Mayor stood and approached the Island star.

"May I?" she asked.

She took it, slow and steady, surprised by its fleshy texture. She turned it over, passed it from one hand to the other, and held it up to the sliver of moonlight bouncing from a mirror in the hallway.

"You dug it up?" The Mayor asked.

"Yes."

"And there are others?"

"Yes," Huan said. "Well, I think so. I've tossed many from the Island, but I am certain that there will be more."

"How does he use it?"

"I don't know."

"Well," she said, lowering the star and slipping it into the pocket of her robe. "Let's find out, shall we?"

Huan's eyes stayed on the pocket where the star rested.

"Thank you, Huan. You did the right thing."

He managed a slight smile, then turned and shuffled back out of the mansion and into the night. The Mayor sat in the kitchen, studying the star, thinking on the future of her empire.

Constructing A Simon-Killer

Wilfred was a terrible marksman. This wasn't from a lack of practice or familiarity with all manner of projectile weapons. To the contrary, there were few outside of the military industrialization complex that knew more about the physics of a bullet traveling from point A to point B.

Black powder muskets, .45 caliber pistols, gas-powered semi-automatic rifles, tear gas launchers, period-accurate double barrel shotguns, breach guns, sniper rifles. He'd studied them all, fired them all. On Earth, he had owned an arsenal of superspy proportions.

Yet, he couldn't fire a single one of them with any kind of consistent accuracy. He'd tried eye exercises, prescription shooting goggles, laser scopes, anything to get his vision to work in harmony with his trigger finger, but nothing helped. It was anxiety. No cure for that. His clusters sprawled across the targets like dissipating clouds.

The shame caused him to give up on his dream of military service and/or law enforcement. He was left to distantly dream, study the craft of gun-smithing, and eventually develop his own workshop in his garage where he would develop a masterpiece of modern weaponry. It was a short-barreled, high-powered rifle with a flexing gun stock to minimize kick, a curved extended clip developed for perfect balance, and enough power to shoot through walls and penetrate light body armor. It was tough, jam-proof, and compact enough for close-quarters, house-clearing operations.

It was his contribution to the War on Terror.

He sent a prototype to the Army. He soon heard back from

the ATF. Nothing big, just a search of his house and workshop, a few questions about his ex-wife as well as his frequenting of fiery alt-right websites. They even rehashed a decades-old restraining order filed in Texas.

An office romance gone sideways. He admitted that he wasn't the easiest man to break up with, which was why he had decided to devote himself to a chaste, sober, and Christian life.

He nearly shot a kid a few years later after a misunderstanding over some firecrackers. He was carrying a snub-nosed revolver under his jacket(licensed) and heard the popping then saw a bunch of black kids surrounding a white kid. There was lots of shouting and cussing. He pulled his gun in less than a second, believing himself ready to finally prove himself to himself. The teens didn't react well to the threat, one charged with his hand seeming to reach to a gun stuffed in the back of his pants.

Wilfred fired and missed. Some ran, some laid down prone. The cops came, commended Wilfred on "firing a warning shot" and took the kids to the station.

No charges were filed on anyone. The kids weren't fighting. Just drunk and having fun. The moment frightened Wilfred—the thought of what would have happened had he not had terrible aim. Yet, he kept crafting, kept collecting, kept building up an armory he would never need nor use.

The Rapture arrived two years after he died of heart disease.

New Wichita recruited him quickly after he reached the Wilderness. He'd been boasting of his past as a gunsmith. They needed an army and an army needed weapons. He promised to deliver.

But he could not. None of the minerals on the Island were familiar, nor did he possess the equipment to test their properties. His 21st Century understanding of physics, geology, and chemistry was almost irrelevant on the Island. No sulfur, no potassium nitrate, nothing with an appropriate flash rate. He knew he needed smarter minds to figure this Island out for him, but wouldn't admit it. He enjoyed his position of power and feared losing it if he confessed he wasn't the savior he'd promised.

So he worked in his isolated cave far from downtown. He really just meddled, hoping to stumble onto something useful. He received few visitors and only saw The Mayor when she needed someone to yell at. Wilfred always made for a good punching bag.

But that night she woke him up with a present and a smile. She'd wrapped the Island Star in a blanket, fearing what would happen if she dropped it on the ground. She unfolded it on his stone work table beneath a solar tube feeding down soft moonlight. The Star emerged, glowing a sublime blue. He poked it gently, feeling its odd, soft give.

"And this is what destroyed downtown?" he asked.

"Yes. This is what is giving Simon his power. Huan finds them buried in the Island, so we need to figure this out before anyone else does."

"I'll do my best," Wilfred said.

The Mayor stepped back from the star, glad to no longer being the bearer of such a dangerous, but valuable object.

"You do that, you make a weapon out of this, I'll give you anything and everything you could possibly hope for. The council is meeting in the morning and I want some ideas on how we are going to use this darling little killer."

Wilfred nodded, keeping his eyes on the star, the fear of failure sending subtle tremors through his heart and a familiar tremble through his fingers. The Mayor left Wilfred to his work, her shoes clicking along the stone passageway.

He poked the star again. He had to assume it was unstable,

that anything could set it off. He needed to find a safe trigger. He reached underneath his work bench for a small, wooden box. He dug through it until he found a stone chipped into a sharp, pointed blade. It had cloth wrapped around the hilt as a somewhat comfortable handle.

He held the knife above the star, the point dancing from his unsteady hand. He took a deep breath in, then out, and pressed the point softly against the fleshy exterior of the star. It resisted. He pressed a little harder, grimacing from fear. He held his face back, waiting for whatever came.

The flesh gave, the blade piercing inside. A thick gelatin rose through the cut and smeared the blade. He pulled the knife back out of the star. He brought it to his nose, sniffed, catching notes of petroleum and iron, salt as well.

He examined the smear on the point as closely as he could with the dim light. He stood up from the workbench, crossed to the other side of his cave, held out his hand as far as he could, then smacked the blade against the wall. The blade chipped from the impact, but nothing exploded.

He considered, turned back to the star, tapped his foot and chewed at his lip. He walked back to his bed and lowered to his hands and knees. He reached under the frame, found a bowl and pulled it out. Crusted mud from the pits was left, a few roaches crawling inside. He used an old shirt to clear it all out, then brought the bowl to the work bench. He grabbed the star and held it over the bowl. Again leaning back away as far as he could, he squeezed three drops into the bowl.

He set the star down carefully, walked the bowl over to the other side of the cave, then returned to the bench for some well-worn flint stones. He took them to the bowl and, standing a step away, struck the stones, sending sparks down to the bowl. Nothing. He edged closer, struck the stones. Nothing. He leaned over, struck the stones repeatedly, seeing the sparks hit the gelatin drops, but not igniting.

He sat down and thought.

Hours passed. He slept. He woke. He tried the stones again. Then start a small fire and squeezed another drop onto the flames. The gelatin only sizzled from the heat. He slept. He rolled over on the bed to see the sunlight peeking down the solar tube.

He returned to the workbench again and felt the cut on the star. The gelatin inside had sealed the cut shut, like a scab. He took off his shoe and smacked the star. It bounced off the table and rolled across the cave. He walked over to it and sat down to stare into its mystery for several minutes.

"Fuck you," he told the star.

He wrapped the star back in the blanket and left his cave.

How To Properly Manage A Young Empire
Part 6

"I don't need this shit today," The Mayor told Julia after encountering the mob of malnourished prisoners shuffling through downtown like someone had just liberated a concentration camp.

Julia's proud smirk irritated The Mayor. She'd met the atheist before, a troublesome pacifist that she assumed would be like all other troublesome pacifists. Ignore them long enough and they grow bored and move on to the next cause célèbre. She was merely a stray, a provocateur with a lot of voice but nothing in the way of fangs.

Which is why the site of Julia staging a slow prison break so baffled The Mayor that she couldn't even muster anger or shock. Perhaps a little shame as the morning sunlight bounced through downtown and illuminated the ashen and skeletal faces of the condemned.

"So, what? You're going to run off into the Wilderness with these convicts?" The Mayor asked.

"Yup."

"Create a socialist utopia with thieves and sexual deviants?"

"Sounds kinda fun don't you think?"

Sentries flanked the group, spears held out in more a matter of ceremony since it was clear the prisoners weren't able-bodied enough to be a threat. The Mayor rubbed her eyes, taking a moment to collect herself. The citizens would start emerging soon, she had to clear out downtown before anyone saw the sorry spectacle.

"We are a civil society and justice must be served," The Mayor said. "I have no time for your childish logic so, just stop. Go back to whatever hole you hide in and don't come back to America."

Some of the prisoners cowered a bit, keeping their eyes down, hoping to fade into the group, perhaps slipping into the shadows.

"Have you read the Bible?" Julia asked The Mayor.

"Yes, of course."

"I mean, have you really read it? Not just a few pages out of obligation or the feel-good lines churches hang up in Sunday school classrooms. I have. Twice. What I learned from the Bible is that God is cruel, petulant, unjust, but also very aware of how He is perceived. He wants it to be clear to everyone in His Creation that He is just, kind, and loving. Image control. That's what He's most concerned about."

"And your point is?"

"That He must know what I'm doing right now. He's going to send an angel or an earthquake or some divine intervention to prevent you from stopping us. He will want to reassert His image as the gracious liberator of the weak, friend of the meek and impoverished. If He doesn't, then that means that He is a fraud. So, no matter how this plays out, I win."

"That's really stupid," The Mayor said.

"Doesn't mean I'm not right."

The Mayor sighed. She looked across downtown, seeing figures shuffling out of caves, New Wichita was stirring awake. The council members would be on their way soon for the emergency meeting.

"God doesn't care about us," The Mayor said. The prisoners and the sentries all swung their eyes towards The Mayor. "That's the secret of the Island. That's the thing that all of us know, but none of us want to admit. We failed in the campground. Whatever He wanted from us, we didn't deliver. The Wilderness is Him kicking us out of the house, forcing us to get out of His hair and find our own way. He doesn't care what you are doing and isn't going to care that you spend the next month in an oven. It's up to us to build a society out of this mess."

Julia smiled. She approached The Mayor. The sentries circled in between them, spears nearly touching Julia's abdomen.

"Good for you," Julia said.

"Whatever," The Mayor said. "Get them all back down to the ovens. Her too. We'll sort this out later."

Julia snatched a spear and yanked it out of the sentry's hand. She flipped the spear around and prepared to throw it at The Mayor. The other sentry stabbed his spear into her hip. Julia screamed, hobbled backwards, gathered her feet, then threw the spear at The Mayor. The Mayor dodged away and the spear sparked against a wall and clattered to the ground. Prisoners grabbed Julia, pulled her back into their group, shielding her from the approaching sentries.

"I'm going to bury you!" The Mayor growled as she followed the sentries.

"No one is burying anyone!"

Everyone looked to the cavern opening where I stood. I hated being a pawn, but knew I couldn't just let the moment play out. I hadn't come for Julia; God didn't know or care about the prison break. I was just there to discuss Simon, but I also wasn't going to let anything happen to Julia.

Julia laughed and struggled out of the group. "See! Image control!" She hobbled toward the entrance, waving the prisoners along.

"Bali, stay out of this," The Mayor said.

I stepped in the way of Julia, leaning in close.

"Don't do this again," I whispered. "I'm not going to protect you next time."

"Yeah, you will."

She patted my cheek, leaving a red hand print, then limped past me with drops of blood marking her trail. The prisoners were unsure, but invigorated. They followed her toward the light.

"We are a sovereign nation, Bali," The Mayor said. "Our laws are sacred."

"First, you are not a sovereign nation. Second, your laws are not even written down. You are little more than a warlord. Those ovens of yours are going to be New Wichita's downfall."

The Mayor glared at me. A few citizens were watching from a distance.

Deciding that a little diplomacy would go a long way, I told her "I want you in power here. I need your help getting the Wilderness back under control, but there is a better way."

"We are a sovereign nation, Bali."

"Fine, okay, you are a sovereign nation but I am the devil and God is God and Jay is your savior. You'd be wise to take our counsel so we don't have to intervene when your nation has lost its way. God is in a real fire and brimstone mood right now and Simon's not the only one in the crosshairs."

"That's unfair, Bali," The Mayor said. "We've been doing our best to create a moral, devout nation living by Christian laws. You know this."

"I'm not going to argue with you. You have a council meeting today, yes?"

"Yes."

"Good. Let's get to it then."

I walked past her towards City Hall. I paused, unable to help myself. "Also, if you are going to be a godly nation, you might consider building a church instead of a mansion."

The Mayor glowered. She snapped her eyes to the sentries,

who quickly glanced away. She approached one and leaned in to whisper in his ear:

"Follow the prisoners out, make sure they leave America, and let me know where they settle."

"Yes, ma'am."

Within the woods, keeping to the shadows, Petrov and his dying head watched.

Constructing A Simon-Killer
Part 2

The council was used to Wilfred's irritability, so no one paid the sullen man much mind as they all filed into City Hall. He held the bundled-up Island Star in his arms like a football, but he was not asked about it. No one wanted to get trapped into an exhausting conversation with the weapons engineer.

Instead, they chatted to each other, low and careful, about the prisoner exodus. A few had seen The Mayor talking with the atheist who led the prisoners up from the ovens. No one knew if The Mayor released the prisoners, or just allowed them to go. My presence had been a factor. Wilfred could tell that everyone was afraid that New Wichita was losing its way, but no one was quite ready to voice their fears.

They passed inside the hall. Wilfred fell into step with Martha, now widely known throughout New Wichita as the crazy woman who thought she was going to marry God. Wilfred didn't think she was that bad looking, but there were better options on the Island if God really was intent on getting hitched.

Like The Mayor. That's who Wilfred would choose. Clever, a few shades cold, a few more shades intimidating. He wondered about her often.

Wilfred nodded a hello to Martha, but she kept her eyes forward, her chin tilted up, like she was some sort of royalty.

Workers were using a plaster derived from the mud pits to seal cracks in the walls and repair molding. Seemed like a waste of time to Wilfred since Simon could just come blow it up again, but perception mattered more to some people than it did to him.

The doors to the Great Hall opened and Wilfred saw me seated next to The Mayor, softly arguing the concept of sovereignty. The Mayor looked up as the counsel entered. She stood, walked to the head and sat back down.

The counsel took their normal seats. Martha was offered the chair reserved for distinguished visitors. Wilfred wondered if she was now a permanent fixture on the counsel. Wilfred didn't go for his chair, instead stopping opposite The Mayor's seat.

"Have a seat," The Mayor told Wilfred.

"Don't think I'm staying long enough," he answered, looking to me.

He reached into the bundle, pulled out the Island Star and tossed it onto the table.

"Jesus Fucking Christ!" The Mayor screamed, jumping out of her chair and backing from the table. The rest of the counsel stood up, confused, and ready for whatever. Only Martha and I stayed in our seats, watching the Island Star roll to a stop in front of me.

"Gonna tell me how to make that thing work?" Wilfred asked me.

"What is that?" the judge asked.

I picked it up, squeezed slightly. I'd forgotten how mesmerizing the blue glow was.

"It's the most dangerous thing on the Island," I said. "And, no, I'm not going to tell you how to use it."

I tossed it back to him and he caught it in the bundle.

"Okay," Wilfred said, wrapping the star tight, then looking to The Mayor.

"Ma'am, with your permission, I'm gonna find me some Engineers and see if we can't get this thing figured out."

"I thought you knew explosives," The Mayor said. "You told me that. We find you something that goes boom and you build a weapon out of it."

"I did, ma'am, but I need to find out what kinda trigger Simon used. It's not heat, it's not pressure. I don't know what the hell this is, so gonna call in some help from people who know this Island a bit better than I do."

"The Engineers can't know we have this," The Mayor said.

"Who you more afraid of, Simon or them?"

The Mayor's face sunk ever so slightly. She was tired, frustrated, but fighting to maintain a regal composure. She walked back to the table and the rest of the counsel followed her lead, taking their usual seats.

"This is a bad idea," I said. "If you were smart, you'd bury that thing back in the ground."

Of course, they wouldn't, but I needed to say it for my own conscience.

"What is it?" The Mayor asked.

I drummed my fingers on the table, thinking. God had never instructed me on how to handle this situation. We knew they'd find the stars. We knew they would realize that the stars were special, but I'm not sure if God ever really thought someone would figure out how to use them.

"They are God's power," Martha said, her eyes forward, not looking at anything in particular.

We all glanced at her, curious. Wilfred couldn't tell if she was guessing. If so, her poker face was as unreadable as any pro.

"Is she right?" The Mayor asked me.

"Of course I am right," Martha said. "I can feel Him, no matter where He is on the Island and I can feel Him inside that thing."

The Mayor looked to me again.

"She is right, sort of," I answered. "God's power is His force of will. In Heaven, God is pure will. Here, His will is muffled by the body He's trapped in. Confused by it, to some degree. These are remnants of His will, left behind after the creation of the Island.

These were on Earth too, but were absorbed into the soil long before man learned how to dig."

"So, these things explode for Simon because he wills it?" The Mayor asked.

"Yes," I said. "Simon may not look it, but he is blessed with focus and patience. Heaps of it. He is going to keep pulling at the strands of the Island until he figures it all out. Or until the entire universe unravels."

The Mayor studied me for a few moments. "Do the Engineers know about these yet?"

"Yes, and they've been smart enough to leave them alone. God's will is too powerful to be controlled."

The Mayor considered as she looked from me towards Wilfred. "If they do figure out how to harness the power, they will take over New Wichita."

"But if we don't get their help, Simon will take over New Wichita," the judge said.

Martha stood and announced "I will accompany him. I will protect him with God's favor."

The Mayor laughed.

"We're going to send an idiot, a lunatic, and the most dangerous weapon on the Island right to our enemies," she said to the counsel, then looked back to Wilfred. "No, I don't think I'm going to let you do that. Go back to your cave, keep experimenting, figure something else out."

"My will is strong, Mayor," Martha said, her eyes still pointed forward. "May I give it a try?"

"I'm willing to try anything at this point," The Mayor said, excusing them with a wave of the hand.

Martha stood and followed Wilfred away from the table and back up the stairs.

"Oh, Martha," I called.

She turned and met my eyes. "Yes, devil?"

"Congratulations on your engagement."

A brief smile escaped her face before she went cold again. The Mayor and the council looked to me, surprised to hear that Martha really was betrothed to The Old Man. She turned and led Wilfred up the stairs, waiting until they were out of the Great Hall to talk.

"We aren't going to your cave," she said.

Wilfred was suspicious, but grinned all the same. "The Engineers?"

"No, we are going to the source."

Wilfred paused and watched her stride toward the front entrance of City Hall. Wilfred jogged to catch up to Martha, beginning to understand why God picked her.

Willow and Her Beloved Stump
Part 5

Willow wept. Exhausted. Spiritually spent. She wept and wept and wept.

"Darling, please, you've done enough, you've done more than anyone else would have."

Trevor's own words were weak. The travel had been excruciating for him as well. He'd slipped in and out of consciousness, his brain shutting down whenever the pain became too intense.

Willow tried to speak, but her sobs reduced the words into impenetrable moans and mumbles. She collapsed over him and kissed his face, then hugged as tight as her weary arms could manage.

Sorrow is the only sickness that can cripple our survival instinct, yet is far too cruel to kill us.

Trevor wasn't sure where he'd heard it. He knew that he was young when he'd encountered the quote and, even then, he realized it would be the most true thing he'd ever know. Was it a morose friend from the coffee shop, a teacher, a pastor? Perhaps he read it in a dusty book unearthed from an over-stacked shelf in a cluttered bookstore?

He really did miss bookstores. He'd considered smuggling books onto the Island and opening a bookstore or maybe just filling New Wichita's empty library. Willow would help him keep the shelves tidy and they would drift through the days laughing and reading.

But he would never be able to hold a book again and he would never be able to hold her.

In time, Willow's panicked sobs eased, her breaths settling into pace with his own. He listened to her soft, nasal snore. She slept so he slept. He wasn't sure they'd ever wake again. Perhaps sorrow on the Island was different and would be kind enough to separate them from their miserable lives.

How unfair it was that, only now, at the most wretched moment of Trevor's existence did God deliver to him something so precious. Something he was not worthy of, something that no one could be worthy of: Willow.

Willow.

He woke intermittently as the day passed, the sun skipping across the sky, Willow's body curled against him. She stirred only a few times. He dreamed of arms and legs. Of awaking to find limbs sprouted from his stumps, hands cradling Willow's face, fingertips tracing the curve of her lips. He felt the warmth of her skin. Not imagined, but felt. He rolled her over, held himself over her, his regrown hair falling over his eyes. She laughed, delighted. He wanted it to be true. He willed it to be true, but he woke again to find that he didn't possess the arms to hold Willow nor the legs to walk alongside her as a peer. He was still her burden.

Willow.

Willow.

Willow.

At dusk, Trevor awoke at the sensation of something sharp stabbing into his hip. His blurry eyes found a spear prodding him. He startled, wiggling like a caterpillar, forcing his weight against Willow. She was slow to rise, resisting.

Trevor followed the spear to the hands that held it. A man. Beyond, over his shoulder, a woman crouched in a tree, bow pulled taught, arrow trained on Willow.

"Go back," the man said.

"Barry?" Willow asked, her voice still softened by sleep.

"Who are you?"

"Willow. We were in the campground together. I was friends with Martha."

Barry glanced back at Mary.

"Was," Willow repeated, a little louder. "Simon said he had friends here that would help us. Is that you?"

"We aren't Simon's friends," Barry said. He lowered his spear as Mary returned the arrow to her quiver and leapt down from the tree.

"Simon doesn't have any friends left on this part of the Island," Mary said. "The angels wiped them all out."

"Oh," Willow said, her voice as small as a mouse's.

"You were on a pike, weren't you?" Barry asked Trevor. "We saw you right after we were exiled."

"Yes. Willow saved me and has pulled me all this way. Simon told us we would find help and be safe from the Americans. I know this is a lot to ask, but is there any chance that you might be able to give us some shelter, just for a few days until we can figure out what to do next?"

Mary leaned to Barry and whispered in his ear. He nodded.

"What happened to Martha?" Mary asked. "Where is she?"

"She went a little crazy," Willow said. "She thinks she's engaged to God."

"They were cruel to Willow," Trevor said. "Martha and the others. I understand why you would be suspicious, but I can assure you that neither of us have any interest in ever seeing her or the Americans again."

Mary smiled at Barry.

"Martha and God. Can you imagine what the sex would be

like?"

"Jealous and angry," Barry said.

"So fucking angry."

Mary took Barry's hand and led him a few steps away. They chatted quietly. Willow stroked her fingers along Trevor's scalp. Tears slipped from her eyes and she cleared them from her cheeks.

Barry nodded. Mary walked past him into the forest, following the trail left from where Willow had dragged Trevor.

"Where is she going?" Willow asked.

"Just to backtrack a bit. She wants to make sure no one else is out there."

"I swear that we aren't with Martha or anyone," Willow said. "I promise. Cross my heart."

"Even if you are alone," Barry said. "That trail is pretty easy to follow, so if New Wichita wanted to track you down, you laid out an obvious path to our front yard."

Barry walked toward Willow, bent down over Trevor. Willow tensed, held up a hand defensively.

"I'm just going to carry him," Barry said.

"He's my responsibility," Willow said.

"Look, you are clearly worn out. Also, I'm not going to let you lay down another trail all the way to our shelter. We've gone out of our way to keep it hidden from the Americans, so the only way we are going to protect you is if I can carry him."

Willow didn't move. She looked down at Trevor.

"We don't have a choice, my dear," Trevor said.

Willow looked back to Barry.

"I can't lose him," she said, eyes warm and reddened.

Barry nodded his head, then held out his spear, offering it to Willow. She took it.

"I understand what you are going through," Barry said. "If

someone was a threat to Mary, I'd react the same way, but this is the only way. But I'll be defenseless and you'll be able to stab me if I act funny."

Willow's watery eyes measured Barry for a few more moments. She kissed Trevor on the forehead, then stood up to give Barry room to pick up her greatest love. Barry grunted as he lifted, but steadied Trevor in his arms.

"There are springs where we are going that are good for healing," Barry said.

"Will it grow me some new limbs?" Trevor asked. "Cause that would be lovely."

"Probably not. But it'll heal your skin, close your wounds. I don't know if there is anything we can do for the rest of you."

"It'll be okay," Willow said. "He's perfect the way he is. I just want him not to hurt so much."

Trevor met her eyes.

"I think you're perfect too."

Martha the Believer
Part 9

They found Yulia sitting alone on the beach, wearing a long black robe, eyes cast out toward the other edge of the lake. The sun was casting purple and red rays stretching from where it nestled into the horizon and all across the sky. A grand, sad, and peaceful moment.

Martha had never encountered Yulia, but Wilfred had. She'd dressed him a few nights after he was exiled just as she'd dressed all the others. Wilfred had never had a woman touch him like Yulia. He'd always wanted to find her cabin again, beg her to do it again, but pride held him back.

And the fear of being told "no."

Wilfred hated his fear, hated how much it controlled his life. Even at that moment, Yulia only twenty yards away, he was terrified of getting any closer, terrified of how she might look at him when she knew he was near.

"She's an Engineer," Wilfred whispered to Martha. "She's the one who makes all the clothes."

"How? Where does she get her materials?"

"From your old clothes. It's like magic. She can make anything."

"Anything?"

Wilfred nodded. Martha studied Yulia for several moments before stepping out onto the beach.

"You are the fanatic," Yulia called, not turning from the water. It wasn't a question, just an acknowledgment. Martha tensed and looked around the beach. She arched her back and lifted her chin.

"I am a believer," Martha said. "And I need to talk to you about my clothes."

"We are closed for the day, my dear."

"It has to be now. I am going to my future husband and I need a wedding dress."

Yulia turned to face Martha for the first time.

"Who are you marrying?"

"God. We are engaged and I am going to Him now to seal our vows."

Yulia leaned to look past Martha to Wilfred. Wilfred shrugged.

"Did God actually propose to you?" Yulia asked.

"Yes."

Amused, Yulia stood, wiped the sand from her robe, then approached Martha.

"God killed my friend on this beach," Yulia said, her smile not breaking. "Why would I help you?"

"Because He is still your Father and I will ensure that you are rewarded when I become your Mother."

"You may be lying," Yulia said. "You also may be insane."

Martha's regal bearing faded slightly, the old Martha returning. She forced her spine straight again.

"Just make me the dress," Martha said. "Please."

Yulia walked within a footstep of Martha, her eyes narrowed. She pointed to Martha's companion, hunched, nervous, and several steps behind.

"What's your name?"

"Wilfred, ma'am."

"Yes, Wilfred, now I remember. The weapons enthusiast with the unsteady hands."

Wilfred frowned.

"Yes, ma'am."

"Please give us some privacy. Find a boat for God's lovely bride."

"Yes, ma'am."

"And you, dear," Yulia said to Martha. "Close your eyes and strip."

"Here?"

"You are about to be divine royalty. Now is no time for modesty."

***

The bohemian wedding dress was a thin layering of lace upon silk upon lace, delicately constructed, showing off Martha's shoulders and accentuating her curves. Martha pulled down the sheer veil as Wilfred rowed them across the lake. She now carried the Island Star, bundled in lace and cradled in both hands so she could present it as her dowry. The lights were clicking on in the campground as the night fell. Campers gathered along the pier as the boat approached. Jay and I walked to the shore.

God hid in His rebuilt cabin.

It may be impossible to adequately portray the pure delight I felt as I saw Martha and her wedding dress, carrying the greatest wedding present possible over to the Creator who'd accidentally proposed to her.

"Stop smiling, Bali," Jay said. I looked over at him and could see that even he was having a hard time hiding his amusement.

I also felt a tinge of sorrow for the poor girl. There was no way that this ended with her finding the happiness she was so sure was waiting for her within a private chamber of God's heart.

I walked out onto the pier and Wilfred threw the boat's rope to me. I tied it off and held out my hand for Martha. She remained seated, not looking at me or any of the campers. Eyes forward like royalty.

"Where is He?" she asked.

I withdrew my hand and stepped back from the boat. I

glanced over to Jay.

"His cabin," Jay called.

"Is He waiting for me?" There was a waiver in her voice.

"I am sure of it," I said and reached again to help her out of the boat.

Martha eased to her feet, took my hand, and with great effort, managed to pull herself, her flowing dress, and her bundle up onto the pier. She steadied for a moment, then motioned for me to lead the way.

So, I did. Jay walked with us. The campers were cautious and remained at a distance. Martha remembered her own amazement when adults had appeared in the campground before her exile. She would need to discuss a better way to manage the Island with God. Not right away, of course, but in time. As she proved her usefulness. She would be a good manager of God's creation. It was not an implication that He was not perfect, but even the greatest of men needed help now and again.

The cabin looked much the same as before. An extra room was built into the back. On the side was an entrance to a storm cellar. God's silhouette could be seen through the curtains.

Martha stopped before the stairs. She looked to me, but I didn't know what to tell her. I had no better idea of what God was thinking.

She gazed at the closed front door, considering. She unwrapped the bundle and held up the Island Star.

"My Lord. My Love. Receive my dowry. Tell me how to prove my devotion to You."

She was happy with the words. She'd worked them over in her head all day. Less was more, she decided.

"What is that?" a camper asked, but was hushed by Jay.

God's door remained closed, his silhouette unmoving.

"You know what is in my heart, God. I need only a sign that I am doing Your will."

Still nothing.

"Wilfred," Martha said, not turning back to look at him.

"Yes, ma'am."

"Go back to the Wilderness. I am going to stay here as long as He demands it."

"Maybe He wants you to leave Him alone?" Jay asked.

"Maybe He doesn't," Martha said.

I turned to the campers.

"Okay, everyone, let's get to the mess hall. We still need to eat."

The door opened a few inches. God's face appeared through the crack.

"Do you know how to use it?" God asked.

"Yes, I believe that I do," Martha said.

God inched His head out a bit more, then looked to the Wilderness across the lake. He turned His focus back to Martha.

"Then use it and be rewarded."

Being A Child God
Part 9

At night, I don't sleep, but instead drift as fog. In the world and out of the world. I'd begun this early on as my powers reached divine proportions. If a person should be walking through the Wilderness, they would not know me from the early morning mist.

I am aware but also unconcerned. Well, largely unconcerned. I admit that I'd developed into a brazen peeping tom. In my defense, I challenge any human to possess the ability to freely spy across vast swaths of area and not use it for entertainment purposes. Impossible. Secrets are too delicious.

As I made my listless rounds across the Wilderness, I found a miserable mob shambling away from New Wichita. I followed along, curious in the way that dreams sometimes stir our slumbering mind into a dim attention. They were a ghastly lot. Emaciated, weak, but resolute as they followed the atheist.

Then I was drawn away by something in the far, far distance. A song. I was always a sucker for a sing-a-long, so I swept away from New Wichita and flew towards the lake. It was an old, country hymn I vaguely recalled. The woman's voice was a lush, slow-drawn mezzo-soprano. I knew it was a mezzo-soprano because I'd once lived with a singer who sounded so much the same that I initially believed it to be her. A new exile perhaps. The voice pulled me faster through the woods, south beyond Rawlings, within eye shot of the fishing villages and their boats crawling sadly across the moonlit waters. I saw the singer sitting in a boat, eyes closed, voice raised.

Martha.

An American was rowing the boat towards the shore.

Captivated, I settled within the tree branches, listening. I finally placed it. "God Is Going To Cut You Down", but without the expected righteousness. Martha's voice was gentle, like she was singing a nursery rhyme.

I recognized the American. The weapons engineer. The man who was trying to kill me by tinkering around in his little cave. I felt his unease, but in my semi-lucid state, I didn't recognize the danger.

The boat met the shore and the American helped her out into the water. She walked to land, then unwrapped a bundle to reveal an Island Star. My mind snapped awake, all of it. I swirled to the ground, materializing in her path. She kept her eyes sealed tight, unconcerned, still singing.

"How thoughtful," I said. "You brought me a present. And here I am, empty-handed."

She didn't respond but her face did twitch from nervousness. I didn't understand the moment. The wedding dress, the star being presented as if she was trying to buy my love. Anat hadn't followed me. She never does, just sleeps through the night as I wander like a curious runaway.

"Martha?" I asked, but she only approached and sang even louder, more aggressive now.

"Go tell that long tongue liar,
go and tell that midnight rider,
tell the rambler, the gambler, the back biter,
tell 'em that God's gonna cut 'em down."

It was a threat.

She dropped the cloth and held the star in her bare hands. She was only a few paces away.

"Martha?"

She stopped singing, opened her eyes and sneered. She squeezed the star. It's flesh budged and broke.

The fire came too quick for me to react.

I Cannot Die
Part 16

We waited for the explosion together. The three of us sitting on the edge of the pier. The Father, the Son, and the Damned in the best seat in the house. The fireball was impressive. The shock wave was startling, even at this distance. I saw it shimmer the water on its way to us. It seemed larger than Simon's in New Wichita.

God was pleased, clear from the admiring smile. He could have been watching da Vinci painting ceilings, Ali besting giants, Beethoven constructing masterpieces. But no. God was watching humans kill. This was His beloved art form. These were His true champions.

"Another devoted human You sent to die in Your Name," I said, but knew He wouldn't answer.

"Is Simon dead?" Jay asked, anxious to get off the pier and back to the safety of land.

God closed His eyes and took in long, slow, meditative breaths. He frowned. He grunted, then opened His eyes.

"Yes," God answered, then lifted His legs from the edge and stood. He watched the angry red flames dissipate on the distant shore. He returned to His cabin, leaving Jay and I. Jay pulled his legs up to his chest, but stayed on the pier. I was impressed. We watched the fires still burning in the surrounding woods.

"We are on the wrong side of this," I said. "You do know that right? This isn't like Earth."

"Still trying to tempt me, brother?" Jay asked.

"If the truth is tempting, then yes."

Jay considered. His eyes lowered to the water below our feet.

"I wish I were a real human," Jay said. "I've always wondered what it was like. Just to be able to swim when I wanted, to walk through the day only thinking of small, petty things."

"Small, petty things like survival and a confused God?"

Jay looked to me, shrugged.

"Still small and petty compared to what He's stuffed into my brain."

"Point taken."

How To Properly Manage A Young Empire
Part 7

CeeCee arrived in the morning along with four sentries with the enraged and gagged Julia in tow. The Mayor met them in the town square.

CeeCee motioned for the sentries to hold as she walked to The Mayor. "There was an explosion last night."

"We heard it," The Mayor said, then looked to Julia and sighed. The Mayor motioned to the sentries. "Take her to the ovens."

They pulled Julia towards the caves as she bucked, squirmed, and yelled through the gag.

"What a waste," The Mayor said, then looking back to the sentry. "Where was the explosion?"

"By the lake."

"Okay, thank you. Gather some men and go see if anyone survived."

She waved CeeCee away.

Martha and Wilfred had fled New Wichita at some point during the night. The Mayor was furious at first, but the explosion meant they'd discovered a trigger. As long as someone survived the blast, The Mayor would then have her weapon. She would have leverage over the rest of the Wilderness. Perhaps even over God.

The Mayor considered the atheist again. The Mayor would have to behead her. Julia was feral and would only provoke New Wichita again if she ever escaped the ovens. The Mayor admired the strength of purpose, the resilience, but also knew that fanaticism could never be contained. Fury was a flood that would, in time, top every wall and wash away every foundation.

Constructing a Simon-Killer
Part 3

Small chunks of Martha were scattered around the blast crater and for several hundred feet in all directions. Wilfred had washed up on the shore, unconscious as scavengers flocked to the beach to clean up the mess.

A raven pecked at Wilfred's arm. He awoke enough to cough out water. Then he vomited. Then he coughed. Then he vomited. The raven cawed its annoyance before skipping out over the sand to find less troublesome meat to pick on.

The world was tumbling and turning with colors and high-pitched whines. He fell back into it and slept.

As the Americans pulled him away from the lake, he had nightmares of the water filling his desperate and burning lungs. He remembered the panic. He remembered waking at some point, unable to swim, drowning again. The cycle seemed eternal. Terror after terror after terror.

He woke, flailed his arms and legs, but the sentries held tight until exhaustion swept back over him.

And he slept.

Yulia Creates So Many Lovely Things
Part 4

Did she send the girl to her death? In a way, yes. But Yulia didn't feel any regret. All of the grief belonged on God's shoulders.

Yulia did feel rage though.

After the fiery bloom eased, Yulia saw body parts raining. She couldn't say for certain that you were dead. She considered examining the scene, looking for evidence of a dead magician, but opted to return to her people instead. They'd already lost one leader and could not afford to lose another.

The animals of the Wilderness were uneasy as they migrated toward America. Toward Rawlings, Yulia guessed. That is where Sophia slept. She would be a powerful Engineer someday if Yulia could just lure her away from the soldier who would hold her back in the guise of protecting her.

Another woman wasted on love.

Five Engineers met Yulia in the eastern Woods. Their aged, naked bodies were marked with black ash in stripes, circles, and crosses. They flanked Yulia and escorted her silently towards the temple. The Engineers had never had to mourn before, so all ceremonies were new and deeply personal. Yulia had left them to find her own solace on the beach. She'd considered returning to her isolated cabin to resume her place as an ambassador to all the new exiles, the Americans, and the outliers of the Wilderness. But now was a time for solidarity. A time for caution. A time to draw battle lines.

The ground wilted into a gentle slope as the Engineers walked onward. The trees grew thicker, taller, and more sparse as they approached The Sanctuary. Few exiles would ever get this close. This space was only for the Engineers along with a few selected guests and trusted laborers.

This valley did not exist at the birth of the Island. This was the Engineers first great creation.

Walking down through the last, dense cluster of trees, they reached a hidden valley stretched out for hundreds of yards with towering trees the size of red oaks standing like pillars holding the living ceiling aloft. The red oaks were limbless until they reached the canopy where they then stretched out their great branches in a web to conceal The Sanctuary from above. The forest was sparse within, just enough of the giant trees to hide the temple from God's jealous eye.

A number of smaller statues and temples dotted the valley, all built with bricks forged from the mudpits. Each structure possessed its own meaning to the Engineer who created it, representing an expression, an individual belief. There was no shared religion among the Engineers. They were more scientists than mystics, all prodding and poking at God's new physical and metaphysical world.

In the center was a pyramid built in the Mayan tradition, constructed out of massive, dried mud blocks. Layered, square bases gradually narrowed up to The Great Salon seated on the top. The circular structure had entrances on all sides, but a dense roof and walls. All voices were welcome inside, but none were allowed to spy from the outside. Not God. Not Simon. Not even me—or so they thought. A long set of stairs scaled the side facing the lake. Entrants must turn their backs from God to reach the Great Salon, but the stairs were also an invitation to God to join the discussion should He ever have the courage to face His abandoned children.

Engineers from across the Sanctuary approached Yulia and fell in line with the escorts as the procession approached the pyramid. They scaled the stairs, reached the top, and, as Yulia stepped within the darkness of the Great Salon, she felt the presence of outsiders.

"Tabitha," Yulia said.

A squat woman with a slight hump to her back stepped past Yulia. Her long, silver hair nearly reached the floor and caught glints of sunlight before disappearing into the shadow of the Great Salon. She walked to the center where a tiny, malnourished tree withered from a lack of sunlight. Tabitha gathered her hair, tied it into a ponytail, then sat cross-legged in front of the tree.

She hummed a low, gentle melody, almost like a lullaby. Blue flames sparked alive on the tree's limbs. Small at first, then crackling into a hearty fire. The branches lifted like snakes waking and looking to the sun. The trunk stretched, thickened and rose almost to the ceiling as its branches stretched across the room. The tips of the tree's branches glowed with blue fire and revealed Edward and Tommy on the far side of the Salon. They ducked away from the branches, fearing the flames though they cast off no heat. Glowing white blossoms cracked and spread open at the tips of the branches as if casting off bedsheets. The room was illuminated. Twenty-three Engineers surrounded the base of the tree with Edward and Tommy being the only outsiders. Yulia approached them.

"Strange times for a pastor."

Edward looked from the flaming blossoms to the Engineer.

"Strange times for us all," he said. "We need to discuss Simon."

Constructing A Simon-Killer
Part 4

Wilfred wasn't a whiner or a malingerer. He wasn't one of those punks who faked injuries in high school when the summer football two-a-days started to lose their appeal. Wilfred believed he was a tough son of a bitch, but also wasn't in a hurry to get off the improvised stretcher as he was carried back to New Wichita. He appreciated the exalted status it afforded him. The man who risked his life to build a bomb.

Even after being blown up and drowned, Wilfred felt good. Exhilarated even. He could've walked into New Wichita, but why waste the opportunity? He felt like an astronaut, a sports hero, a brave explorer who'd just unraveled the secret to New Wichita's independence and security. From his discovery, they would build a sovereign empire.

Through the trees, Wilfred caught a glimpse of The Mayor striding from the cavern towards the procession. Towards Wilfred, the liberator. Wilfred fixed a weary smile, seeming to wilt into the stretcher. It was important that they saw he was still managing, bravely, even giving The Mayor and the other council members a thumbs-up.

"So, it worked?" The Mayor asked.

Wilfred waved her close for, you see, his voice couldn't carry very far because he was so feeble from the explosion and drowning and everything. The Mayor sighed, knelt down and put her ear close to his lips.

"Simon is dead," he said, really playing up a gravely tremble. "And I know how you will rule the Wilderness."

Being A Child God
Part 10

It started as a distant, muffled thump. A scraping. I slept. I awoke, the thumping was closer. I slept. I awoke. I slept.

Then a new sensation. Air touching my cheek. My eyes opened. I couldn't breathe because of the weight on top of me. My face was tilted up. I was a child trying to swim but it all felt up and down. Gravity was everywhere and nowhere. I saw only black ink, the hallucinations looming, great shadow monsters swallowing me whole. It was my mind giving form to dread. I wanted to die again, to sleep, to stop feeling.

A small tinkling bell sang like a tiny songbird. I saw movement, but also could have imagined it. I blinked, feeling dirt fall out of my eyeball. No moisture. Movement again.

Then I was cold. So, so, so cold. My face felt tight, different. I tasted dirt on my lips.

A pulley squeaked high above. A golden light descended. A lantern, I decided. It arrived and I knew what I saw was real. Huan unhooked it from the tattered rope and held the lantern down to me. I squinted away from the too bright light.

"What are you?" Huan asked.

I winked back. It was all I could do.

Less is more, my boy! No joke is as funny as the one you don't have to tell.

***

The work was slow. Huan gently dug around my face, my head, my neck, my shoulders. He would have been a good artist or surgeon had he been born in a less racist time and place.

Patience was not my strongest personality trait, but I managed well enough. Not being able to talk was the worst. He often looked down at me, a sad pity in his eyes.

"I am sorry this has happened to you," he said more than once.

The first tiny breath came as he dug around the front of my chest. The air was cool and delicious. I hadn't swallowed much dirt since I'd just materialized inside the Island. My lungs never had the opportunity to draw in earth. I closed my eyes, felt energy sparkling. Another breath, the rest of my body awakening.

I burst into mist, fled my grave and sped upwards. I rematerialized at the lip of the hole, looking down at Huan.

"Gave the crazy girl a bomb, huh?" I called. "No hard feelings, buddy. Find me another Island Star and we'll call it even."

"Simon?" Human asked.

I didn't understand and hesitated. "Of course I'm Simon, who else would I be?"

I heard rustling behind me and I turned to find to two thin, malnourished men lit by another lantern. They watched me in horror.

"Can you point me out of here?" I asked, but noticed the

sounds weren't coming out of my mouth quite right. My cheeks were too tight, my tongue was slow and sluggish. I wrote it off to dehydration.

One of the men held his skeletal arm up, a trembling finger pointing behind him.

I transformed, but quickly materialized, facing the men. "Give me a little time, then all this will be over. No more prisoners on the Island. Sound good?"

Their eyes were hollow, bulging. One nodded, still terrified. I chalked that up to unearthing a god.

I burst into mist and swept away. The tunnels twisted and twisted and twisted. I looked for air flows, for difference in temperature, but I often found more chambers with more of Huan's diving holes.

A scream echoed through the tunnels and I turned toward it. Winding, probing, feeling warmth, turning for the sound. I heard a brash woman's voice, a man's growl that I recognized. The Cook. That miserable bastard that deserved the ovens far more than any of their current residents.

Then I remembered the exodus. I'd watched them ambling through the woods, aimless and weary.

So, the ovens were empty and in need of new batch of condemned.

If we were without our wars and our prisons and our shopping malls, what is America but a utopia?

Fallimento really was my John the Baptist.

I turned a corner to find the glow of a solar tube illuminating a long tunnel. It led to the ovens. I'd been down here before, wondering how I would execute a prison break should it ever fit into my plans.

I raced on, curious. I turned into the first vein and saw the Cook, shirtless, his overalls unsnapped and hanging to his sides. He dragged the Island's lone atheist by the hair as she shouted the foulest string of expletives I'd ever heard. And I lived in Vegas. She was blindfolded and hands were bound in front of her. She kicked violently, trying to rip her hair free. I swept past them and materialized underneath a solar tube.

The Cook stopped, stunned. Julia tilted around, unable to see but still pointing her face at me.

"What the hell are you?" the Cook asked in a damaged rasp. A long, gnarly scar ran across this windpipe.

"I am Simon!" I shouted, but then realized that he didn't ask "Who the hell are you?" but "What the hell are you?"

"What?" he asked.

"What?" I asked.

That was when it dawned on me that I might not have come through the explosion entirely unscathed. The drama of the moment seeped out. I thought I'd be received as both a menacing devil and a righteous savior. Instead, I panicked at what the cook actually saw before him.

"Is it..." I began, touching my face, feeling the bulges and ripples of scars. "Is it bad?"

"Are you going to save me or not?" the blindfolded atheist asked.

I watched the Cook watching me. "Hold on," I said to Julia. "This is important."

I lifted my other hand, the left, to touch the other side of my face. I then saw that the hand possessed only one finger. I looked over the nubs, then my arms which were webbed with burn marks and shreds of cloth burned into the skin where a shirt had once been.

I began to properly panic. Screaming. Feeling the scars across my face, the bald scalp where hair should have been.

"What are you?" the Cook asked, his grip of Julia's hair loosening.

"Who! You mean 'who!'"

I focused, changed my form back to a child, hoping the skin would clear whatever monstrous wounds that had so shocked the Cook. He flinched backwards, nearly tripping. Julia freed her hair from his grasp and crawled away to a wall. She ripped off the blindfold.

"Is this better?" I asked, hating the moment more than any that had come before. Even being blown up and buried.

"Simon?" the Cook asked.

"Do I look okay?" I insisted, moving to Julia.

She held up her hand, defensively.

"Look at me! Do I look okay?"

"Yeah, whatever."

"Don't lie to me! What do I look like?"

"A child," she said.

"What are you?" the Cook asked.

"Hey, kid," Julia said. "I'm not sure what's happening right now, but I could use some help."

I looked at her bound hands, then the half-naked Cook.

"Oh, yeah, right."

I searched the cave for options, then settled on a nearby oven.

"Get in," I said.

"What?"

"Did you see what I did to your City Hall?"

He was slowly inching the opposite direction of the oven. "Yeah."

"Do you want me to do that same thing down here?"

"No."

"Then get in the oven."

It took him several moments. We were all being super awkward and I hated it. I wanted to be an elegant god. Instead, I was the Mr. Bean of divinities.

The Cook was still inching away, palms up in surrender.

"I am being super serious right now!" I yelled and I couldn't believe that "super serious" just escaped my mouth. I mean, goddamn it, really?

"Okay, okay," he finally conceded. It took him a few heartbeats to finally move towards the oven.

He was my first captive.

I would lock him in his own prison.

I would never tell anyone how un-amazing it had been.

He opened the heavy door and it took quite a deal of wiggling and adjusting and crawling for his large belly to squeeze inside.

Julia strode past me, slammed the door, and locked it.

"Fuck you dude!" she exclaimed, brandishing dual middle fingers.

"So, do I look okay?" I asked again.

"Yeah, I guess. So, you're the one everyone is fussing about?"

"Heh. Yeah. I've heard a lot about you too." I'd been curious about the atheist for quite some time. I knew God wouldn't put an atheist on the Island unless He had a good reason. And here she was, indebted to me. Without a better plan, I offered her my right hand, the one with the appropriate amount of fingers. She looked at it.

"Trust me, I'm married."

"But you're a child," she said.

"I'm complicated."

She grinned, then took my hand. I consumed us both in mist, then we swirled up the solar tube and out into the Wilderness.

The Girl Who Doomed God
Part 10

I found my queen gazing over the edge of the Island to Heaven below, as if looking for the followers that had been cast down into the quilt of souls.

If I gotta burn, I hope Mark Twain and Oscar Wilde are cooking right next to me in Satan's cauldron. The three of us will clink our mint juleps and drink to the God that didn't deserve us.

"I found you a friend!" I said, presenting Julia and feeling ridiculous. I was focusing on the sound of my words, aware that there was a slur if I wasn't careful. I both needed to see what happened to my face and was terrified of seeing what happened to my face.

"I don't need a matchmaker, Simon," she said, turning to me. "And why are you a child again?"

"It's complicated."

Anat tilted her head, eyeing me curiously, then passed her gaze onto Julia.

"I'm sorry for him," Anat said, walking to Julia and offering her hand.

"He's not that bad. He just saved me from a redneck, so I'll give him a pass."

"Julia's an atheist," I announced.

Anat kept her grip on Julia's hand.

"How? We know God exists."

Julia shrugged. "Old habit, I guess. Also, fuck that Guy, am I right?"

Anat nodded, slipped her hand away, and turned back to

Heaven.

"We're going to take over," Anat said as she walked to the edge, motioning for Julia to join her. "Did Simon tell you that?"

"No, but I am intrigued. How exactly do you plan to pull it off?"

I followed them to the edge but kept my distance. "We are still in the planning phases, but we are recruiting. I bet we can find a spot on our starting lineup for a strong-headed atheist."

"I'm not a joiner," Julia said. "I'm more a freelance freedom fighter and chances are good I'll end up turning on you too."

Anat looked to Julia, then turned to me.

"I like her," Anat said. "You did good, Simon. Now stop being a child and join the adults."

Julia met my gaze briefly. She hadn't seen what the Cook had seen, but she must have known it was bad.

"I'm actually going to go do some things. Errands, you know? Checking out things. There was a bit of a kerfuffle last night, I'm sure you saw the explosion and, well …"

I was like a fish trapped on the shore.

"It's complicated?" Anat asked.

"Yeah," I said and, for some reason, I pointed double finger pistols at her and said "pweh, pweh." "Anyhoo, I'll be back. You two talk."

Anat saw through me. She never missed a thing but what else could I do?

"Find the prisoners," Julia said. "Bring them here, okay?"

I nodded. My heart was tight in my chest, bracing for the abandonment sure to come. Anat would reject me as soon as she knew her king was a monster. I knew it with the same certainty that I knew my own name.

On Earth, I always smelled rejection coming. I was an escape artist in magic and love. Anything to slip away from the hurt.

That was exactly what I was going to do this time too unless I found another way.

"Go Moses," Anat said. "Deliver her people from bondage."

I feigned a heroic smile, chest jutting out, my fists at my side, my phantom fingers tingling.

"As you wish."

Then I was gone.

"He's kind of a weirdo, huh?" Julia asked.

"Yes, but he's my weirdo," Anat said, then turned to Julia. "You would be so powerful if only you believed."

"The Island already has plenty of witches and sorcerers. And at least one too many gods."

The Huddled Masses

They were camped not far from New Wichita, gorging themselves on a mudpit. They turned wearily as I approached. They were all so thin, so tired, so defeated.

My new army.

I exhaled mist that swept across the crowd of escaped prisoners. They cowered but were too fatigued to run. I swept them up and returned to the heart of my universe.

I Cannot Die
Part 17

God sat at the arts and crafts table. Alone. The beads were neatly arranged into bowls along the table, strings cut to size. But there were no campers. No little fingers to choose the beads that defined the children and their love of their Creator. The bright, lettered beads reflected off God's mirrored sunglasses so that I could almost spell out His thoughts.

We thought the news of your death would lift his mood, but it had affected him in a way neither Jay nor I understood and certainly had never seen before.

The campers hid in their cabins, watching through the windows. The whispers would start soon. I guessed we would see our first child grow into an adult that night. The exodus would be fast after that. Growth would be an escape from the anxiety of the campground, which was for the best. The campground was now a failed experiment. God's focus was not on the campers anymore. It was on the Wilderness and the way the unknown loomed over Him for the first time in the history of His time and space.

I kept my distance as God gazed across the beads. Jay passed by me on his way to the volcano. He would be bathing himself for the first time. I worried that he wouldn't be able to survive the experience, so I sent angels along with him, just in case.

I walked to the arts and crafts table and sat opposite God. His head tilted up just enough to see that it was me, then looked back down to the beads. He rose his hand, reaching across the bowls for a letter "L". He grabbed a string and ran it through the bead. God then grabbed an "O", strung it, then an "S" and a "T". He knotted the string, holding the beads in place, then hung it from His neck.

"Take that off," I said.

His hand felt the beads.

"Take that off," I said again. "The children cannot see you with that."

A tear escaped from underneath his sunglasses.

"Go back to Your cabin and get Yourself together."

He nodded. Another tear. The necklace burst into flames around his neck. The beads melted, the string broke and it fell to the table. He stood up from the table, stepped back over the bench and walked, head down, back to His cabin.

I waited for His door to close before calling out the children to help me clean up the table and prepare for lunch.

How To Properly Manage A Young Empire
Part 8

The artist was not to be touched. That was the standing order. So the sentries only watched as Petrov painted towering letters across the scorched facade of City Hall.

"SHAME" and "RELEASE YOUR PRISONERS AND REPENT" in dark red—the color of blood, the color of fury, the color of revolution.

Petrov had placed the head on a moist cloth beside a crude, wooden ladder. A few splatters of red had fallen into her stringy, dried hair, but she didn't mind. She only wished she was further away from the wall so she could take in the full scope of the work.

"Everyone go home!" The Mayor called as she strode through the crowd with CeeCee by her side. "Petrov, get down from there!"

Petrov remained on the ladder, finishing the final "T". The Mayor stopped at the ladder, gazed across the wall, bit back her rage. She turned to the crowd.

"Go away!"

The crowd started to disperse, but resettled once The Mayor turned back to the ladder.

"Come down right now!"

Petrov ran the brush over a few streaks, took a moment to look over his work, then dipped the brush back into the wooden paint bucket hanging from the ladder. He unhooked the bucket, then descended. He didn't address The Mayor as he sat down the bucket, collected the head, looked her into the eyes, smiling. The head smiled back, weak, but proud. Petrov fixed the harness back over her and returned the head to his shoulder. He turned to The Mayor.

"Empty the ovens," Petrov said, soft but certain.

"They are empty," The Mayor shot back. "Aside from one. The atheist staged a jailbreak, violating our sovereignty and endangering the Island by releasing dangerous criminals out into the Wilderness. We are in the process of sweeping them back up. We will bring them back to finish their sentences."

Petrov nodded. He picked up the paint bucket and walked past The Mayor, looking over the wall until he found a blank space he liked. He set the bucket down, took out the brush and resumed painting. The Mayor looked back to the crowd. They again started to disperse, trying not to get caught watching. She walked to Petrov's shoulder not containing the head and leaned close.

"Please don't make me do this to you," she whispered.

Petrov paused, considered, but continued painting.

The Mayor dipped her head.

"Take him," she said.

The sentries moved uneasily toward Petrov. They took his arms, but Petrov struggled, ripping an arm free and leaning back to paint the wall. The sentries grasped him harder and yanked the paintbrush out of his hand.

"Take him to the Cook," The Mayor said. "But wait for me."

The sentries pulled Petrov away. The Mayor snapped her fingers and pointed to the wall.

"Clean it off."

Digging To Heaven
Part 4

Two more stars. Two more weapons. Two more potential explosions. Huan sat back in his hole. It was sixty feet deep now. He estimated it would need to be another hundred feet before reaching the bottom of the Island. He could just keep digging. The Mayor was having Huan watched. He couldn't escape New Wichita with such precious cargo and, even if he did, Simon would stop him from throwing them off the Island.

So it only made sense to keep digging. But more workers were manning more holes throughout the caves. The first priority of New Wichita was now to find Island stars. They were stockpiling for war.

Huan wished, for the first time since reaching the Wilderness, that he could return to God and seek His advice. Huan missed prayer, he missed the solace of a great and mysterious plan.

Huan turned the star over in his hands, admiring its glow, wondering at its insides.

Huan did not know the better way forward, he only knew that he was now committed to New Wichita. Because of this, he rang the small bell three times to call for the rope. It would pull him from the hole and allow him to deliver the frightening stars to a woman he could only hope wouldn't misuse them.

***

The council was meeting in the weapon engineer's cave, standing bedside as if he was royalty. Huan waited in the back of the group for his chance to talk to The Mayor.

"I don't understand what you mean," The Mayor said.

"Belief," Wilfred said. "That's the trigger. Bali was right. The stars are will. They respond to someone believing in what they are doing, igniting that remnant of God's will, forcing the thing to explode."

"So, you think happy thoughts and it goes boom?" the judge asked, more than a little haughty.

"Yes. So we can't just have anyone make it blow up. It's gotta be someone with a sense of purpose."

"How do we weaponize belief?" the judge asked.

"Find people willing to be told what to believe," The Mayor said. "And, if this thing can destroy Simon, it can definitely bring the Engineers to their knees."

Huan was startled by the comment. He had no idea that Simon had been struck. Huan only knew that he'd dug up the magician from the bowels of the Island.

"Perhaps we can even use it as a deterrent against the angels," The Mayor continued. "We can't use it as a suicide bomb again, though. It must become some sort of projectile so we don't just burn through all of our believers. Can you do that?"

"Maybe," Wilfred said. "I'll need some volunteers."

"You'll get them. Someone get me Huan."

Huan backed up a few paces, his hand instinctively going over the bag as he reconsidered his alliances.

"He's here already," the judge said as the council turned to the miner.

The Mayor stepped through, looked at the bag, seeing the lumps held within. "You brought me a present, I assume."

"Simon is alive," Huan said. "I saw him today."

"That's a lie," Wilfred said. "I saw him die."

"He's hurt," Huan said. "The explosion scarred him terribly, but it did not kill him."

The Mayor considered, looked back to Wilfred.

"Then we still know we can hurt him," The Mayor said. "I can work with that."

Son of God

Jesus hated hymns. Jesus hated Christmas. Jesus hated children's choirs for the most part. Jesus hated people who smiled too much unless they were very old or very sick. Jesus hated anyone who owned more than one house. Jesus hated payday lenders. Jesus hated people who nicknamed everyone they knew. Jesus hated his own nickname, "Jay," because it sounded so American. And Jesus hated Americans.

While alone on the top of the volcano, Jay was free to confess the worst of him as he settled into the spring, feeling anxiety seeping out of him along with a frightening amount of blood. He was free to let go. A ritual suicide that never quite managed the job.

The steaming water swirled with the life dripping out of wounds in his wrists, his scalp, and his feet. Here, Jesus allowed himself weakness. He allowed himself hatred and jealousy. He allowed himself to be human.

God would normally sit next to him, holding His son above the water, allowing Jesus to steep in unhappiness. But God was out of sorts these days and Jesus didn't want his time of confession overshadowed by God's own emotional baggage.

This was Jesus's space. This was the present his Father bestowed to help Jay endure another human body. A reward for loyalty. An apology.

And, to be fair, my brother wasn't all morose bitterness.

For instance, Jesus loved watching women move when they thought no one was looking. Jesus loved watching women move when they knew someone was looking. Jesus loved when dogs accidentally slid into walls. Jesus loved when the Green Bay Packers lost. Jesus loved old men who had trouble with umbrellas on windy days. Jesus loved that God loved him best.

Also Jesus loved magic tricks and had wanted to be closer friends with you since we pulled you out of Heaven. He felt a kinship to all magicians, but would never admit it unless he was bathing in the volcano spring. If you want to inspire a genuine smile from the Savior, practice your slight of hand. A good card trick always tickled the Lord.

Jesus deeply resented that you never tried to be his friend.

He wasn't always so sullen on the Island. For the first few rounds of campers, God openly introduced Jay as His son. Jesus did his best to be welcoming and exude the bright light all late Christians expected of him. He smiled though he detested how fake it felt. He laughed at jokes. He pretended to enjoy their off-key and saccharine worship songs. He shook hands and listened to stories of Jesus saving their souls individually by appearing in road signs, fluffy clouds, and burnt pancakes. They thanked him for all the little miracles he had placed into their paths like mile markers on the way to Heaven.

Jesus wasn't behind any of those little miracles and he thought materializing in inanimate objects was low and inelegant magic. He never said so because his own Father had once appeared in a bush. A burning bush, perhaps, but a bush all the same.

Jesus quickly grew tired of his role as God's PR department. His dramatic allergy to life and water didn't help with the moodiness, but I think he would have been fine had God given him any indication of how long we would be on the Island. God didn't because God enjoys vagueness. He swam through it as a fish swims through water.

So, we waited. And we waited. And we waited. As Jesus withdrew from the children, God leaned on me. God was confused and hurt by Jesus's spiritual rejection of the Island, but neither of them were particularly good at expressing feelings. They were aces at dictating other people's emotions, but managing their own was always a shaky proposition.

And communication? It would take vulnerability and both had too much pride to grant the necessary humility any entry.

God did ask me for advice from time to time. I told Him to allow Jesus to go back to Heaven. God rejected the idea. I told Him to allow Jesus to grow and marry, start the family that was denied him in the previous life. God rejected the idea. I then suggested giving Jesus another name and another role. To also give Jesus a release where he could speak freely, bleed off the anxiety, and escape, if only for a brief time, the struggle of being trapped in a mortal form again.

God went with the latter in God's normal, bumbling way. He allowed His son to fade to the background of the campground as a mopey "yes" man, and conceal his identity from the future waves of campers. Once a day, God and Jay scaled the volcano. Jay bathed, bled, and confessed how pained he was to be entangled again within the mortal coil.

And let me say this before we get too far, I love Jesus. Genuinely. I respect Jesus and have never questioned the validity of his anger. If anyone had a right to be furious, it was Jesus. He deserved better. We all deserved better, but Jesus most of all. His existence was hard and he was doing the best he could considering he still carried the weight of thousands of years of human sin within his very frail heart.

And when life touched him on the Island, the wounds of his Earthly life reopened, exposing his hurt for all of creation to see. How humiliating that must have been.

As Jesus sat alone within the volcanic spring, he wondered what drowning in his own blood would feel like. He knew he wouldn't die. He knew God wouldn't allow him to leave the Island behind. Yet he still yearned for oblivion.

His mouth was below the water, his nose just above. His skin was a bluish pale, almost a corpse's. The blood stained his cheeks.

Then you appeared. No illusion. No attempt to hide your brutally scarred, mutilated face or the destroyed hand or the divots of flesh burned off or the flashes of exposed bone. It was shocking.

Jay eased up out of the water. "Have a bad day?"

"Oh, ha ha. We have to talk."

"Perform a trick for me first, Simon."

You tried to smile, but the scars in your face only moved like disturbed marsh water. "Heal me first."

"I don't do that anymore," Jay said. "I've retired from the healing game."

Jay smiled as he dipped back into the water so only his eyes hinted the devilish smile beneath.

You eased down beside the pool and sat down cross-legged, careful not to touch the water.

"Listen, sorry about tossing your dad's plane off the Island and all, but I needed to get His attention. I'm a nice guy though. I'm willing to negotiate."

Jay kept watching, his eyes just above the blood. A few bubbles rose and popped on the surface.

"So, is this a tactic?" you asked. "Keep me talking, see how much you can fleece me for? 'Fleece'. That's a Biblical term, right?"

Jay rolled his eyes, then rose.

"You know what is most annoying about Americans and your entire generation of humans? You were, by large, a literate society with many translations of the Bible to choose from, but so few of you actually read it. Maybe you went to church, maybe you'd wear a cross every day, give money to the church or bums on the street when you were in the mood, but rarely read the actual text."

Simon's eyebrow arched. "Okay, so if I read the Bible, will you heal me?"

Jay grinned. "Too late for that. Those were laws for a different time and a different place. Tell me this—why do you care? It's just skin, bones, a few fingers. All these wounds you can mask with your power. I don't see the purpose of healing you."

You didn't answer, keeping your face poker-blank. You looked to the blood and dipped the last mangled finger left on your right hand into the blood. The surface illuminated as the blood glowed. God's burning cabin appeared. You lifted your finger back out of the blood, the image sunk away.

You held up your finger and examined the blood. "Gross." You smeared it across your cheek. "Does it work that way? Can I just take a bucket of blood with me and use it as an exfoliant? Like Miracle Grow for humans?"

"You can try, I suppose," Jay said. "You haven't answered my question. Why do you need to heal when you can simply hide?"

"I'm married," Simon said. "She is very important to me and, even though I can throw up a mirage, her fingers will find my scars. She will be repulsed. I need to be whole for her. I need to be healed, so name your price. I can give you land in the Wilderness, I can promise not to attack your Dad or burn down His cabin again."

"My Father can take care of Himself. But we could use a new airplane."

"Nope. Name another price."

"Take me back to Heaven."

"Damn," you said, throwing up your hands. "I just want some smoothing out. A little reconstructive surgery."

"The only thing I want from you or God or anyone else is to

be loosed from this shell. If you can get me back to Heaven, then I will reward you. It is the only thing anyone on this Island can offer that has any interest to me."

"Back to Heaven by any means necessary? Doesn't matter who you have to deal with."

Jay frowned, looked down to the blood. "Every moment is suffering. Even on the cross, the pain was bearable because I knew that death would liberate me. I can withstand many things, but not this waiting."

You sighed, considered, your head bobbing slightly as you worked out the problem. "Okay. If I find a way, I will send you back tout de suite. Any chance I could get that healing on credit?"

"Go read your Bible," Jay said, then winked. "I'm not a fan of debtors." He then slipped under the water, disappearing beneath the murky pool. You gazed at the swirling blood.

"Shit."

Being A Child God
Part 11

"I've got a plan."

Anat was naked, glowing a warm orange, and waiting for me beside our bed. I was a grown man in my white on white on white preacher's dress suit. Still an illusion concealing the monster I'd become. The fortress was empty aside from Julia, slumbering several rooms away. Our new army camped under the moonlight, understandably wary of the underground. All the other residents, our followers, had been tossed out into the abyss by angels. Perhaps we should have been mourning them, but Anat was like me, not prone to dwelling on the past.

"Come to bed."

"But this is a really good plan."

"Come to bed."

"And the plan is kinda time sensitive," I said, a little desperate.

Anat walked to me and the shadows danced along the walls as her glow crossed the room. I backed up a step, afraid of being touched. Afraid of her feeling the horror show beneath the mirage.

She paused, sensing my hesitation. Her eyes attempted to pry me open, but I kept up my optimistic smile, like the showman I'd always been.

No matter how great the catastrophe, pretend it's all just part of the master plan. Magic isn't illusion, it's belief. You believe, they believe.

"I've got an idea of how we win this thing."

"Tell me," she said.

"We get Jay back to Heaven." My smile was beaming, but only in the mirage. My scarred skin couldn't stretch that much.

"Why?'

"He's actually Jesus."

"I'd gathered that."

I'd anticipated some sort of impact from the revelation. Before the exile, I'd been shocked when Billy had shoved Jay into the lake, only to see Jay bleed out like a slaughtered pig. The images of our sins glowed on the water and only then did we know.

"Okay," I said. "So, with him in Heaven, God is completely isolated."

"But he still has Bali."

"Yeah, but get this, Bali is the devil. Or Lucifer. Or Satan, maybe. I dunno. Somebody along those lines."

"I also knew that."

I didn't answer straight away. I was angry now. Well, more humiliated.

"How?"

"Because I'm not an idiot." She folded her arms over her breasts and her orange glow shifting to a light blue.

"You're like a mood ring."

"Yes, a mood ring that is losing its patience," Anat said. "So, we send Jay to Heaven, lure Bali along with all the exiles to our side, then force God to step down and let us take over the Island."

"Yeah," I said. "Or something to that effect."

"And how do we get Jay to Heaven?"

"No idea, but I do know who'd know." I held up my good hand like a chauffeur. I had to be very methodical on how and where she touched me until I was healed.

"Who?"

"You'll just have to find out."

"It's Bali."

"Goddmanit, why do you keep asking if you already know everything in the world?"

She smiled, took my hand and leaned in. I inched back, but then settled to receive the kiss. Her lips pressed against my cheek, lingered. She pulled back. I couldn't tell if she registered the scars. Her blue light dimmed.

Not even the darkest chamber of Hell scared me more than the thought of losing her.

I Cannot Die
Part 18

You appeared before us as royalty—a tacky king in a purple, velvet robe and his queen aglow in a dress of fire and diamonds.

A tetherball spun, forgotten, around the pole pit until it raveled tight, then unwound like a lazy hound finding its bed. It bapped a distracted boy on the back of the head. We all gazed at the self-anointed emperors of the Island. A small group of children turned and fled to their cabins. Others followed suit, leaving only about a dozen children still awing at royalty.

"Not here," I said, glancing at God's cabin where the Creator hid out. He must have known you were alive and that you'd returned the campground, but He didn't even bother to look out the window. Maybe He was afraid. Maybe He was ashamed.

Jay had yet to return from the volcano. The Engineers were

quiet and plotting. New Wichita's faith was wavering and unsure. Everyone was adrift. I may not have been the closest adherent to God's law, but I did appreciate a sense of order, especially now that it was absent.

Hand-in-hand with Anat, you strolled to me with a satisfied air. You held out your other hand to me. Your wounded hand. It only appeared perfect within your illusion.

I took it, feeling the long finger curl around my hand. I knew to expect it. I'd seen it from Jay's eyes. I wasn't sure what you were getting at, having me hold it. Perhaps you wanted to see if I already knew, or you were letting me know, on the sly, the fix you'd found yourself in. Whatever your reasoning, the feel of your crippled hand didn't bother me. I'd spent thousands of years on Earth walking through battlefields, morgues, and overwhelmed hospitals. It took a lot to ruffle my feathers.

Your mouth opened and the mist poured out. The children around us gasped and backed away. As the cloud overtook us, I felt my body fade and evaporate. It didn't hurt. Quite the opposite, it felt like dropping a burden, letting the gravity of the Island fall away like an unlocked iron shackle. We lifted as a single entity upward into the sky. We fled far from the campground, far from God, far from the volcano, but not to the Wilderness. We swam with the tumbling clouds. It was freeing, being less than human again. I envied your ability to shed the heaviness of flesh so easily.

And from that great height, I saw how tiny the Island appeared above the eternal expanse of Heaven below. Glorious.

"I am formally registering a vote of no confidence in The Old Man," you said in a voice that was just above a ghostly hiss.

"I've tried that before," I said, my disembodied voice equally shallow. "Didn't turn out well."

"Circumstances are different this time," Anat said. "We have a plan."

"I had a plan."

"Ours is better," she said.

"Touché."

"We want your help," Anat said. "We need to isolate God. He is weak now and, without the plane, He is at our mercy if we unite against Him."

"Jay won't abandon Him," I said, but I knew that wasn't true. Someone had to play devil's advocate and who better than me?

"If we offer him a chance to get back to Heaven, he will take it," you said.

"And you know this because you talked to him?"

"Yes."

"And he does this in exchange for what?"

"Leaving God behind. Leaving God to us." Your voice was just unsteady enough that I knew Anat would notice.

"Not even putting in a request for a farewell gift from the King of Kings?" I was enjoying myself now. Seeding torment and discordance. I rarely had these opportunities on the Island. It was like digging out an old set of golf clubs. It lacked the immediate gratification of the Whisper, but was far more satisfying.

"Will you work with us or not?" Simon asked.

"Under the right circumstances and with the right people, perhaps."

"We can hurt you," Anat said.

"I can hurt you worse and in ways that you will never recover."

"You're bluffing," Anat said.

"Try me."

"Hey, we don't need to do this," you said, softening your hiss to something more like a purr. "Let's just talk it out. All we need to know is how to get Jay back to Heaven."

"Set up a diving board?"

"Simon," Anat said. "Your friend needs a little prodding."

A few moments of silence passed.

Then I materialized and fell. Though I am a demon, I am no more a fan of thousand foot drop than your average human. I flayed arms in wide windmill swings, I screamed out all the air in my lungs, I felt my heart pound heavy and fast.

You caught me with your bad hand. I burst back into mist and returned to the safety of your cloud.

"Let's try this again," you said.

I laughed loud and giddy. My adrenaline spiked from the fall and I was exhilarated from the total loss of control. I'd indulged in a million sins, and nothing was nearly this delicious.

"What would it take for you to join our revolution?" Anat asked.

"How about a healthy round of truth or dare?" It was another seed, something that would wiggle its way into Anat's mind, and grow into something that could split their union like a tree sprouting through a stone. On Earth, they called me nasty things like the Prince of Lies, but the truth was always so much more devastating.

I felt myself materialize and fall again. My breath sucked in and I watched the lake approach quickly.

At terminal velocity, falling into water is only a few hairs better than concrete. When I hit, I felt my bones crush and snap. I was not lucid as I sank beneath the waves, nor as my body resurfaced and drifted, face down.

It was all just dark, excruciating static.

Then the awareness snapped back, my body surfaced, and I turned in the water to find air. The coughs were like bloody ruptures inside my broken ribcage. My shoulders and hips moved on instinct, attempting to swim despite my broken limbs. You and Anat appeared within the mist, hovering over me.

"Do we have your full attention now?" You asked. You

didn't pull me from the water, but allowed me to dip below and reemerge, hacking up lake water tinged by my own blood. My bones struggled to knit back together to give me the ability to swim. Death was close but unattainable. As it has always been for me.

"What will it take to get you on our side?" Anat asked.

Her body began pulsing with heat aimed at me. Steam rose from the lake. My skin was burning and flaking. My right arm healed just enough for me to paddle and stay afloat. I coughed. I laughed. I coughed again.

"Simon is planning on leaving you already," I called up to the cloud. "And Anat is planning on making you her servant once she has the Island. She never saw you as a peer."

The heat eased. I'd created a difficult moment. I was a god in my own right and, when pressed, I can breed chaos that can destroy cities and untangle the tightest of loves. And, in that chaos, comes opportunity. My words pried open Anat's mind like a planet's crust gaping from a quake. I leapt inside.

In her imagination, she was small and sitting alone in a large, empty house. There was knocking on the door, but she wasn't supposed to answer when her father was away. Her focus remained on a small bundle of knitting. Her fingers worked. A scarf. Another gift for her father who would never wear it. The knocking continued, eternal. She was isolated, afraid, and certain that her father worked so many long hours because he couldn't stand her presence. Just like everyone else she'd ever met. She deserved to be left alone.

"Get out!" the little girl screamed.

I was now standing beside her as she continued knitting.

"Most people never feel me step inside," I said.

"I'm not most people."

"No, you are definitely not most people," I said. "You've

chosen the wrong king."

"He is powerful."

Her fingers were moving fast, pulling thread, winding, working.

"Is he powerful enough?" I asked.

"Get out. Please."

I left her mind and dove into yours. There you stood on a darkened stage, no audience, a lone spotlight pouring down. You held two brass rings, clinking them together. Over and over. Clink. Clink. Clink. You were confused. The trick wasn't working. Disembodied grumbling, boos, and heckles erupted all around. You were sweating. Clink. Clink. Clink. Your hands stiffened, burst into fire. The rings dropped. The fire consumed you.

My work done, I dropped back into my half-drowned body bobbing in the water. More bones were healed. I could swim. I watched you and your queen dissolve into the mist. Your cloud darkened to gray and turned onto itself.

"I have burned in a sea of fire," I told you. "I cannot be hurt, I cannot be intimidated, I cannot be bullied. But I can be reasoned with. Unite the Island, Simon. Then we can talk."

The mist swept toward the far shore. There, I saw you and your queen materialize on the sand. You watched me. You tried not to look at each other. It was delicious and shameful.

I turned in the water and began the long swim back to the campground.

Being A Child God
Part 12

I hated you like I'd never hated anyone. I'd lost my footing. I was out of tricks. I was out of words to mend or even conceal the divide between Anat and I. We were exposed and I was enraged.

Misdirected anger, as a therapist would say.

Back at the fortress, we found it devoid of the atheist.

I kinda lost my shit. "Why can't anyone just stay in one goddamn place for one goddamn second? We're housing her death camp survivors. What more do I need to do? Why is everyone so resistant to everything I'm trying to do? Why is this so hard? These fuckers are fighting us every step for what? For that fat sack of hot garbage across the lake who doesn't care about us and enjoys our suffering?"

I kicked at a rock, but it was buried and immovable. My toes crunched. I cursed and railed and acted like a loon. Anat just watched.

"She isn't protecting God," she said. "You know that."

I slumped to the ground. I kicked at the rock with the heel of my foot just to show I couldn't be beaten so easily, then worked on getting my breaths back under control. I hated being angry. I hated everything about the feeling.

"I'm going to be your servant?" I asked.

"Don't let him do that to us."

But you already had. I took my time, measuring my words. "I don't know what to do."

Anat held up her hands, glowing orange, her white dress fading, revealing her beautiful body.

"Come to me, I will make you feel better."

I wanted to. My body urged me on, assuring me that she would understand. She would not judge.

"I can't," I said. "I want to but I can't. I've got to figure this out."

Her orange glow faded to purple. Fire erupted from her skin enveloping her like a robe. She was getting more powerful. I was intimidated. I was sick with longing.

When it hurts. Run.

Sounded like good advice. The Fabulous Fallimento collected divorces like the Yankees collected championship trophies. Retreat was a compelling thought, but it wasn't so easy to run away from a goddess.

Especially on the Island, where there was nowhere to run.

"We have power," I said. "More than God. More than the Engineers. They just won't listen. I can't convince anyone of anything."

"You've convinced me," Anat said.

I looked to her and the anger evaporated. Love is like that sometimes, the sun that burns away the storm clouds.

"Diplomacy is hard," Anat said. "But it must be done. We will find a way. We just need a diplomat. Someone who can reason with them. Someone who isn't bound by a history of faith, someone who is able to strip away the magic and awe and find the logic beneath."

"The atheist."

"You brought her here for a reason," Anat said.

"Maybe I was just hoping for a three-way."

Anat rose an eyebrow, studying me. She looked away, motioning to torches on the walls. Each burst to life.

"Find the atheist."

"Yes, ma'am."

I gazed at the spectacle of her. She rewarded me with a proud smile.

"I'll take her to Edward," I said. "If we can get an atheist and a priest to speak for us, then the Wilderness will follow."

Anat approached me, the flames from her burning robe reaching for my skin like seductive lips searching my body. It was wonderful and agonizing.

"Why are you resisting me?" Anat asked. "Why won't you let me make you forget?"

"I will. Let me sort a few things out. Let me earn it."

She smiled down at me.

"Then go. Ignite our revolution."

The Atheist

Julia followed her heart to the stovepipe. She hated the magical. She resented that something beyond logic compelled her forward, that there was an element of destiny to her life. She didn't believe in the divine. She believed in chaos, the absence of Intelligent Design. Yet, there was a design and she felt it leading her into the woods like a whisper just within earshot.

And it led her right to the artist.

"Petrov," Julia whispered into the pipe. Her voice bounced down the pipe, deep into the earth.

"You found me," a hollow voice returned.

"Of course. Sherlock's got nothing on me. Where's your girl?"

"I don't know," Petrov said. "Wherever she is, she is suffering. They won't know how to care for her."

"And you do?" Julia asked.

"I know that I want to try."

Julia allowed some time for the turmoil within her to calm. She really hated her heart sometimes.

"I'm going to save you, Petrov."

"You will be stuffed inside a stove right next to me if you try, my dear."

"Motherfuckers can try."

"Julia," I called from behind her. I was in my child's form.

She turned and studied me.

"Give me a moment," she whispered into the pipe, then stood and approached me.

"Release him, Simon," she said. "Find the girl's head."

"I'm getting a lot of demands these days, but I'm not seeing a lot of return on investment."

"He's your friend," she said.

"True."

Julia's nostrils flared and her eyes narrowed. "What do you want? And if you ask for a three-way, I'm gonna rip your nuts off."

I smirked and shook my head. "I think I might have an image problem."

"You're a guy. You think like any other guy."

I sighed. "Let's get back on message. I want to dethrone God. You want to dethrone God. We can't do that without the help of the Engineers and the Americans. I want you to be my emissary. I need your help reasoning with them."

"Fuck the Americans."

"Yes, fuck God. Fuck the Americans. Fuck authority. I feel the same way, but unfortunately we need help if we want to bring liberty to the Island."

Julia smirked at the right edge of her mouth. Her eyebrow arched. "You want me to play kingmaker?"

"Yes."

"And how do I insure you won't be even worse than God?" Julia asked.

"I know my limits, Julia. I can't beat the Engineers, the Americans, and God. Not all on my own. This is going to have to be a power-sharing situation if it's going to work. We are remaking reality at its core."

Julia turned to the stovepipe.

"You'll get him out? You'll help him find his girlfriend?"

"If you convince the Engineers to join me, I will free Petrov and I will find the head. Not before. I need you properly motivated."

"You're kind of a dick, huh?"

I shrugged. Julia walked back to the Petrov.

"Simon is going to get you soon," she said into the pipe. "I have to do something for him first."

"Just free her," Petrov said. "I will be okay, but get her somewhere safe. Somewhere she can be cared for. I will be okay. I have survived worse than this."

Julia didn't respond. She stood.

"Find the head first," she said to me, but didn't turn to face me. "Save the head, then I will go to the Engineers. Once I have them on board, then you save Petrov."

I folded my arms tightly. I resented my role as diplomat more and more every day. I was beginning to understand the value of fire and brimstone.

"Okay, fine," I said. "I'll take you to the Engineers, let you get acquainted. I'll fetch the head and bring it to them. The Engineers will know best what to do about her. Deal?"

Julia nodded.

I gasped out mist.

"We'll be back for you!" Julia called to Petrov, just before she evaporated. Even as I swept her into the sky, I felt her pulling back down to the painter.

I'd never carried someone so stubborn.

Edward The Fallen
Part 5

Yulia finally spoke. "Everything you've told me. Everything you've proposed is with the assumption that Simon is still alive."

The burning branches of the tree cast flickering shadows across the room. Tabitha hummed her gentle, endless song. Edward had prepared for a riotous debate, but the Engineers were only absorbing the information. If there was to be an argument, it would wait until Edward and Tommy were gone. Their restraint was inspiring.

"I saw him consumed by the explosion," Yulia continued. "He could be dead."

"He's not," Edward said. "Simon is too squirrelly to be killed by one explosion. And if I am wrong, then we figure something else out. But there are two things that I am absolutely certain of."

Edward paused, searching the faces of the elderly Engineers. He'd yet to normalize their nude bodies, but admired their gentle society, the kind he'd never thought was sustainable outside of the church. He felt more comfortable now throwing in with this group of mystics, even if it was in support of a man/boy sorcerer who was challenging God.

Edward took a deep breath, allowing the words to sort out in his mind before he spoke. Every sentence carried significant weight and he didn't want to rush a single syllable.

"One," Edward began. "God's power has diminished as ours has grown, which makes Him vulnerable, which makes Him scared. This makes Him the most dangerous person on the Island. He has behaved, since I've arrived here, in an erratic and selfish manner. He refuses to share any of His plans for the Island nor do we have any idea of what He expects or wants from us. Aside from another plane and that may be the only leverage we will ever have over Him. Two: the Americans will get worse if we let them. We cannot allow fanaticism to turn this potential Eden into a battle zone."

"Eden?" Yulia asked, then chuckled. A few of the other Engineers smiled and shook their head. "This will never be an Eden, Edward."

"It will if we let it," Edward said.

Yulia took a few moments to study Edward.

"But what you are proposing will only push America into fanaticism," Yulia said. "The Mayor has explosives now. We think we know what she is using, but we don't know how, which means the power has now tipped away from us. Also, if God believes Simon is planning a mutiny, God will respond forcefully. He doesn't respond well to rivalries and carries grudges for a very, very long time."

"All we want is to be left alone so we can study the Island,"

Moonbeam said. "Simon is the disruptive force. Without Simon, we have a genuine hope that God will continue favoring us with His absence. There is still so much we don't understand about this world or God's true power. You are asking us to risk a war waged with weapons we don't understand and against an enemy whose capabilities are still a mystery. I'm having trouble envisioning victory anywhere in your plan."

Edward wasn't in a hurry to respond. He struggled to construct an answer. Every response seemed brittle and short-sighted. He was also in awe of the very fact that he was arguing for the direct challenge of God's divine authority. He'd come quite a long way since seminary.

He felt Tommy's hand touch his arm. Tommy cleared his throat before speaking.

"I get your hesitation. I really do, but you are assuming God will just hide out forever. But He won't. As we argue, He is working out this problem. He isn't just scared, He's pissed, and eventually He'll reassert Himself. Whether or not Simon was smart to toss the plane off the Island, he did and now God is, for the first time in creation, vulnerable. The only certainty is God will now try to tame the Wilderness once He has figured out how and, if history is any indication, we are going to Hell for even considering this."

"You are saying we are already committed?" Yulia asked.

Tommy nodded. "God is jealous and embarrassed. We are all doomed unless we take the fight to Him."

"If we are united," Edward said. "Then we can use our collective strength to persuade Simon to negotiate peace with New Wichita. If New Wichita sees that they are isolated in the Wilderness, they will be forced to give up their ovens and look for a more humane way to deal with their prisoners. Then the Wilderness will become a single front."

"And we will trade the God of the Jews for a manic magician

with Small Man Syndrome?" Moonbeam asked.

"It won't be the same," Edward said.

"Won't it? Pastor, I think you aren't seeing the issue clearly." Moonbeam looked to the other Engineers. Silent nods were exchanged. "Even so, this idea is worth exploring. If we can tame Simon, that would be better than killing him. If we can defeat God, that would be better than submitting to Him. Your plan is foolish, but it may still be our best option."

"If we Defeat God and force Him to negotiate a peace treaty, what are we going to ask for?" Yulia asked. "Who will be at that table? How will the Wilderness make decisions? Are we building a true nation now? Is that what you are really proposing?"

"Yes," Edward said. "I think that is the only way forward."

"You are asking us to give up our freedom," Moonbeam said. "You do realize that? A government always involves a surrender of liberty."

"Yes, but would you prefer to surrender some freedom to your fellow humans or all of your freedom to God?"

Moonbeam smiled. She looked to Yulia.

"I like you, Edward," Yulia said. "More than I anticipated. But we are mourning the loss of a great woman today because we angered God. I am not prepared to put more lives on the line for such a vague, ill-formed plan."

Mutters of agreement arose from the other Engineers.

"Give us time," Yulia said. "Perhaps from this foundation, we can build something worth fighting for. Something worth dying for."

"I understand," Edward said. "We appreciate your time. You know where to find me when you want to talk again."

Tabitha unfolded her legs, opened her eyes and stood. The blue flames dissipated, the tree withered and shrank, its branches retreating. It resumed its bent, weary, and tiny form in the center of the room. Yulia gestured for Edward and Tommy to leave. The Engineers parted, allowing them a path out of the Great Salon and into the dusk. The lovers began walking down the steps. Tommy's hand found Edward's.

"That went better than I expected," Tommy said.

Edward squeezed Tommy's hand. "Thank you for your help."

"Of course, but you did the heavy lifting. They respect you, but this is a big gamble. You are a pastor leading bickering tribes into an all-out war. Regardless of whether Simon is alive or dead, we are marching straight into conflict. You know that, right?"

"Yes. I'm counting on it."

Commotion rose from inside the Salon. Edward turned to look back. The Engineers poured out the door, some leaping all the way from the opening down over the steps, and landing on the ground. Edward and Tommy moved out of the way as Yulia stormed past.

"Show yourself!" Yulia shouted into the trees as the Engineers gathered at the base of the temple.

A child laughed. The same voice laughed from another direction, then another, and another until The Engineers were surrounded by the disembodied voices. The Engineers looked to each other, weary. The shrill laugh grew louder.

Edward smiled.

The laughter stopped. A cloud swirled down like a tornado, touching down only a few feet from the Engineers. The cloud faded and a figure materialized. It wasn't Simon, but a woman he'd never seen before.

"Enchantée," she said with a mocking curtsy.

"The atheist," Earnest said to Yulia, who nodded.

"You've joined the magician?" Yulia asked.

Julia walked towards the temple and stopped in front of Yulia. "'Join' is such an ugly word. But I do know how to spot a winner."

Raul and His Lovely Guitar
Part 4

Not much was spoken, there was no plan, there was only restlessness. The others slept under a slim sliver of moonlight as the musicians slipped away. Edna wondered if Raul would try to kiss her as they crossed the woods. She wouldn't have minded, but he didn't and she thought that was better.

The fishermen were already out that night, their boats quietly skimming over the lake, their lures plunking into the water. One man had a nibble, but nothing more. A beautiful, busty, but hard-edged woman watched Edna and Raul walking along the shore. She pointed toward bushes to where Raul found an unused boat.

"It's got a bit of a leak, but it'll get you to where you're going," the woman said.

"Where do you think we are going?" Edna asked.

"Everyone knows where your people are headed," the woman said. "And you're going to get us all killed in the process."

Raul wasn't certain what to say.

The woman smiled. "And I hope you do." She approached the boat, helped Raul clear away the shrubs and, the three of them pulled the boat to the water. She waved without enthusiasm as Raul and Edna pointed the bow south toward the campground.

Edna couldn't make sense of the stars as Raul rowed. Her mother had taught her rudimentary astronomy back on the Kansas farm as they gazed at the big sky of glimmering stars. She'd dreamed of one day moving to a coast and sailing by the patterns of the night sky. She never made it further south than Dallas.

Since Edna had arrived on the Island, she'd never found patterns consistent from one night to the next. She wondered what a telescope would reveal. Maybe stars blossoming from distant creations? Vague blurs from God's unfinished illusion? Angels hurriedly painting a grand dome set over the Island, their wings flapping, their brushes unsteady, the strokes haphazard. Paint cans strapped to their waists would be dripping and jostling. The drops would fall into the lake and create life. Koi fish and melody.

Unsatisfied with their work, God would tear down the heavens and demand they start again the next night.

Edna's fingers tapped against the edge of the rowboat, imagining ivory keys underneath. Raul watched her and could almost hear the music playing in her mind. He was more anxious to get her to a piano than he'd ever been to lure a woman to bed.

Only the light post burned bright within the dark campground. They'd never discussed the possibility of being caught or how they might escape. Just get to the piano. Raul was without a guitar and knew that he must create music or die.

The boat clunked against the pier. Raul grimaced and looked to God's cabin. No lights blinked on. No movement seen through the windows. He climbed up to the pier and tied off the boat. Edna took his hand and stepped up onto the pier. They took slow, careful steps across the planks. Once they reached the grass, they sprinted to the cover of the mess hall. Raul cupped his hands against the glass and looked inside. The piano sat where he'd last seen it.

They curled around the building, testing the back door first. It was locked. They ran to the front door, but it was also locked. Edna rose her eyebrows in silent panic. Raul stepped back, looked across the walls, then at the windows. He motioned to a park bench. They grabbed it from both ends, walked it over to the mess hall, and sat it beneath a window. Raul climbed up, tested the window and it slid open. Raul's dashing smile almost made Edna laugh. She stepped up next to him and accepted his boost up into the window. She shimmied through the opening, pausing halfway through to examine the shadows of the mess hall. She didn't see life, so she eased a leg through, keeping her hands locked on the window frame. The other foot took more finesse before it slipped free of the frame and she swung down. She held for a few moments, then dropped to the tile. Raul wormed through with the grace of a cat burglar.

He grabbed a table and slid it to the window, stepping onto it and shutting the window tight.

They stood for a few moments, staring at each other, then at the piano.

"Well?" Raul said.

Edna took a few steps, but stopped.

"They are going to hear and come right away," Edna said.

"Are you really going to tell me we came all this way just to look at the piano?" Raul asked.

"No. Of course not. I'm just nervous. I've never liked getting in trouble."

Raul took her hand.

"Then let's make it worth it."

The piano keys were dusty and cool. It was a Grotrian upright. She knew the brand only because her aunt worked in a music store in Topeka and would allow Edna to play on the pianos when her family visited.

"Play the Grotrian while you can, darling," her aunt said. "It sings!"

And it did. The tone had reminded young Edna of hollowed-out logs, lonely frogs, and the mating calls of giants. So much better than the battered old mule that sat in her own home. Her father refused to pay to have it tuned, so the piano just grew wearier and more discordant with each passing season.

Edna's left thumb settled on middle C. Raul sat on her left and scanned the keys, then found his own position. Edna lifted her hands off the keys.

"I can't think of a single thing to play," she said. She was crying, but not in a sorrowful way. More that her excited, fluttering heart was beating too much giddiness through her body. Some of it needed to escape out of her eyes.

She used her shoulder to dry the tears, then laughed.

"I'm sorry you don't have a true pianist and are stuck with me."

Raul took her hands in his. She looked at him.

"Just play and I will follow," he said.

She nodded. Another tear dropped and imprinted in the dust on a key. She used her shirt to clear the key off and the piano pinged softly. She took a deep breath and settled her fingers down on the keys. Raul's found his keys again.

She began with a fractured memory of a somber chamber score, playing through the blanks with flourishes and improvisation. Raul played around her sound, skilled at the music but unpracticed and unsteady with a piano. That she was better trained gave her confidence. She could make up for someone else's clumsiness for once. She charged ahead into Mozart. She didn't remember the complete music, but filled in with imagination where memory failed. It flowed well enough and Raul followed with energy and passion. They were winding around each other like two dancers: one poised and technical, the other athletic and enthused. Adrenaline buzzed through her skin. She chased a stray thought into a ragtime number and Raul galloped behind her.

Their fingers touched briefly as they crossed positions, then retreated like shy lovers. She began playing a Beatles song that she'd not thought of since she was a teenager. She couldn't remember the words, but that cheeky melody came through as clear as a blue, summer sky.

She became more aware of Raul's heat. His heaviness beside her. The music slowed. It beckoned. *This was … oh who was it?* she thought. One of those sappy ballads her mother adored. Something about lights. She didn't know why she played it, but continued anyway. Raul was right on top of her. He had to know the song. Or maybe he knew her now. Their fingers brushed again. Their shoulders were touching. Then came Beethoven and Edna knew she was treading into dangerous waters.

She lifted her hands. Sweat was on her brow. Her breaths were heavy and her face flushed. She steadied. She laughed.

"I think I need a cigarette," she said.

A hand appeared from behind Edna's shoulder, placing a glass of water on the piano.

Edna jumped against Raul. He held her with one hand, the other hand up defensively.

"Settle," God said. He wore a pale blue robe, bunny slippers, and black Ray-Ban sunglasses. He backed from the piano and took a seat at a mess table. "Please, don't let me interrupt."

Raul stood first, then Edna..

"I'm sorry," Raul said. "This was my idea."

"Yes, I know," God said. "I created you, after all."

"Yeah, right," Raul said, relaxing a bit. "This piano is important. We'll leave, just keep this piano here, okay?"

"But no one is here to play it," God said. "None of the souls I've brought have any passion for music. Aside from the two of you."

Raul shifted on his feet, looking briefly to Edna, then to the mess hall door left open. Jay watched from the other side.

"Can we have the piano?" Edna asked. "Can we take it with us to the Wilderness."

"No," God said. "But if you stay here, with Me, you can play it anytime you want."

"But I thought this side was only for children," Raul said.

"Very soon, there will be no place on the Island suitable for children," God said. "Not while Simon and his witch are alive."

"Are you going to kill them?" Edna asked.

God shook his head. He stood and walked to the kitchen. His bunny slippers made scratchy sounds against the concrete floor. Edna looked to Raul briefly. Raul shrugged. Edna reached for the water and took a drink. Her lips welcomed the hydration. Her body hummed. She only wanted to play the piano again, try to find that moment with Raul again. It felt like love. It felt more like love than anything she'd ever experienced. Not the kind where marriage and sex and kids follow, but the kind where she felt understood. Truly understood and accepted. She didn't want to ruin it with sex or romance. She hoped Raul felt the same way.

God returned with a guitar case. He sat the guitar down by the piano, then returned to His seat at the table. He watched them. They watched Him. The guitar and the piano remained silent.

"What are you asking of us?" Raul asked.

"For you to stay with me," God said. "No matter what happens. As long as you stay, I will give you any instrument you ask for. Don't go back to the Wilderness. I will house you, feed you. All you have to do is play them for Me."

"Where do the instruments come from?" Raul asked.

"Does it matter?"

Raul glanced at Edna, then down to the guitar. He sat so she sat. He picked up the case and placed it on his lap.

"I don't understand," Edna said. "Are you lonely? Is that what this is about?"

"Does it matter?"

Edna looked to Raul, then to the piano. She turned swiveled on the bench to face the piano. Raul unlatched the guitar case and lifted out a Breedlove acoustic. Raul laughed.

"What?" Edna asked.

"This is the most expensive guitar I've ever held," Raul said.

God allowed a proud smile. "I've got a little pull."

"If you can get this, why not get another plane?" Edna asked.

God took a long breath, then propped His elbows up on the table. "I don't have that much pull. Not anymore. Not yet, anyway. But, please, play Me something."

Raul nodded and ran his fingers over the ebony fretboard. "Damn." Raul swirled on the bench so his back was facing Edna, barely touching her shoulder. He strapped on the guitar and threw his lot back in with the Creator.

How To Properly Manage A Young Empire
Part 9

The Island stars glowed from The Mayor's nightstand. Their glimmer caught the mirrors in the room and bounced across the Mansion in an endless loop of light.

She'd fallen to sleep gazing at them, then awoke in the middle of the night to gaze at them some more. In the darkness, more of the life within was evident, moving in lazy curly Q's and slithery S's. Tiny beads of darkness like black crystals, tiny distillations of God's mystery and immense power.

She noticed a dimming. Not in the stars, but in the cave. She glanced out her window to the cavern's opening, seeing the mist pour in, diminishing the moonlight. Her heart soured.

"Damn."

She watched the mist weaving through downtown. She considered rising, retrieving a robe, and confronting Simon. But he was coming to her.

She laid back in bed and waited.

The mist fell against the mansion like a crashing wave, sweeping up and engulfing the facade. Simon's face briefly surfaced, looking into The Mayor's bedroom window. The Mayor met his eyes. The face disappeared and the mist found the cracks in the windows, slipping inside the room in tiny jets of white smoke.

The laughter started as a whisper but grew as the mist gathered.

"Have you come to ravish me?" The Mayor asked.

The laughter stopped.

"What?" Simon asked.

"Are you the faceless attacker from my dreams? The disembodied deviant? Should I fight you or just lay back and allow it to happen?"

"What?"

The Mayor threw off her blankets, showing off her naked body, and leaned up.

"Umm, I'm married," Simon said, shaken.

"Maybe I'm into this kind of thing," The Mayor said, enjoying the sound of Simon on the defensive.

The mist formed the older Simon and his white on white on white suit. With quite a bit of effort, he kept his eyes averted. The Mayor sat up in the bed, threw her legs over the side, and grabbed her robe off the side table.

"You know, I really thought we'd managed to kill you," she said as she stood and covered herself.

"You came close," Simon said. His eyes swept the room and settled on the stars. "They are pretty, aren't they?"

"Power always is. How did you get one to explode without sacrificing yourself?"

"I just wanted it bad enough."

The Mayor narrowed her eyes, then looked to the Star. She pointed out her index finger, aiming at the star, and rose her thumb to mimic a pistol.

"Pweh," she said, playfully shooting the star. Its glow didn't shift at all.

"Didn't want it bad enough," Simon said.

"Then let's work together," The Mayor said, walking towards Simon. He retreated against a wall.

"In all seriousness," Simon said, eyes averted. "My wife is the jealous type and will burn this entire town to the ground."

She enjoyed the leverage, keeping the magician pressed against the wall through her will and his fear. Finally, she turned and walked to the stars. She plucked one from the table and held it up.

"So, if I make this explode, maybe that would finish the job?"

"Maybe," Simon said, watching the star glow brighter in her hand. "But you won't sacrifice yourself for that."

"Are you sure?" The Mayor asked. "I do like to win."

Her fingers squeezed the star. It sparkled as its flesh bulged around her fingers.

Simon burst into mist, flooding the room, then materialized again, holding both stars. The Mayor looked to her empty hand, then shrugged and folded her arms over her chest.

"I'll find more," The Mayor said. "We'll kill you one of these days."

"Or," Simon said, juggling the stars in one hand. "We negotiate a permanent ceasefire."

The Mayor studied Simon. She walked back to the bed and sat down on the edge.

"You will leave us alone?" The Mayor asked. "You'll respect our sovereignty?"

"Not as such," Simon said. "We are going to unite the Island and vote out The Old Man. Me, you, the Engineers, the outcasts, the fishermen, everyone. One Island."

"Under your rule?" The Mayor asked.

"No. I lack the motivation and the organizational skills to be a proper dictator. I was thinking more a constitutional democratic monarchy."

"I don't trust you with that much power, Simon. We aren't going to just change the way we do things because we are afraid of some magic tricks and the rogue explosion. We are a moral people. We will rule our land how we choose."

"But that's the thing. That morality is based on the hope of impressing a god that doesn't give a shit about you. You're hoping to impress Him for what? To get sent back to Heaven? To be given more power?"

The Mayor held her hand out for the stars. "Maybe He will sweep our enemies off the Island?"

Simon rolled his eyes, then lowered his hands. Both stars floated in the air. They drifted towards The Mayor. She reached for one, but it darted out of the way. It swung towards her face. She held her ground, but did turn her face slightly away from them as they approached. The white intensified in the stars, then a red flooded and swirled like storm waters. Within moments they were hovering blood moons.

"If you fight me," Simon said. "It's going to get very ugly."

"Can you cut me a better deal than God?" The Mayor asked.

"Maybe I can," Simon said. The stars cooled back to white and floated past The Mayor. They landed softly on the nightstand.

"You are just going to leave them here?" The Mayor asked.

"Like you said, you'll find more," Simon said. "And consider it a show of goodwill."

"In exchange for what?"

"Petrov came here with a severed head. I need it."

The Mayor sat back on the bed. "Why?"

"Leverage."

The Mayor titled her head and smirked. "Okay. She's downstairs in my sink."

"You put her in the sink?"

"Where else does one put a living severed head?"

Simon couldn't think of an answer, so instead shrugged.

"Take her," The Mayor said with a wave of the hand. "She doesn't mean anything to me."

"Then why did you chop off her head?"

"Ask her. She'll tell you all about it."

"Yeesh. Low blow, Miss Mayor." Simon moved to the bedroom

door. "Funny, but really low." Simon opened it a crack before looking back at The Mayor. "When we take this Island away from God. We can rewrite all of the rules. We get to create our own morality. All the laws of the Bible become irrelevant."

"Your point being?"

"You won't need the ovens anymore."

"You sweet, naive little boy."

"Just think on it," Simon said, then evaporated. His mist fled through the cracks of the bedroom door.

The Mayor looked back upon the stars. She rose her hand like a pistol again. She focused, aimed at the stars carefully.

"Pweh."

The light wavered toward pink. The Mayor smiled.

Yulia Creates So Many Lovely Things
Part 5

The atheist removed her legionnaire jacket and sat quietly along the wall of the Salon. Tabitha sat before the small tree, began humming, and the fire bloomed. The tree stretched, sprouting out its glowing limbs, and filled the room with light. Julia watched, unimpressed.

Yulia and the Engineers surrounded Julia, looking down upon her, waiting.

Julia said nothing.

Edward sat down and Tommy followed. The Engineers eased down to the ground. They were left with only the crackling of the fire within the branches, the dancing shadows, and Julia's curious, silent gaze passing across the group.

"I think it is time for new clothes, my dear," Yulia said.

Julia glanced down at her gypsy dress and picked at the fabric. She shrugged, then eased back against the wall.

"So, are we going to talk?" Earnest asked.

"Shhhh," Julia said, pressing her finger to her lips. "Be patient."

Some muttering arose, but Yulia held up her hand. The Engineers settled as Edward watched the atheist. She met his gaze, smiled, then closed her eyes. She leaned her head back against the wall and seemed to sleep.

Tabitha's back arched. Her eyes opened and she stopped humming. Earnest took in a quick breath and said "Simon!" The tree shrank and the Engineers ran out of the Salon.

At the foot of the steps was the severed head. Her beautiful eyes, now deeply sunken but still alive, looked up at the Engineers. Above, Simon's mist swept away.

Yulia and a few other Engineers ran down the steps, surrounding the head. Her eyes watched the naked mystics looming above her. She attempted to smile, but her pale, gray and blue skin was too dry. Her muscles were too weak. Yulia bent over and picked up the head.

"You poor thing," Yulia said.

"Good," Julia said from the door of the Salon. "Petrov wants the head cared for. Do what you have to. I am now ready to discuss the future of the Island."

Yulia looked from the head to Julia. Yulia handed the head to a heavy woman with a shaved head.

"Take her to Barry and Mary."

The Engineer nodded, cradled the head carefully, then sprinted at a shocking speed toward the northwest. Yulia scaled the steps slowly, studying Julia.

"Who was that?" Yulia asked.

"Someone who is very important to someone who is very important to me," the atheist said. She turned and walked back into the Salon.

***

Julia stood in front of the flames. She reached out her hand, testing for the heat which wasn't there. "A fistful of rope lights would be so much easier, you know?"

"We are suckers for spectacle," Yulia said. "What does Simon want?"

"I don't know," Julia said. "I know what he told me, but I have no idea if he is being straight with me. Why don't you tell me what you want first?"

"To be left alone," Yulia said.

"God's not going to do that, right?"

Yulia shrugged. "He will if Simon stops provoking Him."

The atheist looked at Edward.

"What do your people want?" Julia asked.

"To find our place," Edward said.

Julia nodded.

"You know what I want? I want to stop living by laws and moral codes constructed by misogynist, racist xenophobes thousands of years before I was born. That's all I've ever wanted. There is absolutely no reason why our perception of proper morality should have carried over to the Island. Those ovens in New Wichita only exist because we are hanging onto old ways that have zero bearing on our current existence. But we can't move on until we remove The All Powerful Pretender and start anew."

"With Simon on the throne?" Yulia asked.

"Yes, and do you want to know why?"

Earnest laughed. "Please, enlighten us."

"Simon is a pussy. He can be hurt. He can be angered and defied. The people on this Island do not see him as salvation. Will he be a king? Maybe. But kings come and kings go. Unlike gods who tend to linger for long past their relevance. Also, we have Anat, who is even more powerful. Have you met her?"

The Engineers rustled and murmured.

"No, but we know what she can do," Moonbeam said.

"Then you know she'll be a pretty potent counterweight," Julia said.

"Perhaps," Moonbeam said.

"Do you really think we can overthrow God?" Edward asked, the question feeling absurd and vile as it left his lips.

"Maybe? Who cares? We can try and what is the very worst He can do?" Julia asked.

"Send us to Hell," Moonbeam said.

""I've been there and it's not so bad," Julia said. "Also, can

He? How is He gonna get us there? Maybe He can toss us off the Island and maybe we blink into nothingness, but who knows?"

"God does," Edward said. "How do you know He hasn't planned this all out as some elaborate trap?"

"Then we lose," Julia said. "Then He sends us to Hell or maybe somewhere even more horrible. But maybe we win and then we are, for the first time in all of creation, free. Truly free. No more ovens, no more idolatry or religious fanaticism. We rule this Island on reason. On justice."

"With Simon and Anat in charge? You are insane," Earnest said.

"They will know we can do to them what we did to God," Julia said. "Here is the truth. We don't know what's possible on this Island. Maybe we can get back to Heaven or wherever we came from. Maybe we can build the Island bigger. Maybe we can build rocket ships and travel to the stars. We won't ever know with God looming over us. He has always held us back as a species. His rules. His jealousy. His need for worship like some desperate debutante who feeds only on adoration and diet Red Bull. Fuck that. Fuck Him. It is our time, right now. You are afraid of Simon? Well, organize. Form a government. Checks and balances and the threat of rebellion will keep Simon in place."

"And the Americans?" Yulia asked.

"They are horrible people, but they are people. They are part of us, even if we don't like them. War is coming. There is no doubt about it, so the decision isn't about whether or not to fight. It is about who we are fighting. The God who betrayed His promise to you and is holding you hostage or a second-rate magician turned second-rate demigod and a phoenix goddess? I've seen what God had to offer and it led to endless wars, slavery, institutional sexism, homophobia, and brutal tribalism. Let's go another route. We have the chance. Let's fucking take it."

"Can I just vote for you instead?" Tommy asked.

Laughter wafted through the room.

"But I'm serious," Tommy said.

"I'm not politician," Julia said.

Moonbeam stepped forward.

"You are sure we can control Simon and Anat?"

"No," Julia said. "But we can turn them against each other. Anat is our nuclear option and he will fall in line if he fears losing her. We get her on our wavelength, Simon will always follow."

Yulia whispered into Moonbeam's ear. She nodded and stepped out of the Salon.

"Tell Simon and the Americans we want a meeting," Yulia said.

"God will sense the uprising," Edward warned. "He will come."

"Let Him," Julia said. "Let Him try. The sooner the better. Aren't you ready to be free, Edward?"

Edward looked at Tommy. Took his hand.

"More than anything."

Barry And Mary and Domestic Bliss
Part 4

The spring waters possessed an odd, warm, tickle. An all over tickle. It unnerved Willow, felt impure, but Trevor was doing so well that she carried on. She held his body so his face remained above water. His beautiful face. No more burn marks, no blemishes. His black hair was growing back. Not his arms or legs, but Willow didn't mind. It made her feel safer. He couldn't leave her. She knew it was a horrible thing to be comforted by, but she decided to just let it be. Shame never did her any good anyhow.

"A three bedroom Tudor in New England," Trevor said, his eyes closed, absorbing the energy of the spring.

"I don't know what that is."

Trevor pried open one eye and looked at Willow. Her beauty always surprised him like the glory of a sunset.

"A house. A cute, simple house. That would be good for us, I think. A simple life with simple things in a simple area filled with interesting, kind people."

"That sounds nice," Willow said. She smiled easily with Trevor.

"Perhaps we retire and spend a half-year in Chicago or New York or Barcelona, but we always come back to the simple house."

"I'll bake you apple cinnamon pancakes and I'll dress like *Little Shop of Horrors*," Willow said. "No blood or scary plants, though."

"No, of course not."

Her smile grew as she imagined. "And we'll build one of those big machines like in *Pee Wee's Big Adventure* so that you can cook me breakfast and all you gotta to do is hit a button with your nose and watch the machine go!"

"Sounds like a perfect plan," Trevor said.

Willow pulled Trevor close and pressed a kiss against his lips. He leaned into it. Willow would miss being held, but this was good too. More than good. It was the best it had ever been for her.

"You kids are adorable," Mary said as she walked in from a side cave.

Barry followed with a severed head.

Willow shrieked and pulled Trevor tight against her.

Mary giggled, pulled her skirt up over her head, then folded it neatly and laid it on the ground. She stepped down into the springs, then motioned to Barry for the head. He handed it gently to her. Mary lowered the head into the water so only the neck was submerged, keeping the woman's chin just above the water. The woman's tight, anguished face warmed. Her grimace softened. Her eyes closed. Her face flushed from greyish-blue to a soft pink. Her dry, brittle hair softened to a dark blond.

"Who is that?" Willow asked, trying to stay calm, but edging a little further to the opposite side of the spring.

"I don't know," Mary said. "A friend asked us to care for her, so that's what we are going to do."

"How is she still alive?" Willow asked.

"How am I still alive?" Trevor asked.

Willow frowned. She leaned Trevor back, steady against the edge. She stepped through the water to the head.

"May I?" she asked. Mary eased the head to her like a newborn baby.

Willow took it softly. She lowered in the water so she could look directly into the head's eyes.

"What's your name?" Willow asked, though the head couldn't answer. The head's smile emerged, weak, but warm. "Can I give you a name?"

The head blinked once. Willow took that as a yes.

"Michelle," Willow said. "It was my sister. She was beautiful and took good care of me when I was a young 'un. She died before I could return the favor. Can I call you Michelle?"

The head blinked once again.

"Michelle," Willow echoed. Barry sat beside the spring and placed a hand on Mary's shoulder. She turned, kissed it, then folded her hand over his. Willow carried the head back and sat next to Trevor.

"Would you be willing to look after her for a little bit?" Mary asked. "Barry and I have something we need to do."

Willow didn't look up from the head. "Ya'll go on. We're good here."

"And don't get too attached," Mary said. "Petrov is going to come fetch her before long."

"Then he can stay with us, too," Willow said. "We'll be a family. He'll paint the walls all pretty, we'll dress like the Brady Bunch, bake apple pies, and play Monopoly when we don't have to get up too early in the morning."

Digging to Heaven
Part 5

More workers poured into the mines. More collapses as the inexperienced worked too fast, driven by fear and greed. The Mayor had promised estates on the surface as well as grand caverns—whatever it took to lure Americans down into the mines to find her Island stars. They would be given servants, they would be given a place on the council. They would be given reprieve.

The gold rush was on, but the progress was actually slower now. Too much time spent digging out lost souls. Huan stayed safely in his only lonely hole with his indentured helpers. He did not care for Island stars, but promised that he would give the slaves whatever he found. They would exchange the stars for freedom.

Huan dug down. Down. Down. At times he thought he could hear sound from the other side of the dirt. Other times he would feel a phantom wisp of wind.

So he dug. And dug. And dug.

The rope descended and Huan stopped his work. He waited for the little bucket to arrive. In it was a note. Huan flicked a match to get light.

"A meeting has been called. Everyone is to come. Everyone!"

The final "Everyone" was underlined three times. Huan crumpled the note and tossed it back into the bucket. He waved out the match and let it drop to the dirt. He kicked the shovel into the earth as the bucket rose up.

Then the earth fell.

Huan jumped from the collapsing floor and lunged for the rope. His hand slipped but finally held to the braid. Men called from above as the walls crumbled, the floor crumbled beneath him. Huan was dangling as dirt rained down around him.

He waited for the grave to consume him.

But the earth did not pile up around him.

It kept falling.

And falling.

And falling.

Then he felt the wind.

A warm red light glowed through his eyelids sealed tight from terror. He adjusted his grip on the rope. He squinted, allowing the light to seep in slim shards as his eyes adjusted.

Beneath him was Heaven. Above him was the Island.

Huan laughed and laughed and laughed and laughed.

Being A Child God
Part 13

Don't go big on your own dime, boy.

The first lesson from The Fabulous Fallimento.

OPM. Other People's Money. That was how you made it in magic. Never risk your neck on a show. Play on house money. Mommy, daddy, a sugar momma, a corporate sponsor, whoever you can get to bear the risk. That way, if the crowds don't show, if the trick doesn't pan out, or if your promoter runs aways with the profits, you just stroll away from the gig without a care in the world.

Following *Buried Alive On The Strip!*, I never tried to go big again. I died a failed magician. A scared magician.

An eternity later, I awaited the tribes. They were all coming to witness my greatest trick of all. I kept to the trees, out of sight, waiting in the wings as the audience filed in. Edward's group arrived first, following the former pastor out of Rawlings and toward New Wichita. The Mayor greeted them with a cold, practiced smile. They stepped into the maw of the cavern like an offering of virgins to a B movie deity.

The Engineers arrived a little later. Old, naked, and proud. Julia assured me they were on board, but I still feared them the most.

The fishers were late to the party, as always. They were an afterthought. The awkward neighborhood kids you only invited because it would be cruel and petty to leave them out of the mix.

No Barry or Mary. I wasn't surprised. In fact, I was relieved. They would be powerful allies, but they were unpredictable. Perhaps as dangerous as the Engineers.

I sent our own haggard tribe forward out of the trees. My new followers. They were a bit healthier, a little sun on their face, the blisters and scars clear. Even the weakest of them managed to keep a lively pace, pushed onward by the joy of walking back within the grips of their now impotent oppressors.

They were untouchable.

"Are you ready, my king?" Anat whispered beside me.

I looked behind us to the distant lake beyond the trees. I was certain I could feel God's eyes on me. The angels would descend soon. Their Creator's imminent doom could not come unchallenged. Our mist settled from the trees to the ground where we materialized. I ran my fingers over a burlap bag tied to my waste. I looked to Anat and allowed a proud smile. I evaporated and spread across the land like a morning fog enveloping the earth. I twisted tiny tornadoes and sent ahead waves. A full show. Sparks of lightning within the mist. My laugh. My true laugh in my true voice.

The tribes watched from within, awed and afraid. All but Cabin Five, who were amused. I laughed harder, then shot ahead, straight at Billy and his smug grin. He dodged out of the way as my wave swept over and past him. I swirled within the cavern, the light from the hole in the ceiling sending a halo down upon me. I formed a giant image of my face. Laughing and looming. The great and powerful Simon.

Then I turned into a boy wearing a glistening, chrome suit. Part armor, part Armani. I wish I'd had this budget back in Vegas. I would have killed. Killed!

I knelt to one knee, bowing my head. The tribes watched, confused. But then they felt the heat. They turned back to the cavern entrance. A vast column of fire approached, twisting like a water spout connecting a sky to an ocean, a fetus to its mother.

And at its base, Anat, my love, walked forward.

She stepped through the cavern entrance and the water spout snapped and flared out into great wings. They flapped, then burst into thousands of flaming feathers that swirled throughout downtown. The weak fled into caves. The rest marveled.

I rose and approached Anat. I held out my good hand. She took it and we led the tribes toward City Hall. The Engineers followed first. Next came Edward, Tommy, Sophia, Ossie, and Billy. The Mayor and her council were the last to fall into the procession. None of the fishers found the courage, but we'd never really needed them.

We reached City Hall and scaled the steps. Anat turned to address the crowd.

"New Wichita is under my protection!" she declared. A red glow burst out from her, spreading out across the cave and forming a dome throughout the cavern. A few Americans who'd fled to the caves approached the dome from the other side. They held up their hands, shielding themselves from the heat, then fled back underground. They were left to the angels, should the angels care enough to dig them out.

We walked into City Hall. The leaders of the tribes followed.

I Cannot Die
Part 19

Throughout the morning and into the afternoon, Jay sat cross-legged at the edge of the pier. His hopes were high, which worried me. I'd considered telling God, but what would I say? His beloved child was desperate to leave and may very well betray Him? What parent can understand and accept that?

The angels lifted into the air from all across the campground. To the children, they only saw the dust clouds stirred up from the giant wings. But then the swords burst into great, angry flames, held aloft, ready to smite. A chorus of enraged screeches erupted as the angels rallied for war against the exiles.

They began their flight across the lake. The fury of Heaven against the resilience of man.

God appeared beside me and I flinched slightly. He didn't

seem to notice.

"I need more instruments," God asked. "What do you have left?"

"What, like cannons and missiles?"

"Musical instruments."

I looked out at the flaming swords streaking towards the Wilderness. "You're really asking me for musical instruments right now?"

"Yes, why wouldn't I?"

"My mistake," I said. "Um, no. No more instruments. I gave you the last guitar."

"Oh. What about those little guitars?

"Ukuleles?" I asked.

"No, the other ones with more strings?"

"Mandolins?"

"No, I think they are called something else. Oboes, maybe?"

"That's a wind instrument, Father."

"Piccolo?"

"Also a wind instrument."

"Okay. Well, can you figure it out for Me and see if we have one?"

"Father," I said. "Humans invented thousands of stringed instruments, so I may never divine what it is you are talking about. Even if I did, I assure you that we don't have it. We only have the piano and that last guitar."

God took in a deep breath. He looked at me and shook His head, then gazed up at the sun. "That's too bad."

"It is."

"We should have brought more instruments to the Island while we had the chance."

"You're right," I said. "But we didn't, so here we are. One piano. One guitar. Thankfully, we only have two musicians so we should be fine."

"Could we make some?" God asked. He took off his sunglasses and watched, with his pupiless eyes, the flock of angels nearing the other side of the lake. The flames left a trail like a comet breaking into a planet's atmosphere. "Like, if we went over there and grabbed some animals and timber? They made instruments out of animals, didn't they?"

I looked to Him and saw, perhaps for the first time, how diminished He'd become. These were questions God didn't ask.

"Yes, Father, they did. And we could. Once all this has calmed down, we'll see about making some instruments."

"Good. Good."

God replaced His sunglasses and smiled in the direction of the angels.

"This is good," He said. "What we are doing. This is good."

"Only if we win."

God looked down at me.

"I am the Alpha and the Omega," God said. "There was nothing before Me and there will be nothing after Me. They cannot win because I am the Universe and, if I go, everyone goes with Me."

I wasn't convinced nor did I think He was.

"And if the angels fail?" I asked.

"There are more angels, out there in the universe. Millions of them. We will call them home. We will send them after the heathens."

"But, Father, they cannot hear us anymore. Not on the Island. And, without angels, we have no way to reach them. We will be alone."

God's eyes were on the sky.

"The angels won't fail," He said.

"But what if they do?"

"Then I will send you and your brother."

God took one last look at the angels, then walked off the pier. I looked to Jay, who'd turned his head just enough to see us. He turned back to the water.

"Make Me a guitar, Bali," God called. "I don't care what kind, just as long as it plays. I've always wanted to form a rock band."

To My Little Divinities,

I suppose I should apologize. I've been eavesdropping for quite a long time. To be fair, Simon isn't the most subtle. He wants me to hear, I imagine. He wants me to know that he hurts. I've denied him my presence and he wants me to bear witness to his anguish.

So, here I am, Simon. You have my attention. Wail and gnash your teeth.

No? Fine. Allow me to say a few things before I let you boys go back to your gossiping.

Bali.

While on the Island, you entered my mind and my memories without my permission. It was a violation. You crawled through my synapses, wormed your way into my dark corners, and explored my secrets without hesitation, without shame. You felt entitled to my brain just as a defiler would feel entitled to my body. You felt this because God gave you the power.

Just as God also gave men the power to rape, to kill, to beat. So they did.

I have stopped that. Forever.

For the moment, you are beyond my reach so I ask for you to respect my privacy. If you fancy yourself a troubadour wandering the cosmos to sing my praises, my trials, my tribulations, let me make this clear: I don't need your validation and I definitely do not need your help. My name will not leave your lips. Ever. You've lost the right. If you must explain our universe by building up Simon to be the new emperor, fine. Lie. It's what you're best at. You will never again say my name.

If I find out you've broken my trust, I will find you. If you return to our universe and force your way into my mind or the minds of any within my dominion, I will destroy you. Your kind are only a memory in my new universe. The devils. The brutes. The consumers who take, take, take, only because they can. For as long as I sit on the throne, I will never let greed disease the hearts of our people again.

So, don't return. Don't apologize. Don't explain. Just stay gone. I honor your service to the Island and to the peace we won. I did not protest your monument in the lake because you were important to some. Not me. Not all. But some.

And to you, Simon, my silly, magical king.

Finish your story. I won't stop you. You need peers. I know how lonely it has been for you since I left.

But do not embarrass me.

I will keep our stars alight, I will tighten the seams of our galaxies, and I will protect the life and liberty of our universe. I want you to find solace. I want you to find peace. I want you to, at long last, grow up. When you do, come back to me.

Until then, do not embarrass me.

Being A Child God
Part 14

So, my wife.

I Cannot Die
Part 20

Yes. She is quite a woman. Should we continue?

Being A Child God
Part 15

...

I Cannot Die
Part 21

Simon? If we need to stop, I'll understand.

Being A Child God
Part 16

No, of course not. Just give me a little time. She's right. I wanted her to see the hurt. I've grown so powerful, but I still can't overcome loneliness. You can't disappear a void, you know?

I Cannot Die
Part 22

I do. Now you know the mind of God, my friend. Now you know why He created the Earth, the Island, Heaven, and Hell. Now you know the meaning of life.

Being A Child God
Part 17

Heh. How about that?

Being A Child God
Part 18

"That's really your plan?" The Mayor asked. "That's the best you could come up with."

I leaned forward over the long council table and looked at The Mayor sitting at the head. She had a backpack hanging from a strap from the top of her chair. Inside were Stars. I understood the message, but let it pass.

"That's all the plan we need," I said. "We don't know what God is going to do once we get Jay off the Island, so devising some complex scheme is foolish. We just need a vague idea of our endgame."

"How do we get Jay off the Island?" Yulia asked.

I shrugged. "I was hoping you'd have some ideas."

"If we knew how to get back to Heaven, don't you think we would have left already?"

"Some of you, yes," I said. "But most of you want to stay. You are just as curious about the Island as I am. I'm guessing you have, somewhere in your back pocket, a few ideas on how to extend a ladder down to paradise."

"A ladder?" Moonbeam asked.

"Well, a metaphorical ladder."

"If we send Jay back, how do we know he won't just assume God's throne?" Yulia asked. "Perhaps come back to retrieve his Father and undo everything we are trying to accomplish."

"Because Jay is furious. He just wants to go home and he's willing to throw in with anyone who'll get him there and leave him be for eternity. And that's the endgame. With Jay gone, Bali will rebel against God. With the Island united, God will be forced to surrender."

"Or die," Julia said. "Time to fulfill Nietzsche's proclamation. Then we can form a unity government, the first representative government without the oppressive shadow of mythology suffocating our reason."

"And how do you factor in these?" The Mayor leaned back, unzipped the backpack, and pulled out two Island Stars. She rolled them across the long, council table so that it rested between Yulia on one side and Simon on the other. There were gasps from the audience at the ghostly glow.

"Have you all seen these?" The Mayor asked.

"Yes," Yulia said. She reached across the table and picked up the star.

"With that," The Mayor said. "We can destroy God or Simon, just depending on whose side we choose."

The Mayor pointed her finger at the star.

"Pweh."

The star blossomed red and Yulia dropped it. The table cleared aside from Anat, who'd cast a red glow around herself. Wafts of smoke were rising from the red chair that was beginning to singe.

The star didn't explode though.

I looked around me, humiliated. The devil running from a firecracker. If Jay had seen, I'd never hear the end of it. As I walked back to my seat, I scanned the audience and saw Huan. He nodded to me.

"So, Simon, our dear child emperor," The Mayor said. "Maybe we don't need you after all?"

"You find yours, I'll find mine," I said. "I win in this arms race. Every time and in every way."

Yulia picked up the star and sat back down. One by one, the others returned to their seats.

"There were once many more in the Island," Yulia said. "They fed the Island. As they ruptured and were absorbed into the soil, our powers grew. All of our powers. We have Engineers who can sense all the stars in the earth. We've never retrieved them because we'd never even thought about weaponizing them. We just wanted them to continue rupturing, continue feeding the humans the power of the universe. To help us heal, to help us flourish, and to help us assume the Island so slowly that God doesn't notice."

Yulia leaned over the table and grabbed the other star.

"If we want true power," Yulia said. "Not just my Engineers, but all of us, we put these back in the earth and let them disintegrate as intended."

"As intended by a god who wants to keep us trapped here," Simon said. "Does God grow stronger too?"

"Perhaps," Yulia said.

"Angels are coming!" Ossie called from the audience as he stood up and turned towards the doors. "They are coming fast."

"He's right," Earnest said from a few rows away. The Old Man's eyes were closed tight. "All of them, right for us."

"The moment has arrived," Simon said. "So, do you try to kill me, or do we dethrone our Creator?"

The council fell silent. Eyes passed between one another. There were whispers in the audience.

"If we fight God," Edward said. "Will we have to kill Him? He won't ever give up the Island. He has too much pride."

"We'll do what we have to," Anat said.

"How long can you hold the angels out of New Wichita?" The Mayor asked Anat.

"Not long. We will have to face them."

"Is Jay or Bali with them?" The Mayor asked Earnest.

"I don't think so," Earnest said.

"They aren't," Ossie said.

Earnest opened his eyes and looked at Ossie. Earnest bowed his head slightly.

"Okay," The Mayor said. "We will help you fight the angels, but nothing more. We aren't committed to taking down God. Not yet."

The Mayor walked around the table and snatched the stars. Yulia grabbed her wrist.

"Don't waste them," Yulia said. "They are more precious to our future than you will ever know."

The Mayor ripped her wrist away. She looked up at the sentries at the door.

"Order every able-bodied man and woman to the cavern entrance with whatever weapons they can find."

Julia stood and looked to Anat. "I'm taking my people deep into the caves to wait this out. Can you let me out?"

"'My people'?" Anat asked.

"Your people, our people, what the fuck ever. I didn't save them from the ovens just to enlist them as cannon fodder."

"Go," Anat said.

Julia walked to the stairs.

"You are the one that arranged this meeting," The Mayor called after her. "Not even going to join the fight?"

"I'm still not convinced that any of you are worth fighting for," Julia said, turning around. "I promised to bring you together and here you all are. My job here is done."

She pointed at me. "You owe me one Petrov, Simon."

"I do and I promise that I will pay up once I clean up this little mess we have outside."

I stood and walked around the table to Anat. I held up my hand.

"Shall we?" Flames engulfed her dress, then faded to show glowing armor and a helmet adorned with white hot plumage sprouting from the top. She took my hand and we scaled the steps of the hall to face our great enemy.

The Choir Of Angels

I am the bastard son of God. I am the anti-Christ, but I am more angel than I am human. Perhaps this is why I've accepted man and all his weaknesses in a way that Jesus never could. I am apart from them. I see them as innocent fools thrown into a game they were never meant to win.

So, I am not a man, but I am also not an angel. I don't possess the angel's singular purpose, their intellectual simplicity. They are blessed with a clarity that I envy. I once had that clarity too, but God breathed the power of doubt into my mind. The Whisper. The moment He burdened me with my special gift, I could never return to Paradise. I could never again embrace an existence predicated on the infallibility of God's Word.

And, as the angels raced toward a showdown with the greatest threat to God's dominion in billions of years, not one of my brethren possessed a doubt. Their purpose was clear. They didn't understand the Island. They didn't enjoy their menial roles as caretakers and babysitters of the humans, but they also didn't question their lot. There was no other way. There was only God's way.

How I envied them.

My mind left my body and soared after the squadron. Below, the now empty shell of my body stood rigid, eyes glazed. Jay sat near my feet, trying to hide his own mutinous thoughts. God slipped back into His cabin to cuddle His secrets.

I skimmed over the water and swept into the leader of God's great army. The archangel Michael. He released a mighty screech just as the squadron cleared the lake and flew over the abandoned fishing villages. We crossed the forest expanse, the small clearing of Rawlings, the brief flashes of mud pits where animals craned their necks up from their meals, scanning the skies where a cold, vengeful wind blew.

Michael screeched again as, in the distance, the cavern of New Wichita came into view like a howling monster. A red haze emanated within. The angels saw and acknowledged.

"Do you want us to win, brother?" Michael asked me.

"My opinion is irrelevant."

"I know. But I am curious. Do you root for us or humanity?"

"Humanity," I said. "They were chosen by God. I will back them even if it means betraying God. That is how I show my loyalty to Creation."

"I don't understand how you can show loyalty to Creation by defying the Creator."

"I know," I said. "I don't think I'd ever be able to explain to you the difference."

"I don't think so either," Michael said. "I will miss you, brother."

"And I will miss you too. All of you. Enjoy oblivion."

Then Michael led the angels into a dive towards the last bastion of humanity. God's last failed experiment.

Being A Child God
Part 19

I stood at the edge of Anat's fiery barrier. Her bubble of protection that would not stop the angels, but it would at least slow them down. I looked to the far edge of the cavern where Julia slipped through a small break in the bubble. Her army of survivors waited for her on the other side. As soon as she was through, the fire fell back over like a curtain.

"Take this fight out of New Wichita," The Mayor said.

I nodded, looking through the flames to the sky beyond.

"How are we going to fight what we can't see?" Billy asked.

"Leave that to me," I said.

Billy turned to his fellow exiles gathered at the mouth of the cave. "I have no idea what the naked people can do, but for the rest of us, we stay together. Pack up in squads of six people right now. Whoever you trust to keep you alive. You don't have to like them, you just need to know that they won't abandon you. As soon as the cavern opens up, spread out, create distance between you and the rest of the squads. Get into the trees, stay out of open areas. If they grab onto anyone in your squad, get to that person, keep them on the ground. Crawl onto the angels if you have to. They have wings, and if those wings can't flap, they can't fly. We need to keep the angels on the ground, closed in so they can't maneuver. They are bigger and stronger, but we can overwhelm them."

Muttering followed as groups split off. Scared, trembling hands clutched onto spears, axes, and stones. Anything that resembled a weapon.

I felt a tap on my shoulder. I turned to look up at Huan.

"Bring Jay back to me," Huan said. "I can help you."

"How?" I asked.

"I know the way back home."

I smiled and patted him on the shoulder. "I knew you'd come around."

"They're diving!" Ossie said.

"Forty-nine angels," Earnest added.

A fisherman backed from the edge of the cave. "So many." Two of his group grabbed him by the shoulders and held him steady. A woman walked forward and cupped his face in her hands.

"There is no more hiding for us," she said.

I scanned the faces, the fear. I felt sick. It was a horrible thing I was asking of these people. I looked back to Huan.

"Let me take care of our bird problem out there and I'll get you the Messiah," I said. Huan nodded and retreated back into the crowd.

"Well," I said to Anat. "Shall we?"

Anat grinned. The fire opened a path for us, our stage was set, the opening scene underway. I unstrapped the burlap bag from my waist. I untied the opening. Wind gusted toward the cavern, bringing with it a dreadful cold. I threw the bag into the air and a shower of gold poured out. I held up my palms, spun them around and the gold swirled like a cyclone. I motioned outward, sending the gold glitter across the army of angels. Their invisible forms were consumed by sparkling bits of foil. It clung to their feathers in messy splotches like amateur attempts at makeup by a nine-year-old. The angels tumbled and tried to clear the gold from their eyes. Three slammed into the fiery barrier and were engulfed. They screamed and fell into the cavern in a hump of smoke and desperate flailing.

"Get them!" Billy yelled and Americans surrounded the angels, throwing spears into their now exposed bodies.

One angel landed only a few feet from me. It was my first close look at God's errand children. Its glimmering face was almost human, but also avian. It possessed a sharp beak, but also had strong, human cheeks and a brow. It was beautiful and hideous—a mish-mash of parts more nonsensical than the poor platypus.

The angel pushed to its feet and, with pained and clumsy flaps of its wings, it struggled back to get back into the sky. Spears plunged into its side and red blood sprayed back towards the crowd. The exiles gasped and dodged the blood. The angel flailed and limped into the air and back out of the cavern. It flew fifty yards before falling back to the ground. Roars erupted from the cavern as exiles rushed out behind us and ran for the woods.

"You hit them with glitter?" Billy asked as he ran past.

"Awesome, right? It's the herpes of the craft industry."

Billy shook his head, then motioned Ossie, Edward, and Tommy to follow him.

Angels soared above, shaking the glitter from their heads. On the ground, a few angels wiped their faces against the grass. A pack of exiles surrounded one and threw a spear into its side. Red blood spurted out of empty air. The angel cried and attempted to lift up into the air, but the humans leapt upon it, pulling it down to the ground. Another angel swept down and clutched two of the exiles off, lifting them high into the air, then dropping them.

I burst into mist and lifted Anat up into the air with me. She surrounded us with a fireball and we burned across the sky. I found an angel high in the clouds, circling, watching the action below. Only a few patches of glitter had found its feathers. It was clever, more cautious than the others. A leader, if such a thing existed among the angels.

"Let's take it," Anat said to me. It felt wonderful to have her mingled within me. A peer. A partner in crime.

The angel saw us coming and broke into a dive. I broke the mist apart as it plunged past us. The flames caught its wings. We materialized in mid-air. Anat shot a column of fire down upon the angel's back. It screamed and tumbled to the ground.

We chased down the angel.

"They are so beautiful," Anat said. "Could we tame them?"

"I don't think they will ever turn from God."

The angel righted itself and caught the wind to climb back into the sky, smoke billowing from its feathers.

"What a pitiful shame," Anat said as her hands emerged from the mist and shot large plumes of fire into the chest of the angel.

Billy The Warrior
Part 3

Don't look at the mayhem. Focus only on one task at a time. Keep it ahead of you. Keep moving forward.

Angels swept by, glimmering in the sun. Sophia clutched his hand. He didn't look over, just pulled Sophia onward. To the trees. Get to the trees.

An angel soared down behind them, grabbing Edward and trying to lift him into the air.

"Billy!" Sophia screamed as she grabbed Edward's leg. Billy grasped Edward by the waist. Ossie leapt onto Edward's back and the angel fell to the ground. It twisted away, let go of Edward, and soared back into the sky.

Edward's arms bled, but he pushed up and continued running.

"Pretty tough for a priest," Billy said, ruffling Edward's hair. Edward smiled through a grimace.

Squads across New Wichita were reaching the woods. Some had been bogged down and were battling angels in the open, getting ripped apart and lifted into the sky.

Nothing to be done for them. Sophia pulled Billy forward. Focus. Only think of your squad. Push forward.

Two angels descended in front of them. Edward and Tommy slipped past into the trees, Ossie close behind. Billy and Sophia sped up, but the glittering angels closed off their path, landing just ahead of the woods.

Life burst through the trees as thousands of birds shot from the branches. They swarmed the angels who swung their wings around, trying to brush the birds away. A falcon was plucked from the sky by the angel's beak, crushed and dropped lifeless to the ground.

Billy sprinted into cover and the angels followed, still swarmed by the birds. A deer gored one angel, sending it to its side. A horrible roar erupted just as a grizzly bear punched through the brush and tackled the other angel, ripping into its flesh with its fangs.

"When the hell did we get a bear?" Billy asked Sophia.

Sophia shrugged between heavy breaths.

An angel flew in between the trees, cracking branches as it bullied through. But it couldn't stay aloft. It landed just as Ossie and Tommy surrounded it, both holding crude knives made from flint stone. A squirrel leapt onto the back of the angel and the angel bucked, but the squirrel held. Ossie lunged and buried the knife into the angel's breast. The angel screamed and swatted Ossie away with its wing. Tommy jammed his knife into the angel's throat and the angel collapsed. Other exiles swarmed. Splattered blood sparkled from the flecks of glitter. The sounds of death were everywhere.

Yulia Creates So Many
Lovely Things
Part 6

Three angels surrounded Yulia. She didn't need the glitter. She felt their chill. She'd always admired the beautiful and powerful creatures. The angels would have to die for the Wilderness to survive and Yulia hated God for it.

She remembered Mildred and found the anger to move.

She leapt after one angel. It backed and dodged out of the way. Another Engineer grabbed the angel by the neck. Two more shouldered its side. Yulia turned to the other angels. They closed quickly. She spun from an angel's talons, ducked its wing, and punched its head. Her hand broke, but the angel buckled and fell backwards.

A fireball crashed down upon it as Simon's mist swept above. It screamed something both human and inhuman as it died, a clatter of death rattles and shrieks, a thing built to be eternal but screaming at the terrifying realization of mortality. Yulia sprinted after the third. Earnest grabbed its tail as Yulia reached for its throat. Her good hand found the angel's windpipe and squeezed. The beast couldn't scream as it fell.

In the distance, an angel had grasped an Engineer and flew to the edge of the Island. They struggled in the air. The Engineer grabbed a wing and the pair careened over the side of the Island, toward Heaven.

How To Properly Manage A
Young Empire
Part 10

Sentries lined the entrance of the cavern. Huan stood beside The Mayor as she watched a trail of fire follow an angel falling to the ground. She still held the stars in her hands. A group of fishermen were being mauled by a pair of angels. Three Engineers intervened, beating back the angels. The survivors took the opening and ran for the woods. The wounded were left to soak in their own viscera.

"There's no going back from this," The Mayor said. The stars warmed from blue to orange. "Even if I did kill Simon, we are all still doomed, aren't we?"

"We were doomed the moment we woke up on the Island," Huan said.

An angel swept past Engineers and soared toward the cavern entrance. The sentries braced, holding up their spears.

"No!" The Mayor yelled, running past the sentries and holding up the stars. They went from orange to an angry red. The angel slowed and stopped. It landed and studied the stars, then The Mayor. "Get out of here!"

The Mayor stepped closer to the angel and it backed away. It flapped its wings and flew back toward the trees to find other prey. The Mayor watched, adrenaline fraying her nerves, tears in her eyes. She retreated back behind the sentries, holding the stars tight. A weak, calming laugh emerged.

"It's going to be okay," she told Huan and the few other Americans still at the cavern entrance. "It's going to be okay."

The Choir Of Angels
Part 2

"Forget the others," I told the remaining angels. "Focus only on Simon."

I doubted it would do any good, but the carnage on the ground wasn't going to do anything to sway this war. It was only a body count and, if we were going to sacrifice these beautiful beasts, we might as well point them in a direction of some use.

Anat's column of fire pounded into an angel up above and it burst into flames. The other angels swarmed on the mist, dodging Anat's fireballs and sweeping through.

On the ground, the Engineers, the Americans, and the rest of the weary exiles could only watch the dogfight. Simon swirled, dove, climbed, anything to create enough room for Anat to materialize safely and attack.

He swung toward the cavern, with the angels circling all around him, plunging through the mist, grasping at only air.

"Michael!" I called. "Keep it up, wear him out. You have more endurance than he does. I've seen you raze entire cities, send back an army of demons. You can beat one magician."

Elongate the battle, keep Simon fighting until he loses focus, makes a mistake, gives the angels a small opening. We take out Simon and his queen, then the war would be over.

Through the eyes of Michael I saw Simon's face begin to appear in the mist. His eyes terrified. Simon was looking to the ground, he'd made his mistake. I sent Michael into a dive, talons stretched out. Simon was little more than a cloud, but maybe enough to get claws on.

I was going to win the war for God and I hated myself for it.

Then an arrow struck Michael's skull. I felt it. I felt the

electrical mayhem of death flood Michael's mind. The sorrow of the end. The end I had brought the angel.

I leapt to another angel just in time to see Mary standing atop the cavern, arrow pulled taught and aimed. It struck my angel. I felt another death. I retreated away, back over America, past the shore, over the water, and back into my waiting body. I collapsed upon the pier and wept.

"They are dying," I gasped. "All my brothers!"

I stood and turned toward God's cabin. "Do something!"

"You still have me," Jay said, standing to his feet.

Being A Child God
Part 20

I saw the first arrow strike the angel behind me, but didn't know where it came from. With the second arrow, I saw Mary and Barry standing beneath a cluster of trees sprouted over the cavern entrance. I swung away from the flock of angels and towards my favorite sexual deviants on the entire Island.

Mary notched and fired arrow after arrow until she'd emptied her quiver. Angels rained to the ground where the exiles descended and mauled the wounded creatures.

Mary and Barry then leapt off the edge of the cavern and fell upon an angel. Barry drove his spear through the back of the head of an angel while Mary drove her knife into its back. Crippled, the angel spun towards the ground. The lovers were thrown and crashed far away. The angel stood, staggered, and began to flap its wings. Yulia tackled the angel and grasped its neck, pulling its head back until its spine cracked. It spasmed violently as Yulia held on, its life draining away in a frenzied shiver.

Only a handful of angels remained and were being picked off by Anat's flames. The fight was over. The adrenaline was gone. It now only felt sad. It was a massacre.

Soon, the miracle of angels would be over. At least on the Island.

"I don't feel good about this," Anat said to me.

"Neither do I. Damn God. That miserable Old Man."

I Cannot Die
Part 23

The last of the angels were falling like comets. One by one. Bright, brilliant stars reduced to ashes. One day, humans would forget that these angels had ever existed as anything more than myth. And then, they would forget the myths too.

My brothers.

I let myself cry alone on the pier. Jay had left for God's cabin. Maybe they were planning, scheming, looking for ways out of this desperate situation. I lacked the energy to search their minds and find out for myself.

I hated the humans at that moment, but not nearly as much as I hated God. It felt sick. Hot. The hatred was more intense and more eternal than Hell. A useless, impotent hatred.

I felt a presence. It was the children emerging from the cabins.

They were streaming past God's cabin, toward the waterfall, toward the Wilderness. They were abandoning us. Hours passed and night fell. I had no more tears left in me.

"Let's go face our fate," God said.

I hadn't even noticed their presence. We were all now lesser beings.

We climbed into a boat and pushed off for the Wilderness.

The Atheist
Part 2

"Don't make me go back in!" the Cook pleaded as Julia's army marched forward. He cowered against a wall, hands held in a childish surrender.

"Where is Petrov?" Julia asked.

The cook lowered one hand and pointed toward the right vein of ovens.

"Third on the left."

The iron door was still warm from the fire. Petrov's once pale skin was a purplish red. His skin was tight, dehydrated. It seemed he'd lost fifteen pounds he didn't have to lose.

"Where is she?" Petrov asked, his voice as brittle as dead grass.

"Safe."

Sister Sophia
Part 5

Carnage was not new to her. She witnessed the aftermath of too many massacres throughout Africa. She tended to maimed and mortally wounded, sat with the dying for hours, hearing the priest say time and again that "a watched pot never boils."

But this was different. Death on the Island was different because there was no true death. Life didn't escape as it did on Earth where the soul floated up into Heaven and left behind only a husk. The exiles that were ravaged by the angels—their flesh shredded, limbs severed, skulls cracked like dropped eggs—life still clung to them. A quieted life. A shredded flag unable to wiggle its way free of the cold, lonely pole.

Some would heal, but some would not. It would be eternal suffering. Confusion. Pain. Sorrow.

The wounded animals died naturally. As on Earth. Muscles tightened and curled. Eyes glazed. Organs closed up shop. The brain flicked off the lights. Their story was over.

It was the soul that was the problem. The soul was the curse of man.

"Collect them," Huan said. "Bring them to the tunnels. The angels too."

"We're going to bury them alive?" Billy asked.

"No. There is another way."

Then she felt the panic of the fish far away in the lake. Birds flew into the air.

"Ossie?" she called.

Ossie turned to the south.

"God's coming. With Jay and Bali."

The sky darkened from blue to gray. Then from gray to black.

The sun was swallowed. Silver clouds formed and swirled. Thin tornadoes dropped all across the Wilderness. Distant now, but their roars approaching.

"Get everyone back into the cavern!" Billy said.

"Simon," Huan called.

"Get back into the cave," you said. "We'll take care of it."

Ossie and Billy grabbed a mangled fishermen and pulled him toward the cave. Sophia closed her eyes and called out to the life around her, sending them toward the edges of the Wilderness. To safety.

I Cannot Die
Part 24

God flew ahead of us, His body upright, formal, an emperor intent on pacifying His restless people. His pupiless eyes glowed a blood red. Tornadoes swept across the land—leashed dogs leaping at the end of their chain, snarling, enraged.

Jay and I walked calmly behind. We didn't speak, for the roar of God's fury would eclipse any other sound. Also, we were terrified.

The trees in our paths were uprooted and tossed to the side. We walked in the wake of destruction. Life carved out of the Island, a giant, ugly gash sliced into a masterpiece.

We reached the cavern, fire blooming within, glowing bright under the dark skies. Anat was trying to seal us out, but it wouldn't work. The tornadoes swung and crossed over the cavern entrance. Trees were plucked and sucked into the sky, then dropped like spilled matchsticks. Those that hit the fire burst into flames, but did not break through into the cave. A massive bonfire collected in front of New Wichita.

Beyond the fire, you stood with your army cowering behind. Safe, for the moment.

God landed in the clearing before the cavern entrance. With a wave of his hand, the debris, the dead angels, and the wounded exiles all swept out of the way.

"Come out and bow before your God!" It was a booming voice, far too large for His human frame. The ground shook from His terrible timbre. Not the Voice that could destroy and create as It had in Heaven, but impressive all the same.

"Nope," you called, so small in comparison that it was comical. "This is negotiation time."

"We will never bow to you again!" Anat said.

God closed his eyes. The earth rumbled and split open, a fissure cracking from His feet all the way to the cave.

"I would sooner tear this Island apart!"

The cavern roof began crumbling, and falling against the fire, tumbling along the fiery barrier and falling to the ground. Jay looked at me, worried.

Anat clasped your hand and led you out of the barrier. The rumbling ceased, the tornadoes faded and climbed back into the sky.

Yulia looked to the other Engineers. She frowned, then leapt through the fire. She stood, a few black scorches on her skin, but otherwise unharmed. Edward considered. He grabbed The Mayor's backpack, then ran for the fire. He covered his head and jumped through. Flames engulfed his clothes and the backpack. Anat looked back, waved her hand and the flames gasped away. Edward rolled to his back, grimacing in pain, then pushed himself to his feet. He picked up the backpack and slung it over his shoulder.

Billy took a step for the fire, but Sophia grabbed his hand and pulled him back to the group.

God studied the small assembly. The leaders of the rebellion.

"And this is how you plan to defeat me? A magician, a witch, a nudist, and a priest."

"I know, it sounds like the start of an awesome joke," you said. "But I think we've got Your number. I think You know that too, hence all the sound and fury."

"I've faced worse than you, small one," God said.

"It's not the size that matters, Old Man," you said. "It's the loyalty."

You looked past God to Jay.

"Deal still on?" you asked.

God followed your eyes to His son. Jay looked up at God, then quickly away to me, then to you, then to the ground.

"Yeah," he said.

"What deal?" God asked, striding toward Jay. Jay flinched away and kept his eyes lowered.

"What deal?" He shouted down at Jay. A line of blood trickled out of Jay's ear that faced God. God rose his hand to slap Jay.

For the first time since receiving the gift of the Whisper, I successfully leapt into the mind of God.

Lord In Heaven
Part 2

Chaos. Lights. Planets. Circles. Collisions. Screams. Rapturous moans.

And God in the middle of it all. Overwhelmed, terrified, and small.

I Cannot Die
Part 25

I fell out of His mind like a trapdoor plunging out from underneath my feet. I was back in my body. God stood over me, eyes black with streaks of lightning crossing within.

He grabbed me by the throat.

"Never!" He yelled, the force of His voice disintegrating the earth around me.

Then He threw me.

Time slowed to almost a stop. My body soared into the sky. I saw The Old Man, his hand following through like He'd thrown a football. I was too stunned to scream or to call for help. I kept my eyes on my Father and He, in turn, watched His bastard son fall away for the last time.

He grew small. Smaller. Smaller. I lost sight of Him as the Island, in its entirety, shrank until it was swallowed by the great expanse of Heaven. The last prick of darkness against the massive swirl of warm red souls swimming within Heaven. Then the brightness of Heaven dimmed. Dimmed. Dimmed. Dimmed. Then was gone.

And my role in your story was done. Cast away, not knowing how the second rebellion fared against our diminished God.

Until I heard your voice, Simon. Please, hurry and finish for me. Your voice is growing thinner as the presence of another holy spirit blooms within this new creation. Tell me, how did you win?

Being A Child God
Part 21

Yulia screamed as we watched you shoot from the Island like a rocket streaking towards oblivion. Anat moved her hands up, the bubble evaporating within the cavern and reappearing over God, trapping Him. Jay backed away, shielding his face from the heat. Edward opened the backpack, took out the stars, and ran for the bubble.

Anat looked to me.

"Let him through," I said.

A small opening in the flames appeared and Edward leapt through, a star in each hand. He tackled God and they fell against the ground. Edward held the stars against God's head and grimaced. They glowed red, then purple, then sparks leapt about within. Edward screamed from the heat.

"No!" Jay shouted.

Edward's hands burned, God's temples were blackening.

"Stop!" Jay's voice was unlike anything I'd ever heard. A shout, a whisper, an octave too low for the human ear, a sound both irresistible and hypnotic.

Edward, tears in his eyes, looked up to Jay. The sparks subsided. The stars cooled back to blue.

"Let me do this," Edward pleaded.

"No," Jay repeated, this time in his normal voice. "That is the old way. Vengeance is not justice."

Edward looked back down to God. Edward let the stars drop from his hands. God gazed up at Edward, shocked and enlightened.

"We are better than You," Edward said. He leaned down and kissed God's forehead. He then pushed off his Creator, stood and walked away.

God waved away Anat's barrier then stood up. The tornadoes swirled back into life.

"I will destroy this Island and everything on it! You are not worthy of My love!"

The ground split, a terrible fault gaping open. Exiles ran from the cavern as the roof began shedding giant slabs of stone. God's eyes crackled with electricity.

"Father!" Jay shouted as he leapt onto God's back. Blood spurted out from the palm of Jay's hand. He held his bloody hand against the forehead of God. "See all your sins, Father! See all that You have done!"

God's flew into the sky, trying to spin Jay off his back. But then God stopped. His glowing eyes paled to white. He gasped. Jay held tight, his blood pouring down over the face of God. The Creator gasped. They fell back down to the Island, landing hard. The tremors silenced. The black clouds evaporated. Jay still clung to God, his bloody hand over God's face.

"See what You've done."

Being A Child God
Part 22

We watched. We said nothing. I was ashamed to be witnessing God's immense sorrow. His wails. His tears. I couldn't imagine what sins God was reliving. How many? All of them, I suspected. Every single sin tracing back to Eve's apple.

Perhaps beyond.

Anat walked to Jay and bent over him.

"He's had enough," Anat said.

Jay grit his teeth, then kicked God away. The Old Man rolled over into a fetal position, crying hard, heavy sobs. Jay put his hands over his face, the blood smeared against his olive skin. He then held his hand up to Anat. She took it and pulled Jay to his feet. Our Savior was weak. He was ready.

"Follow me," Huan called.

Jay looked up, nodded, and followed Huan into the cavern. Jay stopped, turned, and returned to me. He folded me into a hug. My body warmed, then a surge of energy hit. It passed across my skin and through my bones in powerful waves of heat. I lost my breath and nearly fainted. He released me and I fell. I was healed. I was whole. Fingers and all.

Jay walked into the cavern.

We never saw him again.

Billy The Warrior
Part 4

Four Engineers, Billy, Sophia, Anat, and I marched God back to the campground. It was slow and sad. Nothing about the victory felt righteous. It was just over and only uncertainty followed.

God didn't speak, didn't resist. At the waterfall, the waves parted, but not spectacularly. More a divine shuffle to the side. Almost as if the water didn't want to have anything to do with their bested and disgraced Creator.

We reached God's cabin and He took heavy steps up the porch steps. The door opened on its own. God smiled, then He walked inside. The door closed on its own.

And that was the Great Surrender.

We heard music from the mess hall and Billy went to investigate. He opened the door and peered inside. Raul cradled his guitar, plucking strings with a luscious energy, Edna dancing her fingers over the keys. Both had their eyes closed, rapturous. They had no idea what had happened.

Billy closed the door and let them be.

Digging to Heaven
Part 6

Huan stood before the hole. The warm red life of Heaven glowed up from the bottom of the Island. A crowd stretched back into the tunnels leading to the surface of New Wichita. We still didn't know what happened when someone dropped down through the hole. Jay had jumped and never returned. That was good enough for many. Not all. But many.

Petrov and the head looked down into Heaven. The souls twisted and slithered around each other. It made me deeply uncomfortable. Too familiar, I think, but maybe they didn't mind existing in a semi-slumber, an eternal, ignorant bliss. They didn't need to know that the universe had just changed hands.

Petrov's wife was down in Heaven somewhere. As were his daughters. Petrov held up the head. She smiled at him and mouthed "thank you." He kissed her cheek, then dropped her down the hole. She fell and fell and fell until her head was too tiny to see anymore.

Julia stepped up behind Petrov and wrapped her arms around him. She squeezed tightly.

"Damn you," she said, the light of Heaven reflecting in her eyes. "Damn you."

He turned in her arms and leaned into the hug.

"This Island is blessed to have you," Petrov said.

"Sure as shit is." She smiled that cocky smile, pulled away, and cleared away tears. "Damn you."

She stepped back. Petrov leaned backwards, eyes still on Julia. He fell through the hole. Moments passed as Julia contemplated. She shook her head and pushed her way through the crowd.

Ossie stepped from the crowd. He hugged Edward and Tommy,

then Billy, then Sophia. I was surprised when he embraced me. It felt good and I nearly cried. People like us rarely get hugs.

"We could use your power," Yulia said from the crowd. "Just stay. Let us train you. Maybe we can bring your husband to the Island. There must be a way."

"If you can figure out how to bring Isaac here, then bring me back with him."

Yulia nodded.

"I love you all," Ossie said. "Good luck."

He turned and jumped feet first down the hole.

The wind picked up a bit, whistling up from the hole and through the caves. The crowd dispersed and returned to New Wichita. More would leap in the weeks, years, and centuries to come. But more would come to the Island. In time, our collective will would grow the small Island into a continent. An ocean would follow. Then a world. Eventually, we discovered how to bring souls back and forth from Heaven. "Vacationing" we called it.

Few of us ever came back from Heaven, but some did. Enough. Enough to keep this experiment going a little while longer.

I Cannot Die
Part 26

What of Jay? How is he? And God? Was there ever another mutiny? Did Julia ever rise up against you? Did you ever ask God why He made the Island? Why He made any of it? Did you achieve your perfect creation?

Being A Child God
Part 23

A perfect creation? No. We haven't yet and probably never will. There have been no major wars, but there are always skirmishes and minor rebellions when people get a bit too bored. We are human. We like to war. We like to steal and conquer, but we also like to love. It seems we do a bit more of the loving now that we aren't beholden to myths. Anat runs a pretty tight ship and can't abide foolishness. Summer and Livie returned from Hell to be her high priestesses and I kinda got sidelined.

But it's still not perfection. That is only possible in Heaven. That is only possible when our minds are too dazzled to be devious.

But who wants something so boring as perfection?

As for God, I did ask Him the big question. Why the Island? Why humans? Why risk Free Will?

It was back when Edward and I were still close. Years had passed since the war. Edward was a bit of a journeyman, traveling between the civilizations as a student of thought. He no longer had a myth to bind his intellect so sought out ideas with a ravenous hunger.

He'd come to live at our palace for a few weeks and we talked and drank and laughed and annoyed Anat. He asked me if I'd ever talked to God since the Fall. I admitted to keeping my distance so, in a drunken bargain, we agreed to cross the lake for a final accounting of God's divine logic.

I knew that God still lived in His cabin, keeping to Himself. I pushed the day's bureaucratic duties off on Anat and we strolled to the other side of the lake. The cabins were still all intact, but where now emblazoned with colors and murals and designs and statues. Not religious iconography as one would assume, just art and life. It was beautiful in a 60's stoner kinda way.

Music wafted from the campground. On the porch I saw Raul, Edna, and a handful of musicians I only vaguely remembered bringing to the Island. They played that lively porch-stomping bluegrass music that was perfect for the clear days of the Island. Raul nodded to me and slid over to let us walk to the front door. They never stopped playing.

I knocked. I knocked again. The door swung open with a rattle and do you know who was inside?

Martha.

She looked good. She glowed. Still a little frumpy, but happy. Fulfilled. She wore a sundress and her long, long hair was braided in intricate knots. She wore an apron that was dusted with baking flour. She gave me a suspicious, playful smile, then waved us inside.

God bent over His work table, painting a tin army man. He wore a kimono with rainbow cotton socks and sandals. It was amazing. He looked up at me, His left pupiless eye was blown up big by the magnifying glass strapped to His head. It was dark green like a blurry photo of a forest planet. He lifted the magnifying glass off, blinked and rubbed at His left eye. He stood, picked up sunglasses from His worktable and slipped them on. He motioned for us to sit on His couch, still stained with Jay's blood from so long ago. There were tiny, plastic globes scattered on the cushions, but Martha cleared them out of the way.

Edward and I sat shoulder to shoulder, awkward like children at a principal's office. Martha stepped outside to give us privacy. God stood. It was a subtle dominance move, but that was okay by me.

Sometimes it's okay to let the other people feel bigger, especially when you both know they aren't.

"So, Martha?" I asked.

"Yes, she is great," God said. "She's been good for Me. We didn't want to make a big thing about the wedding. So much had happened, so much had changed. We both needed quiet, you know?"

"Yes," I said.

"Congratulations," Edward said. "Retirement seems to suit you."

God nodded, content. "Thank you."

And it did suit Him. He was happy in a way I hadn't seen before. He smiled. Perhaps He might have smiled before, back in the campground, but now He smiled without effort. Without calculation.

"Children?" Edward asked.

"No," God said. "We tried, but no. It's been hard on Martha and it's been a little hard on Me. I don't want another son like Jay. No sire to the throne, but it would have been nice to have a child to adore properly. I never really had the chance the first or second time around. They were vessels of purpose, you see.

I loved them, but I didn't really enjoy them. Does that make sense?"

"Yes," I said and Edward nodded his head. "I always thought you would try to get back to Heaven, take back the throne. But you aren't going to, are you?"

"No," God said and looked at the ground. "I'm tired, Simon. And you seem to be doing fine. You make a lot of mistakes, but I try to remember that I made mistakes too."

"You know that?" Edward said. "You wanted us to believe that You were infallible, but you admit that You made mistakes?"

God took in a deep breath. He picked up a nearby planet and gazed at it. "It's hard to admit frailty when the universe depends on You. Retirement has given me the space to be honest with Myself."

Martha appeared with some lemonade and cookies. She smiled proudly. She deserved it. She'd done a good job with The Old Man. Domesticated Him properly. I waited for her to slip back outside before getting to the heart of the matter.

"As you can imagine, we are here for a reason," I said.

"I assumed."

"Why did You create the Island?" Edward asked.

"Because I am not the kind of guy who lets good ideas go," God said. "I've never been afraid of anything but mankind. I always knew there was a chance that they would find a way to overtake Me. And you did."

"Then why did you recreate us?" Edward asked.

"Do you know how boring eternity is when you aren't afraid of anything?"

"No," I answered, because I was afraid of many things. The Engineers rebelling, a new empire emerging to secede from our nation. But mostly I was always afraid of Anat leaving me. Always.

"That was my Hell," God said. "When I sent every soul to Heaven and to Hell, creation no longer held a purpose. Therefore I no longer held a purpose. I created you the first time because I longed to be loved. I kept you alive for so long because I didn't understand love. When I created the Island, it was because I was tired and longed to be vulnerable. That is why I never understood love. I could not be hurt."

God looked to the door, listened to the music. He smiled.

"I still don't understand love, but now I understand hurt. And I am beginning to see that they are almost the same thing."

Edward and I both nodded at the truth of the statement.

"Do you regret the Island?" Edward asked.

"Yes. Of course. But I accept where I am. This new life is good. Also, I needed to know a bit more about human love. Martha has given Me that. She's taught Me quite a bit. I garden now. Can you believe it?"

"Good for you," I said.

"Do you want a second chance with Jay?" Edward asked. "Maybe a chance to just enjoy him as a peer instead of a servant?"

"He deserves to be left alone," God said. "He deserves to be happy. He can't be happy here."

"I've been back to Heaven," I said. "I looked, but I can't find him."

"He is there," God said. "I know it, but I also think it's good if you don't. If he wants to be found, he'll be found."

We sipped on our lemonade. It was too sugary. The music continued as we touched on governance and my plans to extend our reach to a moon. We'd discussed creating an entire solar system rather than just a fake sun.

"Harder than it looks," He told me and, as it turned out, He was right.

"Was sin really necessary?" Edward asked. "Actually, strike

that. Was free will really necessary?"

God wiped crumbs from His lap, then folded His hands behind His head and looked to the ceiling. "No. I don't think so. Not anymore. I was a young God when I created Free Will. I think that's what I've learned most about the Island. Creating pain to encourage love and devotion isn't fair. It isn't good. I was trying for something that I wasn't quite powerful enough to pull off. I could have created a better universe. I see that now. I just didn't."

He closed His eyes and listened to the music. The moment felt done, so I stood. Edward hesitated, but stood too. God groaned as He leaned forward onto His feet. He wiped His hands on His pants before we shook our goodbyes.

"Please come back," God told Edward as He held the handshake firm. "I enjoyed this. I'm proud of you, Edward."

"Thank you and I will," Edward said.

I didn't point out that he hadn't extended me the same courtesy, but I still left God's cabin feeling more satisfied than I'd expected. There were always more questions, but I had business to attend to. I had a wife to entertain. Edward didn't say much on the way back to the Wilderness, instead just wiping tears away when they escaped down his cheeks.

There is more, of course. So much more, but that is the important part, I think. I miss you. We all miss you. I told you about the statue in the lake, right? Still there.

I Cannot Die
Part 27

I've reached the new universe. I can't tell you much. The creator here is new. Ambitious. Good, I think. She enjoyed your story. If Anat is listening, I was judicious about the details. I tried to be true, but also respect her privacy. If Anat isn't listening, feel free to pass along my message. She need not hunt me down.

The creator told me that, if you are still alive in a thousand years, you can expect to see me again. She said to be ready. I don't mean to seem alarmist, but you might consider digging The Old Man out of the mothballs around that time. I'm certain the meeting of the universes will be peaceful.

But still.

Until then, I will have to end our correspondence. My new God demands my fidelity because that is what gods do. Know that you will always be in my heart. You all will. The Great

Creations that finally snipped God's strings.

Be safe my friend. Be better gods than we were. Your universe deserves it.

Note to the reader,

Following the death of my best friend, I fell into a deep spiritual drift which was reflected in my first novel, *the dominant hand*. My friend had been a devout Christian who deserved a long life with his new bride, yet he died after a senseless accident at a church retreat. Before the accident, I'd been revisiting the God Question. If my best friend could find happiness and solace with religion, perhaps I could too. After the accident, I couldn't forgive the God who'd so failed my friend and all those impacted by the tragedy.

Edward and the Island followed two years later. I was angry and remained angry for many years after. I tried several times to write the follow-up novels to complete Edward's story, but every effort failed.

Then, last winter, the story came into sharp focus.

Having gone through a final editorial pass of *Edward and the Infinite*, I realize that I've allowed myself to forgive my best friend's god. I do not believe in its existence, but I've allowed myself to release the bitterness that's haunted me since the accident.

I understand how ego-centric that must seem—me, a lowly mortal, forgiving the god who created all of reality. Yet I have. I am truly an agnostic now. I have settled the God Question with "Not Applicable To My Life." If He does exist, I understand why He failed my friend, failed my friend's family, and failed me. I have accepted God for what He is—flawed. I will no longer hold God's mistakes against Him nor will I ever again feel compelled to worship Him. This has allowed me a measure of happiness and solace.

I hope this story might help you forgive God too.

—Charles

The Martin & Weinke Continuum

From the escapades of a rock prophet to the global culling of humanity by Mother Nature, the Martin & Weinke Continuum connects standalone novels tracing our stumbling march to the end of civilization and beyond. These satirical, character-focused, and cross-genre stories examine our tenuous perch atop the food chain and what happens when everything else on the planet, both natural and unnatural, decides it's time for humans to be dethroned.

In order of continuity:

- *the dominant hand*
- *Deviants*
- *Pets*
- *Edward & The Island*
- *Edward & The Wilderness*
- *Edward & The Infinite*